KC felt a jolt, and something hard hit her suitcase. She dizzily stopped and stared as her suitcase snapped open, sending everything from ski socks to cosmetic bags to her nightie across the lobby floor. She bent over, feeling rage build up inside her like on a smoldering fire that had just been doused with oil.

"I'm really sorry," a deep voice murmured behind her.

KC turned around, took two steps back, and her anger instantly melted. Standing just three feet away from her was the tallest, most beautiful, dark-haired guy she'd ever seen in her life. In his early twenties, he was wearing a tight-fitting, red ski vest with the words *Briar Ski Team* woven in black on the front. A red headband covered his ears, and his rumpled black hair fell over his tanned forehead and icy blue eyes.

"It's . . . okay," KC stammered, her gaze frozen on his gorgeous face.

FRESHMAN NOEL

LINDA A. COONEY

HarperPaperbacks
A Division of HarperCollins*Publishers*

HarperPaperbacks   *A Division of* HarperCollins*Publishers*
10 East 53rd Street, New York, N.Y. 10022

Cover illustration by Tony Greco

First printing: December 1994

Printed in the United States of America

HarperPaperbacks and colophon are trademarks of HarperCollins*Publishers*

❖ 10 9 8 7 6 5 4 3 2 1

One

....

"So this is mountain desert." KC Angeletti stared in amazement, leaning forward in the four-wheel-drive station wagon as it sped down the two-lane highway. "Snow-covered sagebrush. Look, even the mountains up ahead are bare."

Her best friend, Winnie Gottlieb, turned around in the front passenger seat. "Great, isn't it? We could be in Iceland or Antarctica. Maybe even Siberia."

"We're going to be completely anonymous," KC's other close friend, Faith Crowley, added. She shifted gears as they began to climb the mountain grade.

KC could feel the tension slipping out of her muscles. Strangers in a strange land. That's what she, Faith, and Winnie had in mind when they were back at the University of Springfield, hatching a plan for their winter-break trip to Crystal Valley, a ski resort in the Rocky Mountains. Now, only an hour away from the the slopes, KC could almost feel the snow beneath her skis. She laced her fingers together and stretched her arms over her head. "No dorms. No studying. No deadlines. And especially no guys."

"Heaven," Winnie agreed. She grabbed a yellow, duck-billed ski cap out of her bag and pulled it over her spiky head of hair. "Emphasis on the no-guys part. All I want to do is sleep, eat, and ski."

Faith nodded as the lonely telephone poles whizzed by her window. Her blue eyes misted. "I'm not even going to try to think. After this last round of exams, my brain actually stopped working. And Christmas shuttling between divorced parents was no holiday." She quickly checked her map. "We've got another fifty miles on Highway 26. We'll be there in an hour."

KC pulled her long, dark hair back into a rubber band and bit her lip as the top of the Sugar Mountain range began to appear above the smooth, snowy foothills. The clear air made everything look bright and freshly washed under the fading blue sky. Even inside the closed car, she could smell the sage and wet pavement rushing by. She shut her eyes. Her head was tired. Her shoulders were tired. Even her bones were tired. She felt as drained as if she'd just run a marathon.

She felt a deep pang. So many bad things had happened since she'd started at the U of S: her beloved father's death, the discovery that she'd been adopted—even a brief flirtation with drugs and alcohol. She'd fallen in love, too—twice—but had been bitterly disappointed. It was amazing to her that she'd been able to stay on top of her heavy business and economics course load and her nonstop Tri Beta sorority duties.

Winnie whirled to face KC again. Then she propped her chin up in her hands and made a serious face. "Do you realize, KC, we don't have one thing to worry about for seven whole days?"

Faith nodded. "As long as we stay away from guys. Can we remember this?"

"Tell me about it." Winnie's tiny face turned solemn. KC patted her hand. The spring before, Winnie had impulsively married Josh Gaffey. Something had gone wrong, though, and Winnie had just filed for divorce. "Maybe they have all-girls slopes at Crystal Valley," Winnie added softly.

Faith smiled slightly, one corner of her mouth curving upward. She had a busy life directing university theater productions, but she, too, had her share of troubles, KC remembered. Her high school sweetheart and ex, Brooks Baldwin, had died in a climbing accident, and her parents had split up. "I'm going to wear the same beat-up navy parka, blue jeans, and ski gaiters I've been skiing in since tenth grade. No one will come near me."

Winnie shook her head, making a loud, game-show buzzing noise. "*Wrong.* You'll be surrounded by guys gawking at your neat parallels and daring schusses. What the hell. Maybe we should at least toy with the concept of a totally impractical and very hot, high-altitude, uninhibited romance. What do you say, KC?"

KC tried to look cheerful. She couldn't even remember what uninhibited felt like. Or what romance
was. In fact, all she could remember was her name, her
grade-point average, and the inflationary factors leading up to the 1929 stock market crash. "Yeah, sure,
Win. Let's go nuts."

Still standing on her knees as she faced the rear
seat, Winnie took out a wire comb and began ratting
her spiky hair even higher. "Don't joke. We've all been
on the brink of insanity too many times to make light
of this all-too-common condition."

KC nodded and smiled. She knew she was too
burned out to be on the brink of anything right now.
Something inside her had shut down over the past few
months. Her arms and legs and mouth still moved.
But her heart was like an empty vault that had been
locked up long ago: dark and unreachable.

"Look!" Winnie shouted later, as the highway
steepened and they rounded a bend. "We're up off the
plain. Crystal Valley—here we come!"

KC and Winnie sat up and stared as Faith drove on,
steering the wagon through a narrow mountain pass.
Snow blew across the road, bordered on one side by a
rocky, frozen stream. They turned the bend, and the
yellow lights of Crystal Valley glittered below.

"Look!" Faith exclaimed. "You can see the slopes
from here."

KC stared down at the view, then forgot to breathe.
The white mountains, sprinkled with thin stands of fir,
looked like gently folded mounds of whipped cream

extending for miles to the horizon. Closer, rising straight up from the little mountain valley below, were the Crystal Valley ski runs. Even from this distance, she could see the spidery thin chairlifts inching their way up the steep mountainside. And as she stared, the early sunset was turning the snow into a soft apricot-pink.

"It's beautiful," KC breathed. "More beautiful than I ever imagined it would be."

"Now if we can just get this rig down the grade," Faith said grimly, gently pumping the brakes. "You guys check for directional signs while I watch for ice."

Two miles later, the highway spilled into a narrow, flat valley, bordered by snow-covered farmhouses, barns, and haystacks. Faith turned off Highway 26 at the Crystal Valley junction, where a huge truck stop, restaurant, and motel stood, surrounded by a plowed parking lot and a shack selling tire chains. Dirty pickups with gunracks stood at the gas pumps. Farther on, they passed several strip motels and a big building with a sign that read BIG JACK'S DISCOUNT SPORTING GOODS: HUNTING, FISHING, RAFTING, SKIING.

"Keep going until you hit Main Street," Winnie instructed, bouncing a little in her seat. "Then turn left at that big grocery store."

KC's heart lifted. As they turned onto Main Street, the rough mood of the place abrupted shifted. Crystal Valley was actually a small, European-style town built on a hill facing the ski slopes. A quaint boardwalk bordered the winding main street, which was lined with interesting shops and meandered gracefully toward a massive lodge way down at the bottom of the hill.

Holiday banners fluttered in the breeze, and a tiny, split-level central park was decorated with an iron-rail staircase and a large Christmas tree. Jingling horse-drawn sleds passed. KC rolled down her window. The air was chilly, but she detected the far-off smell of bread baking and coffee beans roasting.

"Okay, turn right now onto Sugar Mountain Road," Winnie called out. She pointed down a snowy lane bordered by rail fences leading away from down-town. Even in the now-dimming light, KC could see suntanned vacationers, bundled in parkas and ski bibs, balancing skis on their shoulders as they headed back toward the huge apartment complex that loomed ahead in the distance.

"Here it is," KC said, checking a map in a bro-chure. "The Sugar Mountain Village. Turn right, Faith."

"It's huge," Winnie whispered, gaping as Faith drove into the lot. Four ten-story high rises were arranged in a square formation, with a courtyard in the center and jammed parking lots spreading in every direction.

KC grimaced. "It looks more like a giant Motel 8 than a ski village."

Faith laughed. "You organized this trip, KC. And only you have enough hard-nosed business sense to find lodging this cheap. We're here, aren't we? Who cares where we crash?"

KC opened her door and breathed in the dry, clean air. Almost immediately, her nose and fingers began to tingle with cold.

"Come on, let's get our bags and boogie!" Winnie

yelled, her green-and-yellow zebra-print leggings blazing against the snowy lot. Faith unlocked the ski rack and the back door of the wagon, pulling their nylon duffels and suitcases out.

Meanwhile, KC was jumping out of the car, her boots nearly slipping on the grubby parking-lot ice. She checked a slip in her purse, then looked up at the massive complex. "We're looking for Apartment 1029," KC called out, grabbing her duffel out of the back. "And, of course, we're looking for our friend, the mysterious Victoria Prudence Headly—who has graciously agreed to share our tacky crash pad."

"Who?" Faith called out, sliding her skis and poles off the car-top rack and hoisting them onto her shoulder. Her eyes sparkled as she gazed out at the mountains rising behind the roof of the complex.

"Victoria," KC repeated. She lugged her stuff across the snow with Faith and Winnie. "You know. Our roommate."

Winnie giggled. "Oh, God. I almost forgot. Poor thing, she's going to have to put up with us for a week."

KC sighed. The only way she'd managed to whittle the cost of the vacation to practically nothing was to get a fourth roommate through a college vacation exchange. All she knew about Victoria Prudence Headly was that she was a freshman anthropology major at Cantwell-Jamison, a stuffy, expensive girls school on the East Coast.

"Can't wait to meet Vicky-baby," Winnie cracked, dragging her suitcase up to an antiseptic-looking glass door labeled Units B & C. "She probably brought her study lamp and nose drops with her. I know all about Cantwell-Jamison. They're all tweedy eggheads with their noses to the grindstone."

"So." Faith tugged her satchel higher on her shoulder, looking around the building in confusion. "Why in the world would someone like that come to Crystal Valley all by herself?"

KC tried to focus as she moved inside through the big door. The hallway was clean, but the cinder-block walls and worn beige carpeting made it look about as romantic as a gas station. The fluorescent lighting gave everything a bright bluish cast. KC stared at the apartment numbers on the mile-long hall to their left. "Maybe 1029 is on the first floor," she mumbled. "Then again, it might be on the tenth."

"Who knows?" Winnie babbled on, standing still as if she were waiting for KC's directions. "Maybe Victoria's studying the courtship and mating rituals of American university students in the northern Rocky Mountain region of the North American continent."

KC laughed and temporarily gave up trying to figure out the room numbers. Digging into her parka pocket, she whipped out a lavish color brochure on Crystal Valley. "We, on the other hand, have come to escape. Look at this." She pointed. "Daily après-ski parties at the Crystal Valley Lodge's famous outdoor hot tubs. Nightly dancing—country or disco—in its vast lodge ballroom."

Faith laughed, her skis and poles rattling. "I'll take the tubs."

"And, *come on down, gals*," KC cracked, "because the famous Annual New Year's Eve Masked Ball will carry on as it has every year since 1945 in the lodge's fabulous ballroom."

"*Ahhhhh!*" Winnie screamed, looking confusedly around at the apartment numbers. "We'll go disguised as three electric appliances."

"No, thanks," KC went on. "I'll be in the apartment, taking a nice, long, hot bath." She grabbed her suitcase, her frustration and fatigue beginning to mount. "Okay, where are we?" she cried. "We've been standing here for five minutes, spinning our wheels." She turned around, and her suitcase abruptly turned with her.

"Look out, KC!" she heard Faith yell.

KC felt a jolt and something hard hit her suitcase. She dizzily stopped and stared as her suitcase snapped open, sending everything from ski socks to cosmetic bags to her nightie across the lobby floor. She bent over, feeling rage build up inside her like a smoldering fire that has just been doused with oil.

"I'm really sorry," a deep voice murmured behind her.

KC turned around, took two steps back, and her anger instantly melted. Standing just three feet away from her was the tallest, most beautiful, dark-haired guy she'd ever seen in her life. In his early twenties, he was wearing a tight-fitting, red ski vest with the words *Briar Ski Team* woven in black on the front. A red headband covered his ears, and his rumpled black hair fell over his tanned forehead and icy blue eyes.

"It's . . . okay," KC stammered, her gaze frozen on his gorgeous face

"Would you let me help?" the guy asked, a concerned look contracting his dark eyebrows for a moment. He touched her shoulder lightly, and for the first time in a long time, KC could actually feel her heart beating in her chest. She drew in her breath, unwilling to break the spell. The sensation of his hand still burned into her shoulder. Winnie and Faith suddenly disappeared. The sterile lobby and her broken suitcase vanished. The only thing she was aware of was the outline of his face and the burning, blue stare of his eyes.

KC kneeled down, not even looking at her clothes. "Awfully clumsy . . ." she stammered.

"Please—let me." The guy stooped and stared back into her eyes, as he picked up a few scattered articles of clothing.

"Oh," KC whispered, "you don't have to do that."

The guy stood up and gave her a long, slow smile. KC stood up, too, and took a step back.

"In that case," he murmured, biting the edge of his lip, "I'll let you go—for now."

KC's spirits soared as he turned and headed quickly into the waiting elevator. They would meet again. KC did not have a single doubt.

"Nice," Winnie murmured, staring. "Very nice."

"We're on the wrong side of the building, KC," Faith said. She was sitting on the stairs, staring at a map of the apartment complex. "We're supposed to be in Apartment 1029, but in Building B, also known as

Winterfest. That's directly opposite where we're standing. See? We're in Holiday right now. It's got the same room numbers, but this building has the privately owned condominiums. Faith pointed across a large courtyard opposite the front door.

KC's heart sank. Their apartment was in the opposite building, not where the mysterious, dashing guy was headed. She finished stuffing her things into her suitcase and slowly followed Faith and Winnie across the snowy courtyard. A few minutes later, Faith, Winnie, and KC were stepping out of an industrial-sized elevator into another identical hall.

"Here it is," Faith called out, bumping KC ahead with cheerful abandon. "Apartment 1029. Tenth floor. Maybe we'll be high enough to see the mountains."

They all stopped at once in front of the door, dropping their duffels, skis, and suitcases. From the other side of the door, they could hear loud, throbbing music. Winnie began banging loudly on the door with her fist.

Several moments passed before the door opened and a girl with a cloud of fluffy blond curls and sleepy blue eyes stood before them. KC stared at her skintight fuchsia ski suit and skimpy white T-shirt. "Um . . . are you Victoria?" KC asked.

The girl slid her arm up the doorjamb, absently swirling a drink in her free hand. Then she ran her glance up and down the three friends. "Oh . . . it's you!" she finally said, her face brightening, as if she'd forgotten about having roommates until that very moment. "Call me Tory," she chirped, banging the door back against the wall and lifting her glass in a cheerful toast.

KC followed Faith and Winnie inside. The living room was narrow, with a low ceiling and a gold shag wall-to-wall carpet. A sagging sofa bed and chair faced a picture window, which looked out over the complex's inner courtyard and the opposite apartments. A tiny kitchen adjoined the main room, separated by a counter and two stools. To the left was a door leading to the bedroom.

KC dropped her suitcase and looked back at Tory, unable to take her eyes off the pouty pink lips, three nose rings, and whitish blond hair. Music continued to boom from her compact disc player, and as she closed the door, she immediately began to twirl and swing her hips to the beat, delicately balancing her drink between her thumb and third finger.

"Classic resort tackiness," Winnie yelled over the music, sitting on the bar stool and twirling it.

"It's fine," Faith commented, peering at a framed picture next to the couch of a giant bull elk standing in a snowy mountain field.

"I got here hours ago on this really dink of a plane," Tory shouted over the music, chugging the rest of her drink, then setting the glass down and throwing her head back with abandon. "So I've had plenty of time to check out the men in this little mountain hollow."

KC and Winnie stared while Faith shook her head and headed down the tiny hall to inspect the bedroom. Tory was perfect, KC thought. She, Faith, and Winnie could find out about all the guys in Crystal Valley without actually getting near one.

Winnie laughed, opening the refrigerator door and looking inside. "Gee, Tory. What's the verdict?"

Tory gave KC and Winnie a sultry look that almost made KC laugh out loud. At first, KC thought Tory was kidding. But as she looked closely into Tory's vacant eyes, she realized the girl was no joke. She was the real thing: an authentic airhead ski bunny. "The verdict," Tory breathed with a long wink and a three-glasses-of-wine smile, "is very, very good for us, girls. I've checked out every hunky ski bum within a mile of this place, and they're all looking very good, very available, and very, very bad."

KC winced, dropping into the sagging couch.

"Gee," Winnie snorted, hopping off the bar stool, "that's wonderful, Tory."

"This place looks like it'll do," Faith said with a cheerful grin, emerging from the single bedroom.

Tory planted a hand on her hip and rolled her blue eyes. "Oh, right," she complained. "The phone in this place barely works, the fridge is empty, and the heating system's so bad it's . . . it's like springtime in Iceland in here."

KC giggled. Back at the U of S, she would have immediately detested someone like Tory. But after running into the mysterious guy in the lobby, KC knew nothing could destroy her fizzy mood. And, after all, watching Tory operate in Crystal Valley would be entertainment. Maybe even enough fun to compensate for a week of loud music and hair spray fumes.

KC put her feet up as Tory bounced into the kitchen and began pouring eggnog from a pitcher into a sloppy line of glasses. "Hey, Tory," KC called out. "How about joining us over at the lodge tonight for the après-ski get-together?"

"Oh." Tory returned to the front room with a wobbling tray of drinks. "Save the lodge for the New Year's Eve bash. I'm checking out the local color tonight."

KC took an eggnog from Tory and gulped it. Instantly, she felt a hot streak of bourbon rush down her throat and settle with a burning sensation in her stomach.

"What kind of color are you talking about, Tory?" Faith asked politely before taking a sip herself. The next second, her mouth fell open in shock. She coughed.

Tory closed her eyes and danced backward. "This town goes crazy every winter break. It's legendary!" she said with a bright smile. "Last year, I hear it was wild. A bunch of townies flashed the New Year's Eve ball, then got arrested for snowmobiling drunk through the Crystal Valley Shopping Village. It's nuts!"

"Nuts," Winnie echoed happily from her perch on the end of the couch. She gave Faith and KC a mischievous grin.

"Hey." Tory checked her watch, then grabbed a sleek black jacket. "I'm outta here. The tavern scene awaits. Break a leg!"

"Bye," KC gasped as Tory swept out the door and slammed it. Turning around to face her friends, KC burst into laughter. "Stuffy old Victoria," she cracked as the three of them got up and dumped their spiked eggnogs into the sink. "How will she ever fit into the valley scene?"

"She'll manage," Faith said with a shake of her head, rinsing out her glass.

KC turned and looked out the picture window that faced the complex's inner courtyard. Night had begun to fall and hundreds of tiny apartment windows stared back, little squares of yellow light in the near darkness. Below, she could make out only a few snow-covered benches and scraggly landscaping. In the distance, however, above the roof of the opposite building she could see the dim outline of white mountains. A black sky full of stars blazed above.

"Beautiful," KC whispered. She raised her arms above her head and stretched her muscles, still sore from the ten-hour drive. As she did, a large apartment window directly across from hers suddenly flooded with light. KC narrowed her eyes. Even from this distance, she could see that the place was big and well-furnished, and as she kept staring she saw a dim, indistinct male figure move through the apartment, flicking on lights as he passed through.

KC squinted, then drew in her breath. The figure moved closer to the window. A guy. Tall, wearing ski gear and a headband. He moved toward the lamp in the corner of the room and turned it on. A red ski vest flashed.

It's him, KC thought, her heart thudding in her chest. The guy from the stairwell.

He stepped back away from the light and stared out

his window. KC shuddered. What was he looking at? Was he staring at her? Quickly, instinctively, KC reached over to the lamp next to her and flicked it off and on again. She stood there, holding her breath, then raised her hand slightly—shyly—as the guy continued to look. Then she saw him reach over to his lamp.

Off. On again.

KC's heart rose to her throat. He recognized her! She reached over and flicked her lamp again.

Off. On. Off. On.

A moment later, he responded.

Off. On. Off. On.

KC stood perfectly still at the window, watching his tall figure pause, then turn, as if he was distracted by a phone call or someone at the door. A moment later, he disappeared. KC's shoulders sagged, and she realized she was breathing again. Her limbs lightened and her head suddenly felt as if it could float off into the dark sky. The man in the window. Silent. Strong. Somehow she felt he was watching over her. Waiting for her.

"Faith and Winnie," KC suddenly called out. "I'll take the sofa bed out here."

Faith walked out, frowning. "You sure, KC?"

KC nodded. "Something tells me this is going to be the best spot in the apartment."

Two

*A*few miles away Josh Gaffey was pushing through a crush of bodies jammed up against the bar of Crystal Valley's raucous Iceman Tavern. Antler chandeliers swung. Country music blared from the jukebox. Sunburned waiters balanced pitchers of beer. And before the tavern's huge stone fireplace, several girls in ski sweaters, tight jeans, and furry après-ski boots were dancing wildly.

He finally spotted a corner table next to the dance floor and grabbed it. Then he swung his duffel off his shoulder and sat on the edge of his chair. After ten hours on a Greyhound bus from the U of S campus to Crystal Valley, his nerves were buzzing like hot wires. His muscles were coiled like tight springs.

"What can I get you, darlin'?" a sharp voice intruded.

Josh jumped. He looked up at the pretty blond waitress hovering over him, holding a tray over her head.

"Relax," she yelled over the music, bodies swirling around her. "I'm not going to bite."

He shaded his eyes against the spinning dance-floor lights and tried to think despite the pounding music. "I'll have a Coke."

" 'Kay," she replied with a wink.

"Crystal Valley," he muttered, squirming in the small chair and wishing he'd taken the all-night special bus. That way, he could have strapped on his skis immediately upon arrival.

He slung his leather bomber jacket over the back of his seat, crossed his ankle over his knee, and began bopping it up and down. Bits of melted snow dripped off his shoelaces onto the wood-plank floor.

He checked his watch, drummed his fingers on the table, and scanned the room for his friend, Davis Mattingly, the easygoing amateur surfer he'd met the summer before in Hawaii. Since the summer, Davis had landed a job with Dolphin Enterprises, a snowboard and surfboard manufacturing company. Davis had dropped Josh a few postcards over the months to stay in touch, and one just before Christmas to let him know he'd be in Crystal Valley demonstrating Dolphin's new line of snowboards. At the last minute, Josh decided to join him, and the Iceman Tavern was where they planned to meet.

"Hi, handsome," a pretty girl in a ski sweater called

out from the next table, blowing him a kiss.

Josh coughed and reddened uncomfortably. He looked across at the bar, where a row of broad-shouldered guys were checking out every girl who passed. The Iceman Tavern was definitely a heavy, winter-break pickup scene, not exactly what he had in mind for his ski vacation. What he wanted now was to be alone with his cross-country skis and the high-tech snow tent he'd rented back in Springfield. To be straining his tense muscles against the snow—alone with the mountains, the trees, the cold.

Still, Josh thought, at least he was away from Springfield, where every building, every street, and every familiar face seemed to ring with painful memories.

Winnie.

Josh propped his feet up against the dance floor's rough-hewn log railing and chewed his thumbnail. The spring before, he and Winnie Gottlieb had married in a spur-of-the-moment-type Nevada wedding chapel. Okay, maybe they were only freshmen in college. Maybe they were crazy and wild and too much in love. But they wanted to make a commitment. They thought they knew what they were doing.

Josh made a fist as his thoughts drifted back. After only a few days of marriage, problems—big problems—seemed to explode at every turn. There was the constant lack of money. The accidental pregnancy. Then the motorcycle accident and Winnie's miscarriage. His beautiful, warm, smart Winnie suddenly turned into someone who scared him half to death. She wanted to blame him for everything, and at one horrible point, she accused him of falling in love with their housemate, Fredi.

Josh paid for his Coke and took a long drink. He *had* gotten briefly involved with Fredi after Winnie left. But what Winnie didn't know was that he'd quickly ended the relationship. He was too hurt and cut off to give anything. He'd even been avoiding his buddies Dash and Mikoto. He hadn't told anyone about the divorce papers that arrived in his mailbox just before he left town.

The good thing about Davis, Josh thought with bitterness, is that we barely know each other.

"Josh!" He heard a deep voice behind him, then felt a firm grip on his shoulder. "Hey—man—good to see you."

Josh turned and grinned as Davis hollered for nachos and a Coke, dragging a nearby chair up to the table. A tall, broad-shouldered athlete, Davis had pale-blond hair pulled back into a ponytail, sea-green eyes, and an easygoing smile. Josh lifted his hand and met Davis's firm grasp.

"Thought you'd never get here," Josh said, casting a wry glance back over the wild crowd. "Guess you already figured out where to find your snowboarding customers."

Davis smiled and shrugged, swinging down into the next seat. "Contacts are everything, my friend."

Josh laughed, trying to relax. With his golden skin and sun-bleached hair, Davis looked as if he'd just walked off the beach. Josh rubbed his dark-circled eyes. Davis was a smart guy. His life was as uncomplicated as a sunny day on the slopes. At nineteen, the guy already had held the title of Hawaii's top amateur surfer. And now he had a hot job selling sports equipment. Josh shook his head. While he was burning his brain out developing intricate computer programs and studying for finals, Davis was wandering the Pacific, searching for the perfect wave. While he was agonizing over Winnie, Davis probably had a beautiful, free-spirited surfer girl in every town he hit.

Davis pulled off his down vest and jean jacket. Then he banged his bare elbows onto the plank table in front of him. "How you been, Josh? It's good to see you," he said, his face exuberant, as if he'd just sped down the highest run in Crystal Valley.

"Hi," a girl with a pink headband called over from the next table, winking at Davis. Her two blond tablemates waved, and a second later all three were standing up, performing a tipsy cancan dance.

Davis looked over briefly and casually raised his hand. "Hi," he said in a friendly but distant way. Then he turned back to Josh and shrugged. "It's something in the popcorn they're eating. Makes them go wild."

"Party time," Josh said quickly, forcing a smile. "Finals are over."

"This town must contain the student body populations of at least ten universities right now," Davis remarked. He laced his fingers together and stretched out his arms over his head as if he didn't have a care in the world. "Sorry I'm late. I'm up here with my boss—the Silver Fox himself—Ron Higgenbothem. When he found out I was meeting you here at the

Iceman, he insisted on giving me a big-time lecture on drinking and debauching."

Josh raked his hair back. "You hardly drink at all."

Davis shrugged and rubbed his peeling, sunburned nose. "Ron goes overboard. He's such a debaucher himself, he knows what it's like to wake up with a hangover. And I've got a big snowboarding demonstration tomorrow morning. Let's just say he wants all my faculties intact while I'm flipping through space on one of his six-hundred-dollar boards."

"Makes sense," Josh remarked, noticing the scar under Davis's right eye. In surfing circles, Davis was known as a risk taker but also as a dependable guy who didn't let his big success swell his head out of shape. Still, there was something about his friend tonight that wasn't quite the same.

Davis grabbed his wallet and paid the waitress as she set down the nachos. "Yeah, sure," he said with a cheerful wave of his hand. "But Ron takes the whole thing too seriously. He's probably thinking the whole resort town's going to show up to watch me jump. But the sport's just not there yet. It's still sort of a teen-thrill thing. People turn out to see Olympic-caliber stuff. Downhill. Slalom." He grinned as he lifted his glass in a toast. "To good times."

"To good times," Josh echoed, straining to sound upbeat. He took a sip, then planted his elbows on the table.

"Hey." Davis nudged him. "Don't look so down. My pay's pretty shabby, and it's not the Olympics, but it's getting me through the slow winter months."

Josh looked off. A group of girls leaning against the tavern bar were openly staring at Davis. "Things don't look very slow from where I'm sitting."

Davis glanced back over his shoulder and gave the group a mild smile. But when he looked back at Josh, his face had turned serious. Josh stared as Davis leaned back in his chair and studied the paper-straw wrapper he was flicking between his thumb and index finger. "Yeah—well," Davis said, his face intent.

Josh frowned. Something was definitely going on with Davis, but he wasn't sure what. His eyes had a troubled, cloudy look he couldn't pinpoint. "Something going on with you?"

Davis bit his lip and looked up, his outstretched arm taut. "I don't know, man. Just seeing you seems to bring it all back, Gaffey."

"What?"

A pained looked swept across Davis's face. "You know. Last summer. Back on the islands?"

Josh stared.

"Faith!" Davis burst out. "It's Faith I'm thinking about. Thought about. Will think about. I can't get her out of my mind."

Josh was tongue-tied. Talking about Faith was no good. Talking about her led to talking about Winnie, and . . .

Davis was leaning forward in his seat now, his eyes eager, his mouth a tight line of intensity. "Did you see much of her last fall?"

A wave of panic swept over Josh. Davis looked as if he were a man on a war mission. Josh wanted to help his friend, but the last thing he needed was to talk about old memories. He picked a nacho out of the basket. "Sure, Davis. Sure I did."

Davis scooted his elbows closer and rocked his broad shoulders back and forth a little, his face deadly serious. "Yeah, sure you did, she's your wife's best friend. Is she still beautiful? Is she still—you know—magic?"

"Uh . . . sure she is, Davis," Josh muttered, rubbing the back of his head. In his letters, he'd avoided mentioning his breakup with Winnie.

Davis chewed on his knuckle, and Josh slowly began to realize just how serious his friend was. It was clear Davis had done a lot of thinking about Faith. Maybe he was even looking for commitment. But he was sounding out Josh first. "We wrote for a while, you know. She was directing some big Shakespeare play. Carrying a full load of credits. Hiking in the mountains."

Josh wished he could open a window and breathe a little fresh air. "Yeah—yeah, she's great."

"Her eyes . . ." Davis stammered, covering his face with his hands. "They were so blue. You know, Gaffey, one day I'm going to run into her. It's going to be the right time. The right place. I'll wait for her. Then, I . . . I don't know what I'd do. I'd probably do something crazy and settle down."

Josh bit his lip and rocked back and forth in his chair.

Davis suddenly brightened. "Hey—speaking of Faith. How's Winnie? Taking a break from each other for a few days, huh?"

Josh felt his face fall. For a long time, he said nothing. He prayed for the wacky girls at the next table to come over and distract Davis again so he wouldn't have to talk. Instead of responding, he picked up a large, gooey, cheese-covered nacho and stuffed it in his mouth. He rubbed his hands together and looked up at the ceiling. But a moment later, he felt Davis's hand on his arm. "What's going on, Josh?"

Something inside Josh tightened up. "Look, Davis. We . . . we split up a few months back."

Davis's green eyes clouded. He didn't seem to believe what Josh was saying. "What? But you seemed so happy last sum—"

"It didn't work out," Josh said abruptly, looking down at the single kernel of popcorn he was picking apart with his two thumbnails. "She had a miscarriage . . ."

"No—that's awful, man." Davis gripped Josh's shoulder.

Josh felt his throat tighten. He couldn't talk about this. He couldn't even think about it. Why did it even have to come up? "She was never the same after that," he mumbled. "One day she left—all crazy. She had no idea how much I . . ."

Davis was silent.

Josh felt a wild, cracked laugh emerge from his throat. "The funny thing is that I did end up briefly with Fredi—but it didn't last. So there's no Fredi. No Winnie. Just a pile of divorce papers."

Davis sipped his beer, oblivious to the wild cheering that had erupted around a girl with fluffy blond hair, dancing to a rap tune while balancing a full glass of beer on her head. Josh cringed. The girl was staring directly at their table.

"Too bad, Josh," Davis sympathized, shaking his head. "I liked Winnie a lot. And I mean that. What are you going to do?"

Josh opened his mouth to say something, then shut it and sipped his Coke, turning away from the dance floor and the staring blonde. What was he supposed to say? He didn't know what he was going to do. That's why he had come all the way up to Crystal Valley. So he could check out for a while. Ski. Think. Forget.

Davis sighed and raked his hair back with one hand. Scanning the crowded room, he suddenly stopped and gazed, his eyebrows arched. "Hey, Gaffey. Someone's trying to say hello."

Josh sucked in his breath as Davis turned around in his chair and looked at the slender blond girl who'd apparently just won the beer-balancing contest. Josh finally looked, too. Wearing fuchsia ski bibs over a minuscule T-shirt, she was now performing a wobbly hip-bump routine with two guys wearing University of Colorado sweatshirts. She waved at Josh and Davis again, and it was clear that she was unattached. Josh's heart sank.

"Davis," Josh warned, tensing.

"Come on," Davis said with a cheerful wink. "She's been staring at you for the last five minutes."

"She's been staring at you, studly," Josh said. He watched as the girl pushed her two dance partners away and hooked into his gaze. Her hands went up to her hips, her eyes narrowed seductively, and her little cowboy boots headed straight for their table. A moment later, her two slender elbows were perched on the dance floor railing. She smiled at Josh, then at Davis.

"Hi!" the girl squeaked, still moving to the music. She ran her eyes swiftly up and down Josh's body, then Davis's.

"Would you like to sit down?" Davis asked politely.

Josh nearly choked. He watched as the girl's blue eyes widened and glittered. Then, in one motion, she pushed herself away from the railing and scampered off the dance floor. A moment later, Josh could see her approaching. Her narrow hips swayed. She wet her lips, then stopped in front of them while Davis pulled a chair out for her.

An intense cloud of perfume wafted over Josh as she draped herself in the chair, arching her back seductively. First she looked at Davis, then at Josh.

"My name is Victoria Prudence Headly," she announced, trying to keep a straight face. But she immediately broke down into giggles. "Can you believe my parents gave me that name? I hate them."

"No," Davis said in wonder.

Josh squirmed. Why did Davis invite her to the table anyway? What they needed to do now was leave. But Davis seemed to want to drown in sorrow by playing with this crazy girl.

"Actually," the girl went on, staring down at her pink nails, "my friends call me Tory."

"Hi, Tory," Davis said with a good-natured grin. "You doing okay?"

"Yeah," she chirped. "Thirsty."

Davis motioned to the waitress.

Tory crossed her legs and let her eyes smolder at Davis. "So. What do you two good-looking bums call yourselves?"

Davis laughed. "Don't look at me, Tory," he teased, rocking in his chair, jerking his head in Josh's direction.

"Oh, but I am," Tory came back quickly, drawing one leg up and clasping her arms around her slim thigh. She nestled her cheek on her knee and winked. "I am looking."

Josh felt sick. He wanted to crawl under the table, he was so embarrassed for the girl. But Davis seemed to be taking it in stride. The waitress stopped in front of the table.

"Two drafts," Tory shouted, laughing and bending sideways until she almost fell off her chair. Josh shook his head. He didn't particularly care for girls who drank, and she looked like she drank plenty.

Davis pointed at Josh. "I'm Davis, but check this great guy out, Tory. His name is Josh Gaffey. He's the one you want to get to know. Sincere guy. And he's had a few disappointments. He needs cheering up, right, Josh?"

Josh cringed as Tory shifted in her seat. Her look of surprise changed quickly. And as her mascara-framed eyes softened, she leaned closer and walked two fingers slowly up Josh's arm. Goose bumps flared uncomfortably on his neck.

"Really?" she cooed. "Is something wrong?"

Josh cleared his throat and managed a short laugh. "No . . . uh . . . actually, my friend Davis here uses that line all the time. You know, to meet . . . uh . . . girls. It's his indirect way of saying that he's interested."

"Not." Davis exploded with a huge laugh, suddenly moving his shoulders to the beat of a new country tune on the jukebox. It was clear he enjoyed this flirtation with Tory.

Tory sighed sweetly and leaned closer to Josh. He took in the tininess of her nose and shiny mouth—the precise way her blue eyes had been lined and fringed with black.

"I don't know, Josh." Tory giggled. "I don't think you're being straight with me."

Josh sat awkwardly in his seat, trying to reach for his Coke over Tory's leg. He wished he knew how to tell Tory to go away. But he was never very good at situations like this.

"Come on, Josh," Davis said with a cheerful grin. "It's hang time. Relax."

Tory looked coy. "Wanna dance? Come on, Josh. I need to loosen up. You should see the three roommates I got stuck with for winter-break week." She rolled her eyes and hung her head back with drama. "Three of the dullest girls I can imagine. I can just see them now back at the apartment. They're probably setting their hair and drinking hot cocoa in their grandma's flannel nighties, giggling over a game of Monopoly."

The waitress stopped at their table and set two beers in front of Tory, which she showed no sign of paying for. Davis pulled out a five-dollar bill and placed it on the table. Meanwhile, Tory had already chugged one beer. She turned the glass upside down, guzzling the last few drops. Then she banged it back down on the table. The waitress gave her a skeptical look, handed Davis his change, then slipped a printed flyer on the table.

"Just a little free advertising for our friends down at the lodge," the waitress explained with a smile. "Big New Year's Eve dance in the ballroom, kids. You'll have a lot of fun."

"Hey," Davis spoke up, reading the flyer. He flicked it across the table at Josh, then rubbed his hands together. "I've heard about this. It's a masked ball. Everyone goes bananas."

Tory suddenly sat up in her chair and began bouncing up and down, making little squealing noises. "I love costumes! Oh, Josh. You could go as the Lone Ranger," she shrieked, grabbing Josh's head with both hands and smoothing down the sides of his hair. "You've got the perfect face for it!"

Davis laughed heartily. "Then it's all settled. You and Tory meet at the New Year's Eve masked ball. It's a date."

Josh cringed.

Tory whooped, pressing her slim body into Josh's side and nuzzling his neck with her smooth cheek. He breathed in the perfumed smell of her hair. Her sharp little nails scratched his forearm. Every nerve in Josh's body went on red-hot alert.

Davis nudged Josh a little. "Come on, man. I'll be

there, too. No big deal. Let's just have some fun while we're here."

Josh tried to force a smile but ended up slumping back in his chair, staring at the mass of writhing bodies dancing, drinking, flirting, and shouting.

What am I doing here? Why Crystal Valley? I should have picked a monastery or a solitary motorcycling trip through the desert. Crystal Valley is all wrong. It's the last place in the world I need to be right now.

Three
....

The next morning Crystal Valley lay under a fresh blanket of powder. The sky was a blazing sapphire blue, and the warm sun was already making the eaves of the big apartment buildings drip with melting snow.

Winnie was the first one out the door. Leaving the others to gather their gear, she rushed to the elevator, rode down to the lobby, and burst out of the building with a whoop. She gulped the cold, fresh air and gazed up in every direction at the jagged gray mountaintops of the Sugar Mountain range.

"Snow," she whispered, grinning at the buried cars. "At least six inches of new powder."

A few early-morning cross-country skiers whisked

through a distant, wooded path. She could hear the far-away sound of someone scraping ice off a windshield. A car struggled to start in the cold, but the sounds were muffled by the deep snow. Nothing could disturb the beauty of the morning. For the first time in ages, Winnie felt her heart opening up and the light pouring in.

I'm never going to let myself be unhappy again, Winnie vowed to herself in silence.

She bent over and scooped up a handful of snow, making a tight ball with her hot-pink ski gloves. Soon, Faith, KC, and Tory emerged through the glass doors, and she threw the snowball, hitting Faith's shoulder.

"Fight!" Faith shouted, grinning and dropping her skis on the ground. She dove for the snow, packing an expert snowball. KC followed, jumping on Winnie and planting a loose wad of snow on her head. Winnie giggled, feeling the light powder melting and dripping down her scalp.

Winnie pushed up her sunglasses and felt a solid kind of happiness wrapping around her. Being in Crystal Valley with her two best friends was like a dream come true. She was starting her life all over again, and this time she was going to do things differently.

Number one: I'm going to think before I act. Number two: I'm not going to lose my sense of humor. Number three: I'm never letting go of my oldest and best friends.

"Come on," KC was yelling, gesturing toward a path at the side of the complex. Her skin glowed from the fresh air and her dark curls tumbled down her bright-red ski jacket. "There's a walking and ski trail this way. It's already been plowed, and it leads to the lodge. Isn't that right next to the place where we're renting our skis?"

Winnie nodded, galloping ahead. She looked over her shoulder. Faith and Tory had brought their own skis, which they were stepping into. Faith took off with a hearty push while pale-faced Tory struggled to keep up. Winnie shook her head. Tory had crashed into the apartment at three A.M. the night before. But just a half hour ago, after she, Faith, and KC had bolted their breakfast, Tory sprang out of bed in a snarly mood, insisting that everyone wait for her.

Still, Winnie thought cheerfully, chasing Faith as she passed on her skis, even bubblehead Tory was incapable of spoiling her good mood. She promised herself not to think about anything serious for the entire week. Josh. Divorce. Her future. She would take a vacation from it all.

The Sugar Mountain Village Trail followed a tiny, buried creek past the Valley Stables, a frozen pond, and several luxury ski homes nestled in the bare aspen groves. At the end of the trail, Winnie stopped and waited for the others. "Wow. We're here already," she called over her shoulder, pointing to a group of quaint wooden signs located at the junction of three snowy pathways.

To the left, one trail led down a gentle slope to the historic Crystal Valley Lodge, a solid, five-story wood structure positioned just to the east of the main chair-lifts. From where she was standing, Winnie spotted a few skiers heading out over the fresh snow, and more clamping on their skis in front of the lodge's huge deck. Straight ahead, a trail led to the Crystal Valley lift lines. Early-bird skiers were already bunched up at the bottom, waiting for the chair to take them up over the ridge line. Distant grooming machines slid up and down the new powder, making the low beginner slopes look like beautifully raked, white lawns.

"Look!" Faith called, stopping and pointing a pole to the right. "Here's the sign for Main Street, just up the hill. That's where the ski rental shop is." She grinned at Winnie and KC, her cheeks rosy from the cold and her blond braid swishing over her shoulder. "Everything's so close to the lodge and the lifts. It's perfect, KC. Just perfect."

"Close?" Tory grumbled, pushing forward with her poles and coming to a stop. Her fuchsia jacket and ski bib glared against the snow. "This is close? It's a quarter-mile away—minimum."

KC and Winnie ignored Tory, shaded their eyes from the sun, and looked up at the impressive network of ski runs slicing through the stands of trees on the mountainside. "Do you remember all those great times we had taking ski lessons up at Jacksonville Ridge Resort?" KC said with a laugh.

Winnie laughed, slinging her arm around KC's shoulders and taking in the mountain view as another group of skiers whizzed by. "The back-home, bargain basement of the ski scene. One chair and two rope lifts. If you don't like it, you can shove it."

KC giggled. "Hey, it was cheap."

"Your broken leg wasn't cheap," Faith piped in with a laugh. "It took four cute ski-patrol guys to get you off that trail."

"Oh, sure," KC replied, winking sideways at Winnie. "I remember those guys sooooo well." She hugged Winnie back. "But this trip is not going to be a repeat of that season. We're in Crystal Valley, girls. One of the hottest college party towns in the world."

Faith laughed. "Oh—so hot, KC."

"We're going to ski perfect powder. We're going to party. And I'm going to have a second rendezvous with the most beautiful man I've ever seen in my life."

Winnie bit the side of her tongue. "The Snow-Tan King. First he knocks your suitcase open. Then he gets away without even helping. Wait a minute. Last night, you were vowing not to even look at a guy this week."

KC gave Winnie a playful bump. "You saw him. And so you know why I've got to find him. And I will, Winnie. You know me. I can do anything I put my mind to."

Winnie nudged her back, then stopped. She fingered the tube of Chap Stick in her pocket and gave KC a curious look. KC could be a dangerously single-minded person when she wanted something. But how could KC possibly know she wanted him? She'd only seen the guy for a moment the day before in the lobby.

"Well, bye," Faith was saying. She was standing next to Tory where the paths separated, giving Winnie and KC a tortured look. Since Faith and Tory already had their own ski equipment, it made sense for them to head for the lifts. Winnie and KC still had to rent their equipment. But it was clear Faith didn't relish being stuck with Tory.

"Hey," Tory squealed.

The three friends stared in wonder at Tory jutting a hip out and pretending to hitchhike as a group of guys on snowmobiles passed, heading for the lodge.

"This won't take long, Faith," Winnie reassured her. "We promise to meet you for hot chocolate at the ski hut."

"It's at the top of chair number four," Faith reminded Winnie and KC. She checked her woolen headband and slipped her pole straps around her wrists. Tory, meanwhile, was smearing her lips with another coat of pink gloss. "Meet you there at eleven sharp, okay?"

"Okay," KC and Winnie shouted back, tramping up the trail until it converged with the bottom of Main Street, crowded with skiwear shops, restaurants, and art galleries. Winnie liked the cozy feeling of the town, with its swinging wooden signs and old-fashioned lampposts. The sun sparkled off the steep, snow-laden tops of the buildings that angled down the side of the hill.

The McGlofflin Ski Chalet was located right at the end of the trail on Main Street, a charming wooden chalet with hand-carved shutters, paned windows, and a heavy wooden door painted bright red.

"Cute," Winnie chirped. "I feel like I'm in the Alps."

KC nodded, her face glowing and rosy. Together, they stomped the snow off their feet on the metal porch-grate and opened the door. Winnie led the way, letting the smell of leather, oil, and old wood waft over her. Then she stopped and looked around the small shop. Shiny skis were stacked against the walls, new ski boots were lined up inside charming armoires, and old-fashioned wood-and-glass cases displayed high-tech sunglasses, watches, and ski gloves. To the right, through a crowd, Winnie spotted a long counter with a sign that read Rentals Here.

"Long line," KC whispered behind her as they took their places.

Winnie laughed, accidentally bumping two guys leaving with their equipment. "It's a law of nature, KC. You eat Christmas turkey with your parents, then you split for winter break. Everyone in the universe carrying more than twelve college credits arrived last night in Crystal Valley."

KC nodded, inching forward in the crowd past a rack of ski wax, bronzers, and sunglasses. "Well, we're sure not going to make our rendezvous with Faith and Tory in time."

Winnie jogged in place and smiled. "They'll be okay. Faith is such a good skier. She'll lose Tory the first five minutes."

KC sputtered with laughter, tickling her in the side. Winnie glanced carefully over at her glowing face and shiny dark curls. Just yesterday, she had to practically shovel KC into Faith's car for the trip to Crystal Valley. Between exams and Christmas, KC appeared to be ir-retrievably burned out. But now, Winnie noticed with a start, her friend's gray eyes were actually sparkling.

"Poor Faith," KC whispered into Winnie's ear, giggling. "Stuck with Tory. A true, reality-impaired airhead."

"Nah," Winnie came back. "She'll work out. Barrel of fun."

KC's mouth dropped as the line inched forward. "Since we arrived here fifteen hours ago, she's been either drunk, out chasing guys, or complaining about her hangover."

"Right. We know nothing of these sins."

"Okay, Miss Psychology Major."

Winnie giggled. "That's right. Give me a little respect." She picked up an imported leather cross-country ski boot and examined it. "Look, KC," she argued, "in high school, I practically majored in chasing guys. In college, I spent my first few weeks drinking too much and getting terrible hangovers."

KC reached over and tousled Winnie's hair. "Oh, yeah, I almost forgot."

"I've made too many bad impressions of my own to start in on Tory."

"Okay, you're right." KC instantly brightened, pausing to peer out of one of the chalet's windows. Winnie watched as KC glanced up and down Main Street. "I've had my moments, too. Inebriated and otherwise."

Something suddenly clutched Winnie's throat. It was at unexpected times like this that she remembered slipping the manila envelope into the mailbox. The envelope with the divorce papers in it, addressed to Josh Gaffey.

In the distance, Winnie heard the cash register

beeping and the sound of skis slapping against the floorboards.

KC leaned into Winnie's ear, as if she knew right away what she'd been thinking. "You know how much I've always liked Josh. But it could be you two weren't ready for each other—for marriage."

"Maybe so," Winnie said calmly. "The important thing is that I've accepted it. And I'm looking ahead."

Winnie looked up with a small tear in her eye. But suddenly KC wasn't there. Winnie stood on tiptoe in the crowd and finally spotted her friend climbing over the Austrian ski-sweater display next to the window, trying to look out. KC turned around, agitated. She called out over the crowd. "That was him!"

Winnie frowned and waved at her to come back. The rental line was moving fast now. In fact, they were only a few customers away from the counter. "That was who?"

KC looked back with wild eyes. "The guy," she had to practically yell. "The guy I bumped into. Mr. Wonderful."

"Mr. East-Coast Preppie Tan?"

"Yes," KC whispered loudly, looking back through the window. "There he goes toward the lodge."

Winnie opened her eyes wide with alarm. "Get back in line, KC."

"No, I'm going."

"No, you're not."

"Yes."

Winnie grabbed the back of KC's red jacket just as she was bolting. "You're crazy."

"Let go." KC's eyes were on fire.

"You can't chase him on foot. You need skis anyway."

Winnie looked back over her shoulder at the cash register. "KC. We're next. It's almost our turn."

KC remained in line, temporarily subdued, but was bouncing on the balls of her feet. "He must be headed for the lift lines. If only I knew which chair . . ."

Winnie tried to look into KC's eyes. What was going on? Did she actually know this guy from somewhere else? Why was she flipping out over him like some kind of sixth grader?

But KC turned and raced back for another look through the window. She let out a suppressed squeal and hurried back, her hand over her mouth and her eyes sparkling with excitement. "He is headed for the lifts. I saw him. I need those skis, Winnie."

Winnie tugged at KC's jacket. They'd finally reached the front of the line at the counter, where a tall, copper-haired guy was waiting patiently, his two hands flat on the glass.

"We have to go," KC hissed into Winnie's ear, pulling her away.

"KC—*control yourself*," Winnie heard herself snap back. She looked up and saw that the guy behind the counter could hear everything. Her heart sank. His eyes were twinkling with a wry mixture of humor and contempt. It was exactly the kind of look that always drove KC Angeletti wild.

"That's right," the guy spoke up, grinning from ear to ear. "Control yourself. I can't help you unless you're under control."

Here it comes, Winnie thought desperately. Here it comes.

KC placed her hands on the counter and faced him, her eyes blazing with anger. "What did you just say to me?"

Winnie cringed, expecting the worst.

"Okay. Let's start over," the guy said, his tone brisk. His eyes sparkled at KC. "How may I help you?"

Winnie watched with embarrassment as KC's mouth dropped open. "We want to rent ski equipment," she suddenly barked. "We're in a big hurry."

"KC . . ." Winnie warned, nudging her, then looking up at the guy. "Look," she tried to apologize, "she just can't wait to hit the powder."

But Winnie could tell her words had no effect. The guy didn't even look at her. He was too busy glaring back at KC, his blue eyes burning, ready to fight. Winnie sighed as the guy crossed his arms across his chest and rocked back on his heels a little, as if he suddenly had all the time in the world. She'd seen it all before: KC's impatience and the crazy way it made people react.

"A little impatient, isn't she?" the guy came back with a half-smile.

Winnie's heart sank.

His face dropped suddenly into a look of mock-concern, and he held out his hand for KC over the counter. "My name is Sean McGlofflin, nice to meet you. Now. Going skiing today?"

Winnie could see KC's jaw tense. "Yes," KC replied between clenched teeth. "And-I'm-in-a-hurry."

Sean's eyes grew round with feigned surprise. "You are?" Planting both hands against his side of the counter, he flexed his muscular forearms.

Winnie nudged her head in his direction, as if to break the line of angry connection between the two. "We'll need the works. Downhill skis, poles, and boots."

But Sean didn't unglue his eyes from KC's infuriated face. He swung open the waist-high door that led behind the counter. "Please come this way."

KC marched ahead to the fitting area in the chalet's back room. Winnie's eyes adjusted to the dim light while Sean ambled down a long row of skis piled between wooden slats. A wooden workbench hung with tools and rags stood against a window. Neat rows of ski boots were arranged against the walls.

"Beginner, intermediate, or advanced?" Sean asked, crossing his arms over his chest and staring at KC.

"What difference does it make?" KC snapped, straining to see through the window. "Advanced."

Sean smiled. "If you were advanced, you would know that we need this information when we're adjusting the tension in your binding."

KC narrowed her eyebrows. Winnie felt the air crackling.

"We have a large selection of demos," he said politely, stopping and setting one hand up on the ski rack.

"Just give us the top of the line," KC snapped, "and get us out of here."

Winnie gasped. Had KC gone insane? This guy was perfectly nice. Did she still think she had time to hook up with Mr. Dreamboat out there? He was probably already on the chairlift.

Sean draped his body a little over the ski rack. Then he swiftly pulled a set of skis out and stood them next to KC. "Try these today. You'll like them in the powder."

"I'll take them," Winnie said, anxious to avoid a war. "We're about the same height."

"And try these size eights," Sean said calmly, almost ignoring Winnie as he set the boots down in front of KC.

KC thumped down and yanked off her après-ski boots. "How did you know I was an eight?"

Sean shrugged and stroked his freckled chin, smiling steadily at KC. "Most women your height are."

"Well, I am not like most women," KC shot back.

"True," Sean blazed. "Most of the women who come in here have manners."

Quickly, Winnie grabbed a pair of skis and size-seven boots off the wall. "I'll need these for about a week," she said quietly as Sean swiftly adjusted her bindings, glaring at KC every few seconds.

He grabbed a pair of correctly sized poles and handed them to Winnie. "The rate is fifteen dollars a day. And we recommend paying the twenty-dollar insurance fee."

"Don't pay it, Win," KC snarled as Winnie quickly drew out her cash and handed it to Sean. "Those insurance charges are a scam."

"KC," Winnie said with an urgent look. "Come on."

"I'll take the same thing," KC said, dashing past Sean and taking a pair of top-of-the-line skis, poles, and size-eight boots. Reaching into her parka pocket, she pulled out a wad of cash and threw it down on the fitting chair. "Here. I'll adjust them myself. And you can forget about your damn rip-off insurance charge."

With that, KC flounced through the swinging door and rushed outside. Winnie hurried close behind until she caught up with KC out on the snowy road, jamming her boots into the bindings. Tears streamed down her cheeks.

"KC!" Winnie shouted.

"He's gone!" KC cried.

"What?"

"I thought I could catch up with him," KC sobbed. "But he's disappeared, Win."

Winnie just stood there, staring as KC shoved off down the ski path toward the lift lines.

She's finally done it, Winnie observed with a shake of her head. Miss Perfect, Studious, In-Control KC Angeletti has finally outcrazed me. For once in my life, I can say I remained on earth while KC spun out of control, directly toward outer space.

Four
....

Bend knees, shift weight, plant pole, lift up, and turn. Faith felt the old rhythm kicking in again. She stopped and grinned, looking back over her shoulder for a glimpse of Winnie and KC hiking up toward the rental shop. Then she turned and took in the beauty of Sugar Mountain—the snow-dusted peak just above the top of the chairlift. The sky was cobalt against the glittering firs on the ridges above the slopes. The air smelled of clean snow, wet wool, and coconut oil.

"Look out," Tory shouted, whizzing by her on the trail as it fanned out into a wider bowl, ending where the busy lift lines began. A vision in tight, bright pink, Tory's mass of white-blond hair blew over her black headband as she flew down the slope. Faith watched her swift, slightly out-of-control parallels. It was amazing, Faith thought, that Tory could actually stand up, let alone ski. Tory had had less than four hours' sleep, and it was clear she'd been drinking heavily—wherever she'd been the night before.

Faith pushed ahead, catching up with her at the end of the line for the number-four chairlift. By this time, skiers were zooming in from every direction for their first run of the day. She could feel the excitement in the air over the new powder. Laughter rang out. Bindings popped. Skis scraped. Sunglasses glinted. The chairs clanked as they rattled around the bottom of the lift's engine room.

"Over here, Faith!" Tory screeched, clambering sideways up an embankment to the line. She yanked up the liftline's cording and ducked underneath. Then, stepping heavily all over the skis of two women in Norwegian sweaters, she maneuvered into place. Faith ignored Tory's shortcut and slipped in where a sign said Entrance.

When she finally reached Tory, she had already clamped a pair of headphones on and was busily bopping to a faraway song. Catching Faith's eye, she turned and slipped them off. Then she snapped her gum and blew a large bubble in Faith's direction.

"You should have come with me last night," Tory said with a mischievous wink.

Faith leaned on her poles and stared, in awe of Tory's amazing energy level. "Where did you go?"

Tory clomped forward on her skis and giggled. "The Iceman Tavern. Where else?"

Faith just stood there nodding and staring at her reflection in Tory's mirrored sunglasses. She had no idea what Tory was talking about.

"I met two of the cutest guys you've ever seen." Tory gripped her poles and dug them into the snow for emphasis. "Unbelievably good-looking. One dude was this pro skier. Blond. Built. Buns. The works. He was smart, too. . . . I think."

"Gee," Faith said gently, turning with the line. The crowd pressed forward toward the loading zone.

"I'm going to the big New Year's Eve ball with the other guy," Tory said matter-of-factly. "He was even cuter."

Faith cleared her throat. "Let me get this straight, Tory. You arrived in town only a few hours before we did. But you already have a date?"

"Uh-huh." Tory pulled out a tube of sunblock lipstick and applied it carefully to her small mouth. "This other guy—I wish I could remember his name—he was kinda shy, with this long, lanky bod and these totally deep green eyes—"

"The date was for what?" Faith interrupted.

Tory look stunned. "The New Year's Eve bash at Crystal Valley Lodge. You know. The big masked ball."

Faith nodded, moving forward between the lift line's yellow cording. Some of the skiers were pulling thermoses out of their packs and pouring steamy cups of hot chocolate. Others were checking their bindings, applying sunblock, or laughing at the wisecracking lift operator up ahead.

"Oh, yeah," Faith replied. "The ball. We read

about that in the brochure. I guess the costumes get really wild."

"Yeah."

Faith paused, then looked over. "You have a date with him, but you don't even remember his name?"

Tory jabbed Faith in the side. "I'll never forget that face. And I'll certainly never forget the bod. I'll recognize him okay."

Faith stared in amazement. Tory looked and acted like an airhead, but at least she knew what she wanted. And she seemed to have success.

"Get going, cowboy," Tory began teasing, stabbing her pole playfully in the direction of a blond guy wearing a black jacket and a two-day stubble.

Faith observed carefully. Tory had absolutely no grown-up social skills. Yet it didn't seem to bother the cute blond guy at all. In fact, he was happily poking her back, obviously enjoying Tory's happy spontaneity. Faith pursed her lips and pondered her own situation. Were she, Winnie, and KC just getting too serious about life? Was that why they always had so much trouble with men?

Faith continued to stare as Tory slipped a small, shiny flask out of her pocket. Her head jerked back as she took a quick swig, screwed the top back on, and put it away. Tory gave Faith a bold grin. "Just a little wake-up call, Faith. Don't look so shocked."

"I didn't say anything."

Tory tossed her head and fixed her gaze on the two red-vested ski-patrol guys who were skirting the line, headed for the chair. "Ah, you ski-patrol boys," she shouted, reaching out to pat one of them on the butt as he passed. "Must be nice not to have to wait for a chair like the rest of us unimportant folk."

"Tory . . ." Faith started to protest, trying not to look at the stares Tory was attracting.

Tory staggered back a little on her skis, obviously feeling the effect of whatever she'd just drunk. "Look, I'm dying of dullness waiting for the stupid chair. Plenty of other resorts have quad lifts that go a lot faster."

"Hi to you, too, handsome!" Tory yelled at a guy near the back of the line who was winking at her as he scooped some snow up in his glove.

Faith clomped closer to Tory, her curiosity building. They stopped, and Faith used her pole to toy with the snow on her skis. Suddenly, she had a million questions. For instance, how exactly did Tory meet the two guys at the Iceman? Did she just walk right up to them? Or did they come to her? Did they ask her to dance? Faith was beginning to realize how serious she'd become at the U of S, where studying, deadlines, and pressure had become a way of life. Had she actually forgotten how to have fun?

"Aaahhhhhhhhh!" Tory's sudden shriek interrupted her thoughts.

"What?" Faith cried out, looking around at the other skiers, also startled by Tory's shriek.

Tory was jumping up and down on her skis, waving one pole in the air. *"Hi!"* she yelled over the crowd, bursting into laughter, practically knocking Faith over with her elbow jab. "It's them. I can't believe it. Just as I'm talking about them, they show up . . ." Tory kept turning around, following the path of the two moving skiers. "See, Faith? See?"

Faith laughed, too, as she twisted at the waist, straining to look.

"There," Tory cried out. "The guy in the jeans and red jacket. He's with Mr. Blond ponytail in orange."

Faith's heart sped up. She was actually quite curious to see whom Tory had picked up while she, Winnie, and KC had been sound asleep back in their quiet apartment. She twisted in the other direction, following Tory's pointed finger. But just as she did, a blinding white flash of cold hit her square in the face.

"Ouch!" Faith gasped.

"Hey," Tory shouted happily over the crowd to the guy at the back of the line. "Hey, you little flirt, you. You got lousy aim there."

Faith's eyes were burning from the impact of the freezing cold snowball. She pressed her gloved hands against her closed lids, on the verge of tears.

"Step up, please," the chairlift operator was calling out when Faith opened her eyes. She and Tory hurried forward and stood in the path of the approaching chair. Her eyes still burning, Faith slipped her poles into one hand and held out the other to grab the chair coming around behind her.

"At last," Tory said with impatience as the chair swung up into the air.

Faith felt her shoulders relax as she sank back into the chair and took in the view as the lift took them higher. She was sorry she'd missed her view of Tory's two hunky guys. But now she was happy just to stare at the beautiful scene. Everything was white, soft, and quiet as the chair sped them past snow-laden trees and granite rock formations. Though the slopes to the left of the chair were busy, the fresh snow muffled the sounds of the occasional whoop and laugh. As they reached the top, Faith spotted the ski hut, located on the summit, just to the right of the lift. It was surrounded by a huge deck, where hundreds of skiers already were gathered in the morning sun sipping coffee and hot chocolate.

"Let's boogie," Tory shrieked as the chair reached the unloading area and the two slid off a ramp to the left.

"We've got to wait for KC and Win," Faith reminded her.

"They can catch up with us," Tory yelled over her shoulder, shoving off. "We'll go slow."

"Yeah, right," Faith muttered with a patient smile. She strapped her poles on as she skied ahead, then slipped her goggles over her eyes. Pausing at the top of the bowl, she watched Tory shift from a series of knifelike parallels to an out-of-control schuss that nearly sent her careening into the woods. Grinning, Faith pushed off, too, her heart beginning to beat with excitement.

She picked up speed and felt the cold air blow through her hair. Way below, she could see the lodge nestled in the fir and aspen groves. Just behind it was winding Main Street, smoke rising in spindly columns from its scattered chimneys. She breathed in the sharp smell of fir and ice, then focused on her first turn. She bent her knees, planted her pole, and shifted her weight. Her rhythm began to kick in as if she hadn't spent a day off the slopes. It was like flying again. The crisp air flew against her face. The packed snow hissed against the edges of her skis.

Tory and her guys, wondered Faith as she flew past a line of skiers waiting for their lesson and an older man in knickers who was gracefully skiing a mogul-filled stretch of the bowl. Maybe she's making the whole thing up. A row of tiny kids sped past her, one by one taking a small jump that had been formed at the edge of the run.

Pausing, Faith scanned the area for Tory. She spotted her several hundred yards away, taking another swig out of her flask.

"She could be making it up," Faith whispered out loud, "just to impress me." She watched as Tory appeared to finish off whatever was in the flask. Then she smiled and shook her head. "Anyone who needs to drink like that couldn't feel too good about herself."

Tory took off again, zooming recklessly down the bottom of the bowl like a streak of pink, ignoring the other skiers. Some of the beginners crashed in her path. Other shook their fists at her in anger.

"You're going to kill yourself, Tory," Faith whispered to herself, planting her poles and pushing off, determined to catch her and slow her down. Faith zoomed ahead over a long series of moguls, her knees bobbing and her breath coming quickly. Sweat began to trickle down her back, and her ears went numb with cold. But it didn't seem to matter. Several guys pausing at the edge of the run whistled, and Faith smiled quietly to herself. But as she cast her eyes down the busy slope, she finally caught sight of Tory, sprawled on her back in the middle of the run, laughing hysterically to herself.

"What happened?" Faith called out, sliding to a stop next to Tory.

"I saw him," Tory cried out, before collapsing into hysterics. "I saw my New Year's Eve date—and I got so turned on I wiped out—right into this really bitchy woman."

Faith stared in amazement.

"Look!" Tory yelled with delight, getting up and pointing to moguls just under the chairlift. "There he is again."

Faith turned and squinted through her goggles. The sun fell brightly on the clumpy powder at the edge of the run, where a lone figure stood. Faith felt her breath quicken. The guy was leaning casually against one pole, watching a freestyle snowboarder take a small jump located in an unpopulated stretch of powder. She stared at the familiar wool sweater worn over jeans and gaiters. The long neck. The dark-brown bangs that slipped back off his face with a casual toss of the head.

"Oh, my God," Faith whispered.

"Oh, yes sirree." Tory giggled. "Does he have cute buns or what?"

"It's Josh Gaffey," Faith cried softly, just as he waved to a snowboarder below and took off, not seeing her.

"Now I remember his name," Tory drawled absently, taking another sip from her flask and digging her elbow into the snow. "His name is Josh Gaffey."

Josh Gaffey. Faith's thoughts began to spin wildly. She whipped off her ski glove and pressed a cool hand to her forehead. Josh Gaffey here in Crystal Valley? What is he doing here?

"Don't look so jealous, Faith," Tory cried out, suddenly giggling wildly. "I mean, I know the guy's a stunner."

Winnie? Does Winnie know?

". . . but you'll find something warm to lean up against New Year's Eve," Tory babbled on, falling back into the snow, laughing hysterically. "Actually, you're pretty good-looking, Faith. Just get rid—of—those—dumb blue jeans," Tory jabbered, still giggling, "and you'll do fine."

"Josh Gaffey is your date for New Year's Eve?" Faith asked, her voice quiet and stern, staring down at Tory, still lying in the snow.

Tory giggled and huffed. "Yes. I met him at the tavern last night. How many times do I have to tell you?"

Faith could barely move. Josh Gaffey was here. Winnie was here. What could this possibly mean? Winnie would have told her if she'd known he was coming. In fact, Winnie never would have come if she'd known about Josh.

Winnie didn't know.

"So why is this happening?" Faith said softly.

Faith felt tears sting her eyes. She'd never told Winnie this, but she'd always felt that Winnie and Josh still loved each other very much. They just hadn't figured out how to actually live together, day to day. They'd had too many pressures right off. Sure Josh and Winnie had broken up, but maybe now fate was intervening. Maybe it was meant to be.

"Hi!" Faith heard Winnie's voice yelling from up the hill. Panicked, Faith looked up the slope as Winnie's tiny body bobbed expertly down a series of moguls. Faith felt her heart beat faster. Winnie, in her black vest and tight ski pants, looked exuberant. Her spiky hair whipped in the breeze above her leopard-print headband and hot-pink sunglasses. "We caught you," she gasped, slicing her edges in to stop. "Why are you standing here in the middle of the run?"

Faith bit her lip and cast a glance in the direction where she'd last seen Josh. But he was nowhere in sight.

"Let's go," KC was shouting, hurtling down the slope above them. "There's someone I've got to find."

"Her Mystery Man," Winnie said with a patient smile. "Who else?"

"Wait, KC," Faith shouted as KC headed down to where the bowl narrowed and funneled off into a steeper face that followed the chairlift down to the bottom, "slow down!"

Winnie cupped her hands around her mouth, laughing. "Stop, KC!" she shouted.

Faith watched as KC finally stopped at the lip of the ridge, sending a spray of powder into the air. Faith, Winnie, and Tory followed and pulled in next to her.

From where they were now standing, they could see the beginners' slopes, where the snowplowers and kids looked like ants against the snow. Big crowds gathered around the chairlifts.

KC sagged over her poles, looking thoughtful. "You're right, Win."

"What mystery guy?" Tory broke in, nudging Faith. "You've got a hunky mystery guy, too, KC? So do I. Met him at the Iceman last night and just saw him a minute ago." She touched her glove to her forehead, trying to think. "What's his name, Faith. It's—it's—"

"Tory!" Faith interrupted loudly, pushing forward and grabbing Tory by the elbow, dragging her down to a spot about twenty feet below where KC and Winnie were standing. "Please don't say anything."

"Hey." Tory struggled against Faith's grip as they continued to slide down toward a large tree. Her uphill knee bumped up and down as she fought for control. "Let go of me."

Faith stopped and gritted her teeth. If Josh Gaffey was here in Crystal Valley, then it had to be fate. It was too much of a coincidence to be anything other than that. Josh and Winnie were meant to be together. But there is no way I'm going to let Tory blab the news about Josh to Winnie right now. It would be just like Winnie to freak out and jump on a bus back home.

Tory was stomping her ski and trying to wriggle away from Faith's grasp. "Stop it, Faith. What are you doing?"

"Look, Tory," Faith said intently, whipping off her

gloves and brushing a stray hair out of her eyes. She
dug her edges into the snow to stay put. "Just stand
there and listen. It's important."

Tory rolled her eyes and jutted her hip out.
"What."

"I—don't—want—you—to—even—breathe a word
about Josh Gaffey," Faith warned her, glancing over
her shoulder at Winnie and KC, who were giving them
curious stares from their perch up above.

Tory's shiny mouth dropped open. "Why? What's
wrong? You know him? What's going on?"

"You're not to talk about him. You're not to flirt
with him. You're not to hint about him. And you're
definitely not going to meet him on New Year's Eve."

"I am too!" Tory snapped back in anger. Faith
stared hard at her and watched as Tory's blue eyes
began to cloud under her knit eyebrows. She frowned.
"Something's going on."

"Yes," Faith said grimly, glancing over her shoulder
as Winnie and KC approached, looking concerned.
"Something is going on, but I can't tell you about it
right now. Okay, Tory? This is important. Did you get
my instructions? Is it sinking in?"

Tory pouted. "Why don't you just shove it, Faith
Crowley?"

"Faith?" Winnie was approaching on her skis.

Faith's heart sped up. "Okay, Tory?"

"What's wrong, Faith?" Winnie came closer.

Faith instinctively raised her pole and pointed it directly at Tory's tiny waist. The tip glittered, and Faith
knew she was probably just as crazy as Tory. But this

was important. Winnie and Josh had to get back together, and she wasn't going to let Tory ruin it. "Just do it, Tory." She pushed the pole softly into Tory's stomach. "Just do what I say or I'll shove your drunken butt down Sugar Mountain."

Five

The next afternoon KC was finishing a practice slalom-run set up by the Crystal Valley Ski Club near the bottom of chair number four. Her skis clattered all the way down the course, but her edges held and she'd slammed her way through every gate. She flew through the finish line to a smattering of applause from the other skiers.

But skiing was the furthest thing from her mind.

She dug her edges in and stopped on a small ridge overlooking the slope down to the lodge. Then she checked her watch and scanned the crowd below.

Red vest. Dark hair. Red vest. Dark hair.

For the past two days, KC had been scanning the crowds for her mystery man. She'd even taken up precision slalom-skiing, hoping the Briar Ski Team would show up for practice. Her eyes were strained. Her nerves were on overdrive from expecting to see him any second. Over and over, she'd memorized the words she would say to him, only to change the script the next moment. She skied; she ate and talked with her friends. But the truth was she was in her own silent world—the world that contained only her and the guy in the red vest.

She checked her watch again. Five o'clock. She was supposed to meet Tory, Winnie, and Faith at the lodge for hot chocolate on the deck. Instead, she paused on the ridge, scrutinizing the swarms of skiers, spots of color against the snow.

Yellow pants. Red-and-green jacket. Purple hat. Blond guy. Bearded guy. Woman in pink. Girl in blue. Royal-blue jacket.

"KC!" she heard a shout from below. She looked down and saw Faith waving her pole. Next to her, Winnie was hopping up and down on her skis, doing big windmill turns with her arms.

Before pushing her tips off the ledge, she took one last glance behind, then looked down toward the lodge. "Hi!" she called out, bending into a tight, racing tuck, her knees in a deep bend and her poles jammed under her arms. She skidded to a stop in front of them, feeling the low sun burning her cheeks.

"We saw you on the slalom course," Faith was yelling, an amazed look on her face. White zinc-oxide completely covered her nose. "You must have been practicing all day."

Winnie giggled, pushing up her goggles and scooting over to pat KC on the back. "We didn't know you had it in you."

Faith put a finger to her sunburned chin. "This must have something to do with . . ." She gave KC a knowing look.

KC looked back at Faith, confused. It sounded like Faith was referring to her now-infamous mystery man. But she wasn't sure. Since yesterday morning on the slopes, Faith had been acting strangely. It seemed as if she had something private and important to tell her. But every time Faith tried to talk, Tory or Winnie had interrupted, and Faith had mysteriously clammed up.

"Come on," Winnie urged them. "My body is one giant, purply bruise, and I'm going to die if I don't sit down."

"And we have to meet Tory," Faith reminded them, brushing a clump of snow off the side of her leg.

KC followed Faith and Winnie down the gentle slope to the lodge, past the kids on sleds and beginner skiers practicing their snowplows. The massive deck at the top of the lodge's front staircase was packed with sunbathers and picnickers. And below, in the flat, sun-drenched expanse of snow surrounding the building, hundreds more were milling about, taking off skis, meeting friends, and heading toward the dozens of ski lockups located beneath the deck.

"Coppertan row," Winnie joked when they reached the lodge. She gazed up at the deck and tapped her skis together to loosen the snow clumps. Then she pointed off to the side of the lodge. "Check out the snowshoe volleyball game over there."

"The lodge is beautiful, isn't it?" KC whispered, enthralled, mechanically scanning each table up on the deck, then starting in on the crowd below. She punched herself out of her bindings and stood her skis on end in the snow.

Red vest. Dark hair. Red vest. Dark hair.

"Some of the rooms on the top floors have their own fireplaces, whirlpools, and towel warmers," Winnie was explaining.

"What would we want with that?" Faith asked with a smile, hoisting her skis on her shoulder and heading for the ski lockups. "We've spent the last two days skiing, not sitting around."

KC bent her elbow and made her biceps bulge. "Mountain women," she cracked.

Faith's expression was suddenly furtive. She pulled at KC's arm. "Come on, KC, I see two lockups. Winnie." She pointed in the opposite direction. "Look, there's one over there."

But Winnie marched ahead with them, smiling and whipping off her ski hat, revealing a spiky nest of sweaty hair. "Stop trying to get rid of me, Faith. There are plenty over here, too." Winnie grinned at KC. "She is trying to get rid of me, you know. Actually I think she's in love with a mystery man of her own, and knows that only you would understand."

Faith bit her lip.

KC looked closely at Faith's worried blue eyes. What was wrong with her?

Red vest. Dark hair. Red vest. Dark hair.

KC carefully scanned the crowd once again as Faith and Winnie marched toward the lockups. This time, she took in all the trails leading to the lodge, the expanse surrounding the building, and every face on the sunny deck. Finally, she gave her eyes a rest and turned toward Winnie and Faith, who were stepping out of their skis and placing them upright into the skinny, coin-operated lockups lined up along the side of the building and under the deck.

KC strolled ahead and joined her friends, who were now digging into their pockets for quarters. Her leg muscles were beginning to cramp up. "I wonder where Tory is."

Winnie slipped her coins into the lockup. "Tory and her little flask. I think she thinks drinking makes her sexy."

Faith cleared her throat and made a warning motion with her head. "Shhh, look who's coming."

The three turned and stared as Tory hurtled down the same slopes-to-lodge ski hill, toppling several children at the end of a ski-lesson line. In her sleek pink ski-suit and high-tech goggles, she looked more like a metal Barbie doll on skis than a human being. KC, still searching for the red ski-vest, took the opportunity to take another quick glimpse of the crowd.

"Hi!" Tory shrieked, barreling through the crowded area, grabbing the ski hat off a muscular ski-patrol guy who was leaning down to help a girl wearing a University of Washington Huskies baseball hat.

"Hi, Tory," KC said as she skidded to a stop in front of them. She tried to sound upbeat. Tory wasn't exactly her type, but watching her was a lot of fun. And besides, she'd been gone the last two evenings, leaving her, Winnie, and Faith in peace.

Winnie had finished locking up her skis, but Faith was still hunting around for quarters. Tory quickly put her skis away and linked elbows with Winnie, winking.

"Come on, Winnie." Tory slung her arm around Winnie's shoulders, pointing up to the lodge deck. "Let's check out the male specimens up there in the sun."

"Yeah," Faith burst out, her eyes suddenly eager. She dug into her jacket pockets. "You guys go ahead. KC will help me find some change. Save a table for us, will you?"

KC frowned at Faith. Maybe it was the altitude. Or the sun. But there was definitely something funny going on. She watched Tory and Winnie disappear into the crowd, then turned back to Faith, who'd already found her coins and locked her skis.

"KC?" Faith said quickly.

A red jacket whizzed by on skis, and KC turned around.

Blond hair.

KC stabbed her pole into the ground in frustration, but continued to run her eyes over the growing crowd.

"KC?" Faith was nudging her. "We have to talk."

KC gave Faith a vague nod. "Okay." She backed up a little to get a better view of the steps leading to the lodge deck. He had to come into the lodge sometime. Everyone did.

"I have to talk to you."

KC waved Faith away. Where was he? She'd been

looking for two days. Crystal Valley wasn't that big a resort. Was she crazy? Had she really seen him in the lobby two days ago? Or had it all been an hallucination, brought on by overwork and a long car trip?

"K—C!" Faith was insisting.

Red vest. Dark hair. Red vest. Dark hair.

Not a single person in the crowd looked even halfway familiar. The fact of the matter was, KC thought miserably, the only familiar male she'd laid eyes on in the last two days was Sean McGlofflin, the infuriating guy who'd rented her skis at the ski chalet. She'd run into him at a small breakfast joint downtown that morning while they were ordering caffe lattes to go.

"Hey—look out, everyone," he'd whispered to her as they passed in the crowd, "she's in a really big hurry."

Just thinking about Sean McGlofflin made KC feel raw and crazy. She knew guys like that—townies in resort spots who thought she was some kind of spoiled heiress just because she'd scraped up enough money for an inexpensive vacation. He didn't have the right to make assumptions about what kind of person she was.

"K—C," she heard Faith's exasperated voice behind her. "You just walked past a perfectly good lockup."

Red vest. Dark hair. Red vest. Dark hair.

KC bit the inside of her mouth, trying to control her frustration.

Flannel shirt. Crew cut. Navy jacket. Sunburned face. University of Arizona backpack. Girl laughing. Guy waxing skis. Guy skiing with *no clothes on.*

KC gasped.

Faith screamed.

KC adjusted her sunglasses and stared up at the beginners' slope next to the lodge. Then she leaned her skis up against the side of the building so that she and Faith could run out and get a better look. A giggle rose from her throat. Sure enough, the muscular guy streaking down the slope was absolutely naked, except for the woolen ski mask that completely covered his face and head.

"Look," Faith cried, "he's headed for the lodge."

"Aaaahhhhheeeeee!" KC heard Tory's familiar shriek. She looked up and saw Tory and Winnie waving and laughing from the deck up above, surrounded by a crowd of people, all howling with laughter and applauding the streaker. "He's headed around the lodge," Tory yelled.

"He's coming around again for a second exhibition," Winnie shouted through cupped hands. "Come on up."

"A streaker on skis." KC laughed.

"Come on." Faith pulled her away from the wild crowd. "Here's our chance to talk. Winnie and Tory will be glued to the deck until the show is over."

"What, Faith?" KC cried as Faith dragged her along the perimeter of the lodge and up a side staircase leading into the lodge's cafeteria. Once inside, they saw that the place was empty, but they still had to maneuver through a tangle of ski duffels, drying jackets, and dripping hats dangling from every available chair. It looked like everyone had left to watch the naked skier.

Finally, Faith spotted a deserted table near the central fireplace. She let out a long, shaky breath and leaned forward on her elbows.

KC was starting to get worried. "What happened?"

Faith pushed her wild hair off her face and looked KC straight in the eye. "I saw Josh yesterday."

KC's jaw dropped. "Josh Gaffey?"

Faith nodded. Her lips were pursed together, and she appeared very serious. Then she gave the café a furtive look to make sure they were alone.

KC's head was spinning. "Josh Gaffey here in Crystal Valley? Wha . . . What? With Winnie? Where?"

Faith placed a finger on her lips. "Not with Winnie," she whispered. "She doesn't know about it."

"You haven't told her?" KC gasped.

"Wait, KC." Faith was holding her hands up in defense. "Wait."

"Did you talk to him? Did he follow her here?" KC was breathless.

"I saw him yesterday on the slopes," Faith explained. "And I haven't seen him since. And I haven't talked to Winnie—because I needed to talk to you first."

KC was nearly choking. "Why is he here? Do you realize what this could do to Winnie? She's just getting her life together. She—she seems so happy now. Almost relieved . . ."

Faith looked at her hands intently. "I'm pretty sure it's just a fluke that he's here the same time Winnie is. He was skiing with a friend, I guess, when I saw him. A guy."

KC put her hands up to her mouth and tried to catch her breath.

Suddenly Faith reached out over the table and grabbed KC's hands. "But just think for a moment, KC," Faith said, her eyes beginning to sparkle. "Maybe it's a wonderful second chance for them. Maybe it's fate that they both came here at the exact same time. She misses him. I'm sure of it."

KC shook her head.

"Winnie knows she made some terrible mistakes with their marriage," Faith went on, "and she thinks there's no going back. But she still loves him, KC. I know it."

KC had gotten used to the fact that Winnie and Josh had split up. But now, in a rush, she realized how much she wanted them to find each other again. To KC, Winnie and Josh always stood for something. They were young, but they'd found true love. To KC, Winnie and Josh had been an inspiration. If Winnie could find someone as wonderful as Josh, maybe she could, too, someday. . . .

"I need your advice, KC." Faith was whispering, searching her face. "Look, we both know that Win's moving ahead with the divorce and her new life. But I'm also pretty sure Josh ended things with Fredi at the end of the term. She moved out of the house before Thanksgiving."

"And no one ever saw them together after that," KC agreed with a start.

Faith leaned closer to KC, twisting her braid with her finger. "There's another thing," she murmured.

"Guess who Tory's snagged for a New Year's date? A wild guess. Come on. Out of the blue."

KC's jaw dropped. Now she knew why Faith was so agitated. "Josh?"

"You guessed it."

"*Aaagghhhh,*" KC cried, almost screaming.

"Look," Faith explained. "I've pretty much told Tory to keep her bod away from Josh on New Year's Eve." She grimaced. "I had to practically shove her off the mountain to make her understand I meant business. But I'm not going to let that lip-gloss princess throw herself all over Josh—"

"Right in front of Winnie," KC growled, her heart speeding up. "The divorce would be set in concrete if Winnie saw Tory mauling Josh."

"You're with me?" Faith asked in a determined whisper. "We try to get Josh and Winnie together New Year's Eve?"

KC nodded, grabbing Faith's arm. "But we've got to tell Tory the whole story. If she doesn't know the truth, who knows how badly she could screw everything up?"

"Ooohhh," the two friends heard Winnie's familiar voice as she and Tory plunged into the cafeteria. A chorus of shrieks and laughter followed them as the streaker watchers returned in one giant herd. Winnie grabbed a chair and parked it right next to Faith's. "We thought we'd find you in here. Hey, I've never seen one guy get the attention of so many—so fast."

Tory collapsed next to KC. "I love guys with nerve like that. Especially when they have cute butts."

KC suddenly wanted to tear Tory's hair out. She thought of her and Josh together—in front of Winnie. . . .

"KC." Faith gave her a meaningful look. She pointed at Tory and mouthed the words *Tell her*.

KC nodded, clenching her jaw and standing up. It was now or never. She had to tell Tory about Winnie and Josh before Tory messed everything up. "Help me out with something, Tory," KC said abruptly. "I forgot to lock up my skis."

Tory lifted her empty eyes and stared. "So?"

KC bit her lip, forcing a patient smile. "Come on. Help me find a lockup. Who knows? You might get another eyeful of our friendly neighborhood streaker while you're at it."

Tory turned thoughtful and stood up. "Talked me into it."

Grabbing Tory's arm, KC steered Tory out of the cafeteria. As they headed outside, Tory slipped her tiny flask out of her jacket pocket and took a long sip. But as she did, one of Tory's ski boots knocked clumsily against the other, nearly toppling her.

A wave of fury swept through KC. She grabbed Tory's elbow and stood her up. "Come on, Tory," she snapped. "Put away the flask and pull yourself together."

Tory's mouth dropped open, and in the bright sunshine, KC could see how spaced-out she really was. A slow smile spread across her face. "Let me tell you something, KC," Tory drawled, screwing the cap back on the near-empty flask and tucking it away. "I'm on vacation. And I intend to do exactly as I please this week, whether it involves men, vodka, or any other entertaining substance that happens to slip my way. So zip it, 'kay?"

KC felt her face grow hot with rage as they walked toward the ski lockups. She cleared her throat, determined to hang on to the single thread of patience left in her body. "I'm sorry, Tory."

Together they walked down the staircase and around the base of the lodge until KC reached the spot where she'd left her skis against the side of the building.

"Okay," Tory was saying sweetly. "Where did you leave your skis? I've got two quarters I can fork over for the lockup. See how nice I can be?"

KC ran her eyes up and down the side of the building, looking for her gunmetal-gray, top-of-the-line demo skis.

"Where are they?" Tory complained. "Come on."

KC touched her damp ski glove to her lips, frantically scanning the side of the building. A slow dread began to build in her chest. Her skis.

"My skis are gone!" KC heard a woman cry out from behind her.

KC froze.

"Did someone take your skis, too?" Tory was asking. "Is that why you can't find them?"

KC began to sob with fury. "Oh, no," she cried, running up and down the side of the building. Finally, she stopped and doubled over in agony. Her skis were gone. Stolen. The skis she'd rented from the ski chalet were worth hundreds of dollars. Money she didn't have. Money she wouldn't get back either, because she'd refused to pay the insurance.

"KC?"

KC exploded. She whipped around to face Tory's stunned face. "Of course they've been stolen!"

"Huh?" Tory muttered, her eyes glazed. "Are you sure?"

KC pressed her gloves to her face. "I left them right here against the building," she sobbed.

Tory let out a tiny giggle. "You just leaned them up against the wall?" she drawled. "Of course they're gone, dummy. You gotta lock them up. Oh well, insur- ance'll pay."

KC dropped her hands. She could feel the blood pouring through her veins. Sobs welled up from her chest.

"Hey." Tory lifted her sagging chin a little, clearly drunk. Her eyebrows narrowed. "You said you had something important to tell me."

"You make *me sick!*" KC exploded, her eyes blazing with anger. "I'm *not* insured, you little poodle. Take that and stick it in your vodka-soaked brain."

Tory staggered back a little, her blue eyes momen- tarily alert.

Tears poured down KC's cheeks. "A thief just car- ried them off, Tory. And there's no way I can pay for them now. First, a thief," KC railed, plunging her index finger into Tory's chest, "and now, you—you're one notch lower—you're a drunk—and there's noth- ing worse than a drunk!"

Six

"**B**abe—ah, you know I ain't no princess," Tory sang loudly to the music booming from the Iceman jukebox that same night. She threw her head back and swayed her hips, moving across the empty dance floor. "But when it comes to love, I can really give you the thaaaang you need."

She stopped, leaned against the jukebox, and stared at the swarm of people pushing through the front entrance. Already the bar stools were taken, and a group of guys in matching sweatshirts had launched into a raucous college fight-song. Near the edge of the dance floor, a group of girls in expensive, pastel skiwear stood on their chairs and began singing a rival university's fight song.

Davis and Josh—where *are* you?

Tory frowned. The Iceman was getting good and loud, and skiing on the fluffy powder had been great that day. But things weren't working out. Now she had yet another roommate down her throat. First, yesterday, it was Faith, threatening to push her off the mountain if she went out with Josh Gaffey. Then, today, KC, who actually called her a drunk.

To make things worse, she had only glimpsed Josh twice since they'd set up their big New Year's Eve date. And that was out on the slopes—yesterday. He and Davis hadn't shown up at the Iceman last night. It was as if they'd disappeared from the face of the earth.

"Bitchy, bitchy, bitchy," Tory whispered, the image of KC's furious face burning in her memory. "She deserved to get her skis stolen today. And if she's dumb enough not to pay insurance, what can I say?"

She shook her head and danced faster, fixing her gaze on the big moose head hanging over the empty bar. The pastel-clothed college girls stepped down onto the dance floor, too, followed by a sunburned couple, who were locked in a passionate kiss.

People like KC Angeletti are know-nothing prigs. Her mommy and daddy probably told her she'd go to hell if she had a beer. And Faith. What the hell is her problem, besides being a complete and total bully-in-a-braid? The only one in the nutty trio who has possibilities is Winnie. Winnie is okay—so far, at least.

A smile sneaked across Tory's face as the music kicked into hyper disco-drive. At least she'd had those little white pills to take before coming here. She was beginning to feel a buzz coming on. Miraculously, she'd remembered to save some from school. A few of the hipper study-nerds at Cantwell-Jamison had laid some on her, maybe hoping she'd actually study for finals.

She'd saved them, of course, for more important partying occasions like this one, though. The little white pills were great for waking up when she'd had a little bit too much to drink.

Tory stood up straighter, feeling the tightness of her jeans. She swung a little to the music, waiting for the Iceman action to really heat up. The tables that lined the dance floor's semicircle were all full now, and the front entrance was jammed. To the left of the massive bar, tucked in the back, the Iceman's four pool tables were busy.

"'Nother one, hon?" the waitress called out, stopping on the dance floor, still holding a trayful of empty beer glasses. She smiled politely at Tory, but Tory knew she didn't mean it.

"Skip it," Tory said with a tart toss of her head. "I'm okay for now. I'm waiting for someone."

"Sure," the waitress replied, turning away.

The front door swung open again and again. But there was no Josh, and no Davis. She tried to make important eye contact with each guy who came in, but nothing materialized. Anger began to build up inside her. The stupid waitress. The fat matrons who got in her way on the slopes. Not to mention the hundreds of mule-faced creeps back at Cantwell-Jamison whom she'd gone to school with for the past year and a half. Wherever she went, Tory thought bitterly, incredibly depressing and horrid people seemed to surround her.

Tory bit her lip and hurried off the dance floor. She wove through the crowded tables, popcorn fights, and intercollegiate taunts until she reached the pool tables. Then she draped herself in one of the nearby chairs and stared at two tanned, bearded guys bent over their cue sticks.

"Game?" the taller of the pool players asked with an inviting grin. Slowly, he chalked the tip of his cue and stared.

"Sure." Tory smiled back, crossing her legs. "I'll take the winner."

"You're on," the guy said, still grinning. "Two minutes."

Tory waved the waitress over, deciding on another beer after all. No wonder Cantwell-Jamison College was such a bore. They didn't have great places like this within five hundred miles of the campus. Tests, grades, snobby roommates, and ridiculous codes of honor. Tory knew from the beginning she wouldn't fit in.

And look what happened, Mom and Dad—they kicked me out eventually—just like I told you they would.

Tory felt tears building behind her eyes. She stood up and leaned her hips against the pool table, remembering. She hadn't had the nerve to tell her parents yet. They just thought she was visiting some of her darling Cantwell-Jamison girlfriends in Connecticut. No wonder they'd sent her such a small check for winter break.

"Hey, baby," Tory heard a male voice behind her.

She felt two brawny arms wrap around her waist. Brushing a tear away, Tory turned around quickly and felt the arms releasing her. A black-haired guy was standing in front of her, holding a glass of beer in his hand.

Tory stared.

"Take it," the guy said, grinning. His smile was very white and there was a small space between his two front teeth. "You ordered it, didn't you?"

Tory dug into her pocket for the money.

The guy stepped forward, jiggling the beer a little. "It's okay. I got it."

Tory felt her face soften. She took the beer out of his hand. "Thanks."

"No problem," he said, crossing his arms and smiling at her.

Tory smiled back. She'd hoped the arms belonged to Josh—or Davis. But this guy looked like he had possibilities, too. He had a ruddy, open face and a broad chest that bulged beneath his red turtleneck. His eyes were blue and lively and his smile seemed genuine, though there was something hard about his mouth and the slight scar that ran under it.

"Waitin' for someone, beautiful?" he teased, looping one finger into the side of her belt and tugging her gently toward him. He had muscular arms that made Tory realize he was not the kind of guy she wanted any disagreements with. Yet she was also attracted to his rough, almost outlawlike quality. Anyway, he was anything but the typical Cantwell-Jamison date. Her old college roommates would have taken one look at his naughty, blue-eyed glance and jogged to the nearest emergency phone-booth.

Tory pulled away and giggled. The room suddenly felt warm. "Yeah, I'm waiting," she teased back. "Waiting for a game."

The guy swaggered closer, nuzzling her hair a little. "Oh, well, then excuse me. I didn't know you were a sharkie. I'm Eric Briggs. Mind if I stick around and watch you operate?"

"Briggs," Tory echoed, tossing him a flirtatious smile. She narrowed her eyebrows and pretended to study his face. "There's something very familiar about you."

Eric's eyes flashed. Sliding his foot forward, he leaned his hip against Tory's and nuzzled her ear. "There's something familiar about you, too, kitten. And I'm going to find out what. . . ."

The tall pool player walked over and tapped his cue stick on Tory's shoulder. "Your game."

Tory turned around, giggling. Then she tore away from Eric and took a pool cue off the rack on the wall. "Sorry, Eric," she called over her shoulder, picking up a square of chalk and twisting the tip of the cue into it. "Like I said, I've got a game."

Eric persisted, walking toward her and slipping his index finger up her neck. Shivers ran through Tory's scalp.

"Come on, handsome," Tory complained with a light smile. Her pool partner stopped and watched. "You don't know what you're messing with."

Eric stepped back, crossed his arms, and leaned against the wall, grinning.

"Okay," Tory spoke up, eyeing the bearded guy with the pool cue. Eric was dangerous and tempting. But she knew she wasn't in any shape to tangle with him—not now. She needed to get away from him, at least for a few minutes. "Things are way too hot for me in here," she said over her shoulder.

"Hot, all right," Eric retorted quickly. He walked up to her again and pulled on her belt.

"Stop," Tory said, laughing.

"Let's get outta here," he urged. "There's a hot-spring resort just down the road from here. It's great. Just the thing you need to relax." He grabbed her hard around the waist and pulled her close.

"Hey," her pool partner spoke up, walking around the table with a threatening look. "The lady wants to play pool."

Eric shot the guy a fierce look, then bent down to whisper in her ear. Tory tried to push him away, but she soon realized that she was no match for his brawny strength.

"My pickup's right outside," Eric breathed.

Tory wriggled away. "Look," she said sweetly. "I've got a game. Let me go. Okay? Maybe we'll run into each other on a better night."

Eric released her from his grip, but his steely blue eyes remained fixed on her. "Maybe tomorrow," he murmured. "It's New Year's Eve at the lodge, you know. Big things can happen if you let them."

Tory gave him a taunting smile. "Actually, I've got a date to go to the lodge."

Eric's smile didn't falter. Instead, he began nodding

slowly. Under his shirt, she could almost see his chest muscles flexing with tension. "Sure you do, beautiful. I bet you've got a big date."

"Yeah," Tory answered, a little breathlessly. Actually, there was something very appealing about Eric Briggs. Maybe it was his rough, sexy talk. Or the scar. Or his confidence. Something told her she'd be seeing him again.

"See you, blondie," Eric murmured, making a little bow before turning on his heel and heading back to the bar.

"Bye," Tory said quietly, turning back to the safety of the pool table. Her head was buzzing from the combination of Eric Briggs, the little white pills, and the glasses of beer. When her game was over, she knew she was in no condition to be discovered by Eric again. Instead, she slipped on her jacket and went out through a side door into the snowy evening, headed for home.

Seven

A freezing haze hung over Crystal Valley the next morning. The snow, which had softened under yesterday's hot sun, had refrozen into a hard, slippery glaze. Four-wheel-drive trucks slid sideways in the downtown streets. Icicles grew like daggers above the wooden boardwalks. And the cold air stung Davis's face as he and Josh headed out of their tiny room on the busy motel strip.

"It's going to be one frosty run," Davis muttered, hoisting his snowboard on his shoulder as they headed into town. His baggy orange jacket read SnoPro Boards and his loose snow pants whipped in the breeze. Yellow goggles dangled from his neck. "Hope the old SnoPro board doesn't shatter on its way down."

Josh chuckled. "Me too, pal. I don't want to have to scrape you off the mountain." He reached out and gave the board a pat. "Never actually saw one of these things."

Davis swung it down and pointed to its two bindings, which faced off to the side. "Check it out. You stand on it sideways, like a skateboard or a surfboard. Then—pow. Down the mountain."

"Sounds good to me."

Davis took a deep breath. Crystal Valley was his sixth stop on the demo tour, and it was already beginning to wear on him. At first, he'd taken to snowboarding because it was new, it was outside, and it gave him the same challenge and rush that surfing did. But after he unexpectedly won the U.S. Snowboarding Amateur Nationals in Vail, it became more than a sport. Snowboarding wasn't about having fun with the other powder-hounds anymore. It's about having a job, and starting out at the very bottom of the heap, Davis thought with a grimace.

Josh shook his head as they crunched across the street. Unlike Davis, he wore a moth-eaten, raggedy wool hat, jeans, and a giant red down jacket that was smudged and frayed along the row of front snaps. "Why doesn't Higgenbothem schedule these catchy events for the afternoon?"

Davis shrugged. "The resort schedules them. It's part of the Pro Demo Tour, and SnoPro's just one of the gang. The ski industry is running after the snowboarders with their tongues hanging out. It's the wave of the future, Gaffey."

Josh patted him on the back. "Hey, hey, Davis. Coming up in the world. All right."

Davis's heart sank. Coming up in the world was exactly what he'd had in mind when he took this job. But he quickly found out what it meant to be a product demonstrator in the Dolphin Enterprises corporate culture. Back in Hawaii, guys like him who could ride the waves were the glory boys. He couldn't walk through a town in the islands without attracting a crowd of well-wishers. But snowboarding was a different game. In the eyes of the executives down in Los Angeles, product demonstrators like himself were punks. Punks who'd do the job for free.

"I'd take on a snowboard," Josh was explaining, "but in powder. Nice, deep powder a loooooong way away from the lift lines."

Davis pressed his lips together and nodded, trying to ignore his black thoughts.

"Nothing like riding on nice, dry powder," Davis agreed. "Through the trees. What I'd really like is a trip down to the glaciers in New Zealand. It's like skateboarding without all the noise. Surfing without all the water in your face. Pure, silent speed."

"Silent," Josh echoed, his voice turning serious.

Davis turned and focused on his friend's pale face, which seemed to show every long hour he'd spent inside for the past several months, staring at a computer screen. Davis shook his head a little, feeling envious. Josh was a dedicated guy, headed for a college degree. He was smart, and in the hot field of computer programming.

Davis nudged Josh as they slipped their way past a row of western-art shops, cafés, and ski boutiques. The sun was beginning to burn through the frosty haze. "Guess you have your work cut out for you tonight, huh, Gaffey?" he teased. "You and that beautiful blonde."

Josh looked pained. "Is that tonight?"

Davis laughed. "You got it, my man. New Year's Eve at the lodge. Just you and Tory . . ."

"And a thousand other people," Josh said with a panicky look. "Look. I've got to get ahold of her. I can't do this. It's crazy. I don't even know her and I don't really think we have anything in—"

"Common?" Davis chirped, incredulous. "Come on, Gaff—it's just an innocent date. Don't take it so seriously. Just hang."

Josh shook his head. "Yeah, right."

Davis and Josh turned the corner and headed down the winding bottom of Crystal Valley's Main Street. The snow-covered road was dotted with lampposts and trees. Leftover red and green Christmas banners fluttered in the wind. The storefronts and boardwalks twisted along the road until it reached the Crystal Valley Lodge and the ski slopes that rose behind it. Davis suddenly stopped. He felt a grin spread across his face. "Check this out."

"What?" Josh slipped a little on the ice.

Davis looked up the winding hill, then down. He swept his arm over the scene. "Check out this run."

Josh laughed. "Actually, it's a city street, Mattingly."

Davis shook his head. "No way. I see a course. See?

Take off up there, dip over to the left past the lamppost, then swerve through the traffic and down to the lodge. It'd be a ride."

"Stop the damn traffic," Josh reminded him.

"That would be the fun of it." Davis grinned and looked over at his friend. "I don't like it when things get too predictable, Gaffey."

"How about your boss?" Josh wanted to know, as they crunched past a German bakery. The smell of cinnamon, chocolate, and coffee wafted out. "He wouldn't like it."

Just thinking about Higgenbothem's reaction made Davis's stomach tighten. But he grinned back at Josh. "Snowboarding on city streets is totally illegal, but he'd get a good laugh. What a publicity stunt."

Josh nodded. "Fun guy, huh?"

"A blast," Davis muttered. Higgenbothem seemed okay when he met him down in Park City that fall. With his trim body, silver hair, and graceful, old-world skiing style, he'd seemed like the perfect boss. And as Dolphin Enterprise's sales representative for six western states, Davis figured the guy would have no problem with his paycheck. Quickly, Davis learned that Higgenbothem wasn't as interested in snowboarding as he was in cruising all the best resorts during the ski season and checking out the wealthy ski divorcées. Now Davis suspected Higgenbothem was overspending his expense account, because his latest paycheck was already three days overdue.

"Look at those mountains," Josh was saying softly, staring up at the craggy peaks soaring above the lush snowfields. "And you're working. I still can't get over the fact that this is work for you, Mattingly. You've figured it out."

Davis crunched silently ahead, balling his fists up inside his thick ski gloves. He didn't have anything figured out. He'd failed to hang on to his championship status on Hawaii's amateur surfing circuit. He'd soon figured out that he wasn't good enough to go pro. Demonstrating snowboards was his attempt at a new life. But without the glory, without the status. And now, without money. The way things were going, he was going to be stranded in Crystal Valley without having enough money to eat.

A few minutes later, they were passing the lodge deck and were hiking up to the lift lines. Josh was planning to watch the exhibition, then spend the rest of the day downhilling.

"Davis!" a deep voice was calling out from behind. Davis turned and tensed. It was Higgenbothem himself, walking quickly out of the lodge café. A middle-aged woman in a full-length fur coat held on to his arm for a second, then released it, wiggling her nails in farewell. "Davis, my man!" he called out again, catching up. "Ready for your big moment?"

"Sure," Davis said shortly, before introducing him to Josh. After waiting for Josh and Higgenbothem to snap their skis on, the three headed together for the chairlift line. Higgenbothem skied forward in haste and, while Davis and Josh cringed, made a big fuss over being allowed to head directly to the front of the line.

"Exhibition staff!" Higgenbothem made his voice boom with authority. "Excuse us. Exhibition staff here."

Davis checked his watch as the three-person chairlift swung up into the air. "We're early, Ron."

Higgenbothem's bristly eyebrows lifted and his eyes twinkled. "Gotta give 'em a show, Davis. Give 'em a show."

Davis felt his blood begin to boil as the chair floated them up the side of the mountain. Nothing was worse than a screwball looking for an excuse to butt through a ski line.

"Say, Ron," Davis began quietly, checking the date on his watch again, "how's that paycheck coming? We're running three days late on it."

Higgenbothem's lips tensed, and Davis could see that Josh was looking away, embarrassed. Still, Davis was determined to bring it up. He needed the money. If he didn't get paid, he'd have to borrow from Josh for food.

"Now you just hold on there, young man," Higgenbothem said indignantly. "I've been working these Crystal Valley ski shops like a dog the last few days. That means the paperwork is a little behind. Have a little patience, son."

"Sure," Davis said shortly.

Josh cleared his throat.

Higgenbothem nodded his head, his jaw muscles clenching.

Davis gritted his teeth. At times like this, he almost wished he were back in Hawaii with his parents, staring at the deep blue sea.

When the chair reached the top, Davis slipped gracefully down the ramp and waved good-bye to Josh and his boss. The wind gently blew the snow off the treetops, and the sky was a deep blue as he rode down toward the course. Bending down deep, he carved his board through a wide, unpopulated bowl—icy but broken a little by the morning's first skiers.

Spring up. Single twist in midair.

He swung his way down to the bottom of the bowl, where a small jump had been built. A guy in baggy snow pants and a ripped thermal top waved his ski pole and gave him the thumbs-up. The jump site was clear.

Big flip. Twist once. Land—just right.

"Yahoo!" several fellow-snowboarders yelled into the crisp air. Davis kept going, following a yellow sign that said Snowboarding Exhibition This Way that took him through the crusty powder into a clump of woods. Bursting out of the trees, he stopped quickly. His board rattled menacingly against the rock-hard ice. Then he stared down at the mean-looking course the resort had arranged for the competing snowboarders.

The course was a bloodthirsty, twisting pipe that started on a rocky ledge, then plunged down over a nearly vertical face that was solidly studded with glaze-ice moguls. Ski jumps were positioned in the most dangerous spots. At the bottom of the last jump, the course swerved sharply to the left, to avoid a rocky cliff. At this critical point, any snowboarder without perfect control was sure to wipe out—big time.

And I'm doing it for free, Davis thought bitterly. They want me to kill myself for free.

There was a sound of skis traversing the ice directly behind him. Davis turned to look. A burly guy with dark hair and a sleek black ski jacket drew closer to him. Davis took in his big white smile and the space between his two front teeth. A huge class ring was on his third finger, and his multicolored alpine skis and bindings were top of the line. Davis drew in his breath.

"Hey, hey, hey," the guy called out, stopping with a flourish just above where Davis was standing. He held out his hand. "Davis Mattingly. Well, well, well. Never thought I'd get to meet you. Hey, I'm your biggest fan."

Davis shook his hand, then took off his gloves and tightened his ponytail. "Thanks," he said with a casual smile. The guy seemed like a real jerk.

"I'm Eric Briggs," the guy continued, running his eyes up and down Davis as if he was trying to fathom him.

Davis looked at him again, checking out the deep scar under his mouth and the strange glint in his eye. He also noticed the incredibly expensive ski boots on his feet.

"Recognize you from the surfing circuit. Honolulu. July. You were hot."

Davis nodded. "Thanks. That was a tough competition."

Eric's grin widened. "Hey. You're the best. I heard you were pushing snowboards in the off-season. Nothing like the waves, though, huh?"

Davis looked at him carefully. "This is okay," he said shortly.

Eric nudged him. "They don't pay you enough to do what you're doing. Killing yourself on this ice, huh?"

Davis opened his mouth to speak, then closed it again. The last thing he wanted was to let this jerk know how bad things really were. He had his pride to think about.

"Welcome, ladies and gentlemen, to the second annual Crystal Valley snowboarding exhibition," a voice on a loudspeaker blared. "Let's give a big hand to our sponsors, SnoPro, Action Skis, Tuffsport, Crystal Valley Mountain Gear, Thirstquench Sport Beverages, and PolarHigh—the finest in active skiwear."

Eric let out a sarcastic laugh, leaning into his pole and patting Davis on the back. "Right. And those are the people making all the money today. Not our champ here."

Davis gave him a cool stare.

"*AAAANNND* hear this, folks. On the roster for this morning's event is Hawaii's own Davis Mattingly. Hey, folks, he's taking to the snowboarding scene like a duck to water. Let's see how Hawaii's former amateur surfing champion does on this hairy course."

"Gotta shove off," Davis explained, digging in his edge. Below, he could see the clumps of onlookers gathering along the course.

"Yeah, sure," Eric said quickly, staying with him as he traversed across the slope toward the starting gate. "Tell you what. I've got a little bet going, Davis, my man. My money says you wipe out right down there where that little red flag is."

Davis shrugged, glancing down at the final, sharp turn that had made him shudder a moment before. "Everyone's going to wipe out there. The ice is bad, the pipe is a bear, and that's the worst turn."

And my chances are even worse, since I didn't have enough cash yesterday to buy the right wax for my board, Davis thought.

Eric leaned into Davis's ear. "So just do it, Mattingly. I'll split the winnings with you, man. We're talking five hundred here. And all it'll take is a little spill you were bound to take anyway. Like you said."

Davis narrowed his eyebrows and looked at Eric. He'd seen a little betting like this on the surfing scene, but he had stayed clean.

"Look," Davis said reluctantly. "I can't predict what's going to happen on a course like this, Briggs. It's not like a wave. You don't have that kind of control."

Eric shrugged. "Oh, come on, Mattingly. That aging SnoPro fox couldn't be paying you that much. Hey. Big business is profiting today, Mattingly. Not you. Play a little on the side and you can make it work for you, too. It's just an innocent bet. Nothing illegal."

Davis drew his breath in. Eric was right about Higgenbothem. And Eric was right about his needing the money, too. He felt angry just looking at Higgenbothem standing there across the course, shaking hands with all the officials and pretty girls. Betting was unethical, sure. But it wasn't illegal in this game like it was in football. Why was he so uptight, anyway?

Davis took a deep breath. He didn't like it, but he

was going to be practical for once. "Okay," Davis said with a terse look. "I'll do it. I'll wipe out on the last turn."

"Hey, hey," Eric said with a slap on the back. "See you at the bottom, pal."

Davis turned away and gave his board an angry shove until he was at the beginning of the course with the other competitors. Whistles and laughter rang out through the icy morning air. Product banners fluttered in the breeze. The colorful crowd stood out against the whiteness of the mountain, cheering the boarders on. He watched as the snowboarders, one by one, rode the icy course. Some crashed immediately, unused to the icy conditions. Others freaked out at the jumps or crashed on landing. But all of them, Davis saw with mounting tension, wiped out at the final twist in the course.

Davis felt something lift inside him. Maybe it was pride. Maybe it was a call from somewhere deep in his soul.

You can do it, the voice murmured inside his head. You're better than they are. You've got the balance— the strength. Do the right thing.

Davis gulped and planted his gloved hands hard into his hips. Eric's bet had suddenly reminded him of someone else—Phillip Cannon—the sleazy developer back in Hawaii who'd tried to bribe him into keeping quiet about an endangered bird living in a cove destined for his bulldozers. Davis stared down at the snow. It had felt so good to stand up to that guy. So free. So solid. His cheeks suddenly became hot with emotion. Thinking about Mahali Cove made him think about Faith. And thinking about Faith made him remember who he really was. And what he wanted to become.

"Next up, Daaaaaavis Mattingly!" the announcer called out, waking Davis from his thoughts. Squaring his shoulders, he took a deep breath and slipped into position. As his board tip dropped down the mountain, he suddenly realized that it wasn't the money that was important. It was the freedom to do what he thought was right. Faith always understood that.

"*YYYYEEEEAAA!*" he heard the crowd roar as he took on the first jump. His body was pure energy as he took a double spiral and landed perfectly. His board felt like a hot knife as he sped through the slalom that followed, then the second jump, a perfect tail-grab that sent the crowd wild. Suddenly, everything felt so perfect and in control; it was as if he'd been transported back home. The rutted ice had turned, somehow, into a soft, blue-green wave, carrying him powerfully home to the beach.

The final curve loomed ahead as Davis recovered from a final, jaw-jarring, 360-degree twist. Spreading his arms wide, Davis struggled to maintain his balance, shift his weight, and dig his edge into the unyielding ice. He would ride the wave out just as surely as he would someday find Faith again. "He's taking the final turn!" the announcer screamed as Davis leaned powerfully to the left, nearly scraping his ear on the icy surface. A centimeter more and his body would have been a statistic. But his edge held. The finish line rushed ahead, and the next moment, he was speeding forward beneath the huge finish-line banner.

Davis held his fists up in the air, as the crowd cheered wildly. New Year's resolution for the rest of my life, Davis decided with a quiet inner smile. No more self-doubt. No more shortcuts and crooks. This is where my life begins—and it's going to take off.

Eight

"A masked ball," KC cried, making two fists and jogging in place on Winnie's bed back at the apartment.

"One of Western civilization's greatest inventions." Winnie grinned back, grabbing KC's leg and making her fall onto the saggy mattress. "The disguise heightens the intrigue and romance. The eighteenth-century French courtesans were especially good at it—before they got their heads chopped off in the Revolution."

KC threw a pillow at her. If the intrigue and romance of this ball got any higher, she'd probably lose her head, too. The New Year's Eve masked ball in the lodge was less than an hour away. And before the clock struck midnight, she had one single, all-encompassing life purpose: to find the mysterious man she'd been searching for since the moment she'd arrived in town.

"Get out of the bathroom, Tory," Faith yelled. She was brushing her long hair. "We've got bad ski-hat hair to fix."

Meanwhile, KC watched as Winnie flung another rejected outfit onto the floor, already cluttered with discarded tops, scarves, and open cosmetic bags. Damp ski jackets, draped over suitcases, were facing the creaking electric baseboard heat. The room smelled of sunblock, wet leather gloves, and something musky Tory had just sprayed onto her neck.

"Why won't she come out of the bathroom? What am I going to wear?" Faith shrieked, collapsing on her bed.

"You think you've got problems," KC remarked, jumping up and flipping through her closet for the seventeenth time. "I've got to figure out how to pay for a pair of very expensive stolen skis."

Winnie shook her finger at KC. "That's not what you're thinking about. . . ."

"I am too!" KC shot back, laughing and yanking a fluffy white sweater off a hanger. She giggled. "Well, that and—"

"Your mystery man," Winnie and Faith shouted in unison.

KC hugged the sweater to her chest and twirled around, unable to control the impossibly huge smile that was beginning to stretch her face in two. Then, as abruptly as her happiness hit, it washed away, followed by a wave of panic. She sat down on the edge of Winnie's bed. Her stolen skis were a huge problem. Monumental. And sure, there was a good chance she'd find her mystery man tonight. But what would she say when she actually saw him? She knew she was too keyed up to stay cool. What if she burst into giggles—or said something dumb or . . .

"Earth to KC." Winnie was nudging her.

KC looked up and gave Winnie a nervous smile. It was impossible to hide anything from Winnie and Faith, and maybe that was a good thing.

"Hey, KC." Winnie hugged her from the side. "You're a wreck, but we love you. Let's go knock 'em dead tonight at the ball, okay?"

KC stood up and paced. Winnie and Faith must love her. They had missed a whole day of skiing today because of her. Since she didn't have skis, they opted to take a day off to check out the Crystal Valley shops and watch an ice-skating show at the lodge rink.

"Don't worry, KC," Faith chimed in, zipping her jeans. "We'll desert you tomorrow. You can spend the whole day as a lounge lizard in the lodge while we ruin our knees up there on the mountain."

Winnie yanked on a pair of leopard-print stirrup pants and headed for the bedroom door. "Yeah. But meanwhile I'm going to fortify my bod. Anyone up for pre-dance Cocoa Puffs?"

Faith and KC both held their noses while Winnie laughed and did an exaggerated waltz out of the room.

"KC," Faith was whispering, walking forward on her knees in the tiny space between the closet and Winnie's bed. She leaned her elbow up on the bed next to KC, looking urgent. "Tory still doesn't know about Winnie and Josh. What are we going to do?"

KC bit her lip. Tory had come home early the night before, but Winnie had been there, too. And while she, Faith, and Winnie had been sightseeing all day, Tory had been skiing. They hadn't had one moment to pull Tory aside and explain the problem to her.

"All you can do is grab her at the ball, before she runs into Josh," KC whispered, "then pray she doesn't purposely sabotage their reunion." KC looked down and pretended to tie her shoe as Tory emerged from the bathroom, a cloud of platinum hair and eye shadow.

KC and Faith stared as Tory hiked up one of her thigh-high boots. She lifted her arms up, threw her fluffy hair back, and gave them a thousand-watt smile. "We—are—going—to—create a disturbance."

KC and Faith reached over and high-fived her. Chances were Tory hated their guts after KC had called her a drunk and Faith had threatened to push her off the mountain if she mentioned Josh. That's why they were now trying to handle her ego with kid gloves. Winnie and Josh's successful reunion tonight depended on her good graces.

"You look hot, Tory," KC beamed back.

"That's right, Tory," Faith quickly agreed, pulling on a blue angora sweater. "Every guy in town is going to want a dance with you."

Tory slid her arms down from their provocative position and shook her finger. "Oh—but there's only one guy I'm interested in. And that's . . ."

"Winnie!" KC suddenly shouted, panicked, as Winnie strolled back into the bedroom.

Winnie fanned away Tory's perfume, staring at KC.

KC glanced quickly at Tory, then relaxed when she saw her digging into her suitcase and pulling out a belt. The dangerous moment had passed.

"Relax, KC," Winnie was saying, standing in the doorway, her hands planted on her tiny hips. "You're going nuts, you know that? And if you don't run into that studly tonight, I'm going to find him myself."

KC felt her heart speed up as Faith, Tory, and Winnie put on their coats and applied last-minute lipstick in the tiny bathroom. Every emotion and hope she'd ever had in her life seemed to be focused on this one, glorious, crazy night. She had to know him. There was something in his face. Something in the way he stood there in the window. She didn't know what it was. But she was going to find out.

"It's time," Faith broke in, grinning and doing a little pirouette out of the bedroom. Her cheeks glowing with excitement, she pulled on her gloves and threw KC's hat at her. "Eight forty-five on the dot. Come on. Turn out the lights."

KC followed Faith, Winnie, and Tory into the hall and down the elevator into the freezing night. Together they hurried around the building and took the Sugar Mountain Village's shortcut path to the lodge, which was already packed with other partygoers. KC breathed in the icy, bracing air. Up above, the black sky was studded with brilliant stars. Ahead was the dusky blue outline of Sugar Mountain. Her heart was full, and she wondered if her mystery man was in the crowd behind them, or in front.

Winnie was skipping ahead like a pony through the frigid, bluish haze. "I can't figure out why KC's become such a romantic," she shouted into the night. "Every time she meets a guy who's nice, she ends up fighting with him."

"Why?" Tory asked with a blank look.

"Shhhhhh," KC protested.

"It's KC's way of saying I like you," Faith called out gaily. "Then she falls. Think about it. Peter Dvorsky . . . Cody Wainwright . . ."

"Stop," KC broke in, looking around in a panic at the bear suits, pirates, and Robin Hoods whizzing by them on skis, headed for the lodge. Any of them could be her man. "This is different."

"Okay." Winnie turned and skipped backward, her color-tipped, spiky hair bobbing in the dim light, "but let's just forget about being serious tonight, okay? I'm going to dance with as many guys as possible—and I'm not going to feel a thing, for any of them."

"Sounds good to me," Faith agreed. "KC can do all the touchy-feely stuff for us tonight. Okay, girls?"

Once they reached the trail junction, the four girls were swept up in a river of people skiing, walking, and snowshoeing toward the lodge below. Mexican sombreros bobbed. Papier-mâché animal masks wiggled. Marie Antoinette skirts swished against the snow. KC could feel her heart beating wildly now. In the distance, she could see the lodge, like a massive lantern, sending yellow blocks of light over the surrounding snow. All around it, the trees sparkled with lights. Even from this distance, she could hear the thumping of a huge band.

The route to the ballroom was up the lodge's big wooden staircase and through its elegant main lobby. KC wiped her snowy feet on the ten-foot-long mat, then followed the crowd through the big wooden doors into the lobby's carpeted expanse. At night, KC thought it looked twice as beautiful. A fire blazed in the massive stone fireplace. Wreaths hung from the rough-hewn rafters. Lights sparkled from the big indoor trees. The air smelled of cider, fir, and smoky wood.

"Look at the costumes," Faith whispered excitedly, her golden hair caressing her shoulders. "They're amazing."

KC nodded, feeling desperate. Some of the women were dressed in elaborate, full-length Southern belle dresses. But there were also guys in tiger suits. Bunny suits. Santa Claus suits. Knights in shining armor. How was she ever going to find her mystery man? She stopped. All of the fancy costumes were lined up in front of a long table labeled Costume Contestants Register Here.

"Look, here's where we go." Faith pulled her over to another line, where a guy in a white Crystal Valley Lodge turtleneck was passing out black half-masks to the people without costumes. KC noticed the big double doors to the ballroom just behind him.

"Okay, ladies," the guy called out, holding four half-masks. "Rule number one. Everyone has to wear a mystery mask until midnight."

Tory planted her hand on her hip. "Do we have to?" she whined, a pained look on her face. "They're sweaty and awful."

"Have fun, ladies," the guy said, ignoring her.

KC took her mask and followed the others to the coat check. Then, smoothing her sweater and still holding her mask, she walked carefully into the ballroom. She breathed in and touched Faith's arm for reassurance. The ballroom was already a sea of color and motion, and a deep, bump-and-grind number was throbbing. She gulped as they moved ahead, staring at all the disguises. With so many costumes, finding her mystery man seemed almost hopeless. The only solution she could come up with was trying to find someone local, who might point her in the right direction.

While Winnie and Tory rushed off, KC and Faith took in the wild scene. The ballroom's huge, beamed ceiling was hung with streamers and release nets filled with balloons. Costumes shimmered. Suntans flashed. Faith's eyes were sparkling. "Wouldn't it be wonderful if Winnie and Josh got back together—tonight—in this beautiful room?" Faith whispered into KC's ear.

KC nodded, absently patting Faith's shoulder. While Faith darted off to get a Coke, she shouldered her way into the carnival-like atmosphere, half-mask still in hand. She stared at the big band lined up at the far end of the room. Costumes bobbed. Skimpy bikini tops glittered. Her eyes quickly surveyed a group of sunburned guys in suspenders and jeans leaning against the room's huge timbered columns. Disappointed, she scanned the action around the ballroom's giant stone fireplace, where a group of masked couples were dancing.

KC paused next to a big column at the edge of the dance floor, alone. She knew the rule was to wear her mask until the stroke of midnight. But she hesitated. If she could just stand there for a moment, unmasked, maybe her mystery man would recognize her. Sweat broke out on her upper lip, and she had to take a deep breath to steady herself.

"Three hours and counting!" the bandleader called into the microphone to the uproarious cheer of the giddy, sun-soaked crowd. "We're making memories tonight, folks. So make them good ones."

"Good memories," KC echoed softly, her eyes scanning the crowd, her heart pounding in her chest. Slowly, she lifted her mask to her face. Then, the next moment, something made her stop. A tall guy wearing his half-mask, jeans, and a white turtleneck shouldered his way through the tangle of dancing, writhing bodies. KC stopped breathing. She recognized the well-muscled shoulders and the long legs. He moved swiftly, gracefully toward her, and in a split second, she saw the head of dark hair above the mask. Was it him? She stared, and as he approached, she could feel her knees begin to buckle under.

"Hey, check it out," the masked face spoke as it passed, "she's standing still. What's the matter? Forget what all the hurry was about?"

KC's jaw dropped. The guy lifted his mask off, and in a single, infuriating moment, she realized her mistake. He wasn't her mystery man at all. It was only

Sean McGlofflin, the rude guy who worked at his family's ski shop fitting rental skis. She froze. She still hadn't told the McGlofflins about her stolen skis.

"Oh, hello," she replied, her heart sinking.

Grabbing a soft drink from the table beside them, Sean took a long gulp. "No mask, huh?" he shouted. "That's breaking the rules, you know." His eyes were both sarcastic and twinkling. "Better chance at getting a dance this way, huh?"

KC opened her mouth to hurl an insult back at him, but she quickly stopped herself. The stolen skis weighing on her mind had belonged to the McGlofflin Ski Chalet, after all. The last thing she needed now was to start a major war with a family member.

Dropping her mask down over her face, KC forced herself to be pleasant. "No, actually I think the mask will improve my odds," she said calmly.

"Mmmm," Sean responded, stroking his chin, staring straight into her eyes. "She's humble. She's standing still. A change has come over Miss Angeletti." He leaned forward a little and looked closely at her face. "Yeeeees. I think something has brought her back to earth."

KC stared right back, then looked down. "Actually," she cleared her throat, "something did."

Sean smiled. "The rich are so easily disappointed."

KC felt her blood begin to pound angrily in her temples, but she held her temper. "My skis were stolen, I'm not rich, and I didn't pay for the insurance you recommended," KC said simply, praying that her honest approach would pay off eventually.

Sean's face suddenly looked open and boyish. He gave her the warmest smile imaginable. "You're kidding. But you were so convinced the insurance plan was a rip-off. Amazing that you could be so wrong." Crossing his arms over his chest, he gave her a playful look. "Bad luck. What are you going to do?"

KC bit her lip, humiliated. The frustration was actually beginning to make her hands tremble. "I don't know."

Sean gave her a lopsided smile as the music picked up and intensified into a wild beat. "Stop by the store day after tomorrow," he shouted into her ear. "I'll talk to my parents and find out what they want to do."

KC nodded and watched Sean disappear back into the mass of twisting bodies. Then, pursing her lips, she pulled her mask down and pushed forward into the crowd, looking for her mystery man.

Davis walked along the perimeter of the ballroom, followed by Josh. The place was now completely filled with sweating, laughing, dreamy-eyed dancers. He stopped, then smiled at the whole crazy scene. He felt solid and good that night; the snowboarding demonstration that morning had gone well. His run had been perfect, and Higgenbothem had walked off with a big trophy for SnoPro Boards and the Dolphin Enterprises executives back in L.A. It now seemed incredible that he had almost gone along with Eric Briggs's sleazy bet. He'd done the right thing, the honest thing. And he was proud of it.

The band had just moved into a deep, frenzied

disco beat, peppered with something that sounded Latin. The crowd was wild for it; it made Davis want to dance, too. He swayed his shoulders a little, feeling his mood lift even higher. Still, it wasn't just any girl he wanted tonight. The girl he wanted was someone very special and very far away. She was the one whose memory made him change his mind that morning. And her name was Faith.

"You're safe," Davis yelled into Josh's ear, trying to loosen him up. "Tory's probably glued to another manly chest—for now, anyway."

Josh glanced at the dancers, then hid his masked face with the side of his hand. "I gotta get out of here. She's on my trail."

"So she recognized you." Davis laughed and tried to cheer him up, ducking two women dressed as belly dancers. "Find someone else to dance with, man. Loosen up. Have a little fun."

Josh breathed in, then leaned against the log wall. "You're right. I don't know what's wrong with me— except that I guess I need that wilderness trip on my skis. This is all too . . ." Josh held his hands out helplessly toward the crowd, then dropped them down, smiling a little.

Davis grabbed Josh's shoulders and shook him. Then, still laughing, he leaned up against the wall, too, casually checking out the masses of dancers. He swayed his head back and forth and let his eyes drift lazily over the color and movement. His body felt light and fizzy, as if the music had pushed away every dark thought. Suddenly there was no Higgenbothem.

No poverty. No fear. Just music and bodies.

Then, slowly, half-consciously, his eyes began to rest on a girl. He smiled. He could see only her back. But there was something pleasing about her body in the powder-blue sweater and jeans. She was leaning forward slightly and saying something to someone deeper in the crowd whom he couldn't see. Davis sighed. In the muggy ballroom, against the glitter of sequins and neon, the girl was like a breath of fresh air.

". . . get something to drink," Josh was shouting in his ear.

Davis nodded and smiled, still watching the powder-blue sweater sway. It turned. Her hair—long, silky, and blond in the dim light. The masked face—heart-shaped, resting on a long, graceful neck. He stared and felt a clutch at his throat. Something deep inside him began to pound. Her hands lifted into the air in a goofy dance, like a tap dance. Her fingers—long and tapered. Something was making him think of home. The beach. The waves. The beautiful girl from the mainland.

Faith.

"Davis?" Josh was pulling his arm. "I'm going to get another Coke."

Davis's eyes were cemented to the figure in the crowd. She kept slipping in and out of sight. He held up his arm, shooing Josh away. He took a step forward.

Faith.

He was dreaming. His mind was playing tricks on him. The face turned in the swirling light, and she gently lifted the mask from her face, as if to flick something away from her eye.

Faith.

Davis's mouth went dry. It couldn't be. She was hundreds of miles away in Jacksonville. Or at the U of S. She wasn't here in Crystal Valley. It was too incredible.

He stared. Now her face was fully visible. His heart turned upside down. It was impossible, but it was her. It was Faith Crowley—the girl he would never forget. Could never forget.

Davis froze, unable to move. He needed to get his bearings. She slipped deeper into the crowd. Standing there alone at the edge of the dance floor, he felt his whole life contract into that single moment. His face was numb, his chest was swelling with emotion. He would stand there. He would wait for her to appear again—even if it took forever.

Nine

"I did not say that!" Winnie was shrieking happily over the music to the two guys from Innsbruck, Austria, she was dancing with. By a quarter to midnight, the lodge ballroom had turned into one giant, bubbling soup of human bodies. Lights spun. Brassy music blared. Sweat trickled in tiny lines down Winnie's back.

"Oh, yes, you did," one of the guys shouted back in his thick accent. He took her right hand and swung her under his muscled arm. Winnie giggled. Both guys had jobs in Crystal Valley operating the chairlifts. She loved their big, brawny shoulders and heads of blond hair. The Crystal Valley sun had turned their faces barbecue-brown. They could barely speak English, but

Winnie was getting along just fine with body language.

"Winnie," she heard Faith's urgent voice somewhere behind her in the blur of music and lights. "Winnie—I need to talk to you."

Winnie turned around, still bouncing. She'd been bouncing for so long, Faith's head seemed to be bobbing, too, even though she was standing perfectly still. "Not now, Faith!" she shouted between twirls with her Austrian partner. "Can't you see I'm busy? Go. Go find someone to kiss at midnight. You need a kiss."

Winnie danced on. Faith's figure retreated like a shadow into the forest of flailing arms and legs.

"Ten minutes, folks," the silky-smooth voice of the bandleader cooed into the microphone. Miraculously, everyone could hear him over the music. "Just ten minutes to find a partner, make a wish, and make that wish come true."

Winnie boogied harder, grabbing the Austrian guys by the hands and yanking their big arms around. Why did people always have to talk about wishes and resolutions on New Year's Eve? Why wish? It wasn't anything you could count on. What was the use? The world, after all, was a dangerous, complicated place. It was full of heartache and disappointment and failure. Why remind everyone that there were wishes to be made and dreams to come true? Why not just live in the moment? It was the only thing you could really count on.

A moment later Winnie felt Faith's hands on her shoulders.

"Faith!" Winnie shouted, giggling. "Party pooper."

Faith dragged her away, and Winnie gave in to her,

bursting into laughter when she saw the desperate looks the Austrian twins were giving her.

"Come here," Faith ordered, steering Winnie's thin shoulders toward the middle of the dance floor.

Winnie jogged obediently in front of her friend like a bouncing wheelbarrow. Wearing a goofy face, she waved to the curious onlookers who parted in front of her. She looked up at the huge nets hanging from the ceiling, filled with colorful balloons. She checked her pocket for the wads of streamers and confetti. Bodies surrounded her like a blurry maze, but Faith's hands remained firm.

"Now stop," Faith yelled, pushing down on her shoulders, "and wait here!"

Winnie's mouth dropped open, but she couldn't help laughing as she turned to face Faith.

"Ladies and gentlemen," the bandleader's deep voice boomed. "The countdown has begun. Ten, nine, eight . . ."

". . . seven, six, five," Winnie chanted with the roaring crowd. Feeling free, she lifted her arms up and spun around.

". . . four, three, two, *one*," the crowd chanted.

There was a huge bang as a thousand noisemakers blasted all at once and the strings holding the vast nets onto the ceiling were cut. A million balloons rained down and Winnie held her arms wide open, as if she wanted to catch them all at once. The music started in again, loud and nostalgic.

"Should old acquaintance beeee forgot and . . ." Winnie sang in her loudest voice. She spun around, grinning and giving in to the craziness. Couples were whipping off their masks and kissing. Others clung to each other and sang. Winnie felt weightless and carefree as she slipped off her own mask and gazed at the lovers and strangers milling about her. Then she felt a brief pang of loneliness witnessing the kisses—the embraces.

She closed her eyes and tried to think of a wish. A tiny, sad longing flickered through her, but she shoved it away. Her eyes fluttered open, and a split second later she saw the corner of Faith's fluffy blue sweater in the crowd. Winnie squinted. Faith with a guy! No, she was pushing him away, in Winnie's direction, just as the guy was slipping off his own mask.

Suddenly, something made Winnie shiver. Her eyes traveled up the length of the guy's body. She took in the old brown boots with the leather laces. There were the faded blue jeans, patched on the left knee with the small bandanna-print square she'd snipped from her freshman Halloween costume.

Winnie stopped breathing. Hot tears began to build up behind her eyelids. Everything seemed to slow and flatten out. There was no noise, no party, no one—just the guy in front of her with the Harley-Davidson belt buckle and the faded green turtleneck.

Josh.

Her arms floated into the air. She didn't have to look up. She already knew the face that belonged to the body. The long, angular jaw. The funny, lopsided grin. The two green eyes that seemed to have their own, warm light.

"Josh," she whispered. She looked up into his face

for the first time. His face, tanned by the mountain sun, looked down at her in utter shock. His hair—shorter, Winnie thought. He must have cut it before Christmas for his parents, she thought, her mind whirling, not making sense. His mouth opened to speak.

"Winnie." Josh mouthed the word.

Later, Winnie never could remember who stepped forward first. It was if they had joined in a dream and neither had any control over what would happen next. They just watched each other as their arms lifted, their faces drew near, and their lips suddenly met.

". . . in the days of auld lang syne," the crowd roared and boomed into Winnie ears. She felt her body press up against Josh's. His heart beat strong and fast against hers. His arms circled her tightly as they had done so many times before. Winnie let her head fall back, barely comprehending what was happening to her in the middle of the swirling lights and music. All she knew was that a wave of pure love was washing over her. All she could feel was the fierce embrace that surrounded her. She was whole again. She was safe.

Josh felt as if he'd been dipped in a vat of warmth and love. Winnie. Suddenly, from nowhere, she was in his arms, and just the feel of her made him forget everything. The divorce papers back on his desk. The anger. The pain. The past. His knees were weak, and he kissed her harder just to stay upright. What was happening?

"Win . . ." he murmured, sliding his lips along the side of her face and taking in the smell of her hair and skin. Sobs gathered in his chest, and he felt them come forward all at once. He had the strange feeling that everything he'd been holding back for so long was about to burst open.

"What . . . what are you doing here?" He could hear Winnie struggling to talk.

Slowly, Josh lifted his head off Winnie's warm neck. He could feel her step back a little to look at him. Her eyes gazed up into his—two burning dark lights on the tiny brown face. Winnie. Her brown eyes had little golden flecks in them. Her eyes could bore through him and understand everything in his heart.

Something slowly tightened inside his stomach.

"Josh," he could hear Winnie calling from somewhere in the dim light and confusion. He could feel her burning fingertips on his cheek. There she was, just as she had been so many times before. Across the library table. Across the breakfast table. Next to him in their bed. Tears fell down her cheeks. She stared at him, her eyes wet. Did she still blame him?

Josh felt himself stepping back, not knowing why. "Win . . ." he breathed, shaking his head, his breath short and fast.

We'll never make this work, he could hear her low growl echoing back from so many months before. It's too hard. It's just too hard.

Instinctively, Josh stepped back again. Her face haunted him. It made everything in their past together come flooding back. The confusing news of Win's pregnancy. The horror of the miscarriage. The sick feeling that had flooded his body the day she'd packed her bags and left him for good. Why had she accused him of so many crimes? All he had wanted was her.

Josh's hands began to shake. A chilling sweat broke out all over his body, and there was a pain in his chest that suddenly made him wonder if he could still breathe. He opened his mouth to speak, but instead of words, there was only empty air rushing up his throat. He tried to look at Winnie's face, but all he could see was blackness. Groping against the dark, he turned away, not knowing where he was going or what he was thinking.

I'm sorry, the words flooded through his brain. I'm sorry. I don't know what's happening to me, Win.

"Josh!" he could now hear Winnie screaming behind him. Tears rose in his eyes as he wove past bobbing faces, sequined heads, and confetti-strewn shoulders.

What am I doing? Josh thought desperately. What am I running from?

Josh's face was going numb. Winnie. He'd just kissed Winnie. Why was she there with Faith? Pain gripped him. For a moment, when he'd kissed Winnie, all of the happiness she'd given him had come flooding back. A second later, it was gone. All he could remember was the pain. And all he wanted was to get away from it.

His legs pumped ahead through the crowd. A blur of fluffy blond hair that framed shiny lips and eyes darted in front of him.

"Hiiiiii!" the girl cried out, just as Josh rushed forward, smashing into the huge plastic cup she was holding. Ice and brown Coke flew into the front of her tight-fitting dress. Stopping, he looked at her.

The girl stared back, her eyes slowly turning into two slits. Everything was whirling around him. Who was this girl and why was she staring?

"Aren't you going to say anything?" he heard her shout.

He stepped back. There was a vague memory of a girl. The girl. Yes, it was Tory. The girl from the Iceman Tavern. He struggled to speak. "Look . . . I'm really . . . I mean, I'm really sorry. . . ." he stammered.

Tory's face had immediately turned to ice. Slowly, she lifted both hands into the air and shook them, dripping, with great drama. Then she looked up at him and pressed her lips together. "For a minute, I thought you were really enjoying that kiss with my roommate," Tory sneered at him. "But now it looks like you were scared off, you big animal."

Josh shook his head, trying to get his thoughts straight. "Tory? Your roommate? What's . . ."

Brushing off her shiny pink top, which was soaked with her drink, she exploded. "Yeah, I'm rooming with her, you big brute. Whaddaya think you're doing pushing me around like that? And I thought we had a date, you—you—"

"I'm sorry . . ." Josh interrupted, shaking his head in disbelief as if Tory hadn't really happened. Was she an image on a screen or something he'd actually seen? The room began to cave in on him. The walls. The ceiling. The air. He couldn't breathe. He had to escape. "I have to get out of here—uh—Tory. Look, I just can't be here right now," he said in one long breath, before rushing through the throng and out into the cold, clear, starry night.

A moment later, Faith was standing frozen at the edge of the booming dance floor, knee-deep in balloons, tears brimming onto her cheeks. She stared, transfixed, at Winnie, who stood alone and horror-struck a few yards away while Josh hurried away through the crowd toward the door.

Faith clamped her hands to her hot cheeks, sickened by what had just happened. "What have I done?" she whispered. She stepped forward through the noise and confusion and tried to speak to Winnie, but she couldn't. Her mouth was dry and her tongue felt as if it were glued to the top of her mouth.

"Winnie!" a cracked, desperate cry finally came out of Faith's mouth. Winnie's solitary face, streaked with tears, turned toward her, then seemed to collapse. Even in the strange, undulating light, she could see her friend's lips twist and harden. Her eyes looked cold and lifeless. Faith drew her breath in. Winnie's accusing stare was more than she could bear. It was almost a relief to see her rush away.

Faith slowly backed off the dance floor, still in shock. She searched the faces of the frenzied dancers, somehow hoping they could answer the questions swirling through her mind.

But they love each other, Faith thought miserably, brushing away a stray party streamer. Clouds of confetti still fell in wisps from the ceiling. The music suddenly switched to a slow, romantic number. Her eyes wet with tears, Faith shook her head and began to sway imperceptibly to the music. How can two people in love hurt each other so much? Why does it have to be so complicated?

Faith bit her lip, intensely ashamed of herself. She'd intruded on Winnie and Josh's lives. Maybe she had no idea what it was like to be in love and to fight its hard battles. Sure, she and her high school sweetheart, Brooks Baldwin, had dated for years before breaking up their freshman year. But she knew in her heart that her love for Brooks wasn't the deeper kind that Winnie and Josh had from the beginning. What was she doing trying to surprise them? Did she actually think she, Mother Faith, could make everything all better? Winnie and Josh weren't puppets she could control. They were real, live people with feelings she probably would never understand.

Faith's eyes wandered over the swaying lovers on the dance floor. Her tears fell freely now. A filmy blue light filtered down from the ceiling, and her heart sank a little. After she had broken up with Brooks, she'd met only one guy who had given her a feeling of connection and belonging—a guy she could have loved, if there had been time. Brushing her wet cheek, Faith sucked in her breath and tried not to think about that warm summer on the faraway island. The guy with the golden face.

The silky-smooth music soothed her. It was romantic, sad music—all muted brass that made her think of old movies and love letters. She swayed a little, trying not to cry so hard. Balloons bounced gently against her ankles. Then, slowly, as if in a dream, Faith began to turn around. She felt something warm at her neck, as if someone was whispering in her ear. There was pressure at her waist, and she felt a strong hand slip around her, turning her gently in the opposite direction. She looked up and saw the pale-blond hair first. Next, a mysterious black half-mask, below which a sweet mouth smiled. A mouth that was dipping down toward hers in the smoky, whirling darkness.

"What?" Faith whispered softly before her lips met his. She kissed him and felt herself falling into the circle of his arms and shoulders.

What's happening to me? Who is this?

The stranger's lips were warm, and there was something familiar in the firmness of his chest against hers and the tangle of their arms together in that embrace. Something made every muscle in her body go slack as she gave in. She pressed her lips harder to his, trying to remember something . . . trying to get back a feeling she had once before on a moonlit beach on the faraway island. . . .

Her eyes closed, then opened as she let her body sway to the music. She watched as the familiar hand reached up to the mask. Her heart began to pound in her chest, and suddenly, even before his face was revealed, she knew.

"Davis," Faith cried out softly, gazing up into his face.

The lights changed to yellow, then blue again. He was smiling the old, loving, confident smile she'd seen so many times back in Hawaii. What was happening? How could he be here in Crystal Valley?

"It is you," Davis whispered into her ear. His eyes were shining and wet in the darkness. "I thought maybe I was dreaming."

Faith's mouth dropped open, then broke into a huge smile. She touched the side of his face and the tiny scar beneath his eye. "I—I thought you were back in the islands . . ."

"I got a job . . ." Davis stammered, staring at Faith so hard it seemed as if he was unable to focus on what he was saying.

Faith was laughing now in crazy disbelief. "A job? What?"

"Snowboards," he mumbled, stroking her hair gently, "I—demonstrate—them—at—ski—resorts. . . ."

Faith felt herself crying and laughing at the same time. "But how did you happen—"

"—to come to Crystal Valley when you were— here?" Davis finished her sentence as if the two of them were one huge, wonderful thought. "I don't know, Faith," he murmured, dropping his mouth down to her ear and resting his head on her shoulder, "I don't know how I got so lucky."

Faith circled her arms around his back and slid them up until she was clinging tightly to his neck. Davis straightened and gripped her arms as if he couldn't bear to have her pull away. Faith gulped. "I . . . didn't know if I'd ever . . . see you again."

Davis's mouth was trembling. Tears welled in his eyes as he drew near her face. "Now that we're together, Faith, I'm never going to let you go again."

Ten

Tory gritted her teeth together and pushed her shoulder into the crowd of girls milling in front of the lodge's bathroom mirror. In the distance she could hear the steady thump of the band. All she could see in front of her, though, was the huge splash of rum and Coke all over the front of her pink top.

"Stupid freak," she muttered in anger, pushing the paper-towel dispenser up and down and ripping off a piece. She reached for the faucet, drenched the towel in cold water, and began to rub the stain furiously.

"Excuse me." A girl with a long braid pushed into her.

Tory glared at her. "Useless," she muttered, tossing the wet towel into the trash and backing away from the mirror. "And that goes for the whole horrible night."

She marched out of the bathroom and into the swirling lights and booming music of the ballroom. Then she crossed her arms over her chest and leaned up against the rough wall next to the buffet table. For a few miserable lonely minutes, she just stood there, staring at the crowd and the parade of couples heading back and forth. She jammed her tongue into the side of her mouth, barely able to contain the fury boiling up inside her. Staring down at the row of pink nails digging into her forearm, she had a sudden, intense urge to start screaming out loud.

"Josh was actually trying to avoid me," Tory muttered. She rolled her eyes and dug her nails in even deeper. "We had a date, dammit."

She closed her eyes and saw Josh kissing Winnie on the dance floor all over again. And it wasn't just a lighthearted, wishing-you-well, New Year's Eve kiss. It was a long, passionate kiss. A lover's kiss. What was he doing suddenly falling for her dippy, totally wacko vacation roommate when he was supposed to have a date with her?

Lowlife. Scum.

Tory opened her eyes again. Her mind snapped off Winnie and Josh. The lights revolved, and the smell of rum and Coke drifted up from her soaked top. But her eyes were focused on something else.

Davis.

She squinted, taking in the tall form with the broad shoulders and the pale-blond hair. Something twisted in Tory's stomach. His arms—brown and muscular—

wrapped around the girl with the blond hair and the fluffy blue sweater.

Faith!

"What the hell is going on?" Tory heard herself practically shout. Her mouth dropped open as Davis gave Faith a passionate kiss on the lips. Their embrace tightened, and the two seemed locked together in their own private glow on the dance floor. Snotty, bullying Faith ends up with the most beautiful guy in Crystal Valley. Wacko-weirdo Winnie ends up with her date. These girls were even worse than the stuck-up nerds back at Cantwell-Jamison College.

First they write me a flowery letter begging me to be their roommate. Then, as soon as they arrive, they start ruining my life. Faith orders me away from my big New Year's Eve date. KC calls me a drunk. And now Winnie steals Josh.

Tory's eyes darted around the room as she tried to remember where the bar was. She desperately needed a drink.

But just as she was about to wander away, Tory sensed someone approaching her. She sighed, thinking about the big rum and Coke stain. How was she supposed to press up to some cute guy on the dance floor in this condition?

"Hey, beautiful," she heard a deep male voice next to her. "Thought you had a date."

Tory's eyes lifted. She turned her head and felt her spirits bounce a tiny bit. It was brawny Eric Briggs from the Iceman Tavern. She stared, vowing instantly to play it cool with this hotheaded wall of muscle.

"No date?" Eric breathed into her ear, crossing his arms over his muscular chest. A beer bottle dangled between his thumb and third finger. He leaned sideways on the wall, and his huge triceps flexed against the log surface so that he seemed to be doing small push-ups against the building. Eric Briggs was powerful, all right. And in the mood she was in, she was more than ready to latch on to him and his steely blue, bad-boy eyes.

Tory tossed her head. "Did I say I had a date?" she asked with a coy look.

Eric's smile broadened and his eyes never left her face. "I've been watching you, beautiful. I've been watching you since you set foot in that door."

"So?" Tory came back.

Eric's icy blue eyes glittered. "And I watched you rush off the dance floor into the bathroom here." He reached over and took Tory's chin into the palm of his large hand. Then, delicately, he turned her face to his. "You're upset, beautiful."

Tory felt a slow burn in her chest. She bit her lip and looked with longing over at Davis, who was now clamped to Faith like a permanent fixture.

Eric followed her gaze, then let go of her face. He took a long swig from his beer bottle. "Ho, ho." He chuckled. "Don't tell me your date was that lousy, two-faced liar, Davis Mattingly."

Tory's eyes opened wide. She stared at Eric's broad face, comforted. Nothing could hurt that face.

"Actually, no," Tory drawled, snuggling up to Eric a little. "I had a date with his friend, who's a big liar, too."

Eric handed her the bottle, and Tory took a drink from it.

"What do you mean, Davis—a liar?" she asked.

Eric's ruddy face hardened. He took a quick drink and stared into the crowd. "He screwed me on a bet. I lost major mucho bucks. Hey, look at him over there with the blonde. Acting like nothing happened. Damn liar."

Tory's eyes traveled the length of Eric's body. A small smile began to form on her lips. Eric didn't like people who messed with him. And neither did she. She could see the anger in his eyes, like the anger she felt. And she could tell, just by looking at his face, he was ready for revenge.

Just like she was.

"I still love him, KC," Winnie was saying quietly, sitting perfectly still on the apartment bed an hour later. She clutched a Kleenex, but KC could see that it was dry. "I didn't realize it until that moment on the ballroom floor. But I love him more than anything in this world."

"Well . . ." KC began carefully. She stroked the spiky bangs off Winnie's forehead, listening to the electric baseboards come back to life in the chilly apartment. "It must have been an awful shock to see you so suddenly. Maybe he just got confused."

Winnie nodded, her brown eyes staring into the distance. KC's hands fluttered. The snowy walk back to the apartment had been a long one. For a while, Winnie had cried. But then something had happened.

KC remembered her stopping on the icy path next to the aspen grove, then staring up at the starry, frozen sky. Suddenly, Winnie's devastated expression had disappeared, and it was replaced by a look of strength that had made KC think she'd figured out something for herself. Something that no one could take away. Not even Josh.

Winnie turned and looked into KC's eyes. "I thought it was all over. I sent him the divorce papers. I was ready to go on," she said quietly. "Then I saw his face."

KC turned down the bed for Winnie and patted it. "Faith feels terrible about this, Win." Winnie kicked off her boots and climbed in between the sheets. "When she gets back from the lodge, I know she'll want to talk," KC added lamely.

"Okay, KC," Winnie whispered, turning over on her side. There was a pause as KC turned off the light. "Why did he have to run away, KC? And why do I have to feel this way all over again?"

KC gave Winnie a final hug and stood up, exhausted. Then she headed for the apartment's bathroom. She stared at her sunburned face under the harsh light and wrung out a cool washcloth. The night had been a disaster.

"You're a fool," KC told herself, opening the washcloth and completely covering her face with it. Sobs welled up from her chest as she thought about the ball. *What made me think I'd run into my mystery man in a room full of disguises? How could I have been so stupid? If he was there, I couldn't tell. Admit it, KC. He's* an impossible dream, and it's time to forget him.

"And then there was our stupid plot to bring Josh and Winnie together," KC whispered to herself, balling up her fists and leaning them against the mirror. Her head sagged down in frustration.

Faith and I have no idea. Absolutely no idea.

In fact, Josh and Winnie's marriage had always been a mystery to her. They'd met orientation week of their freshman year at U of S. And from the day Winnie had accidentally caught his Frisbee on the dorm green, their relationship had gone from fire to ice so many times KC could never keep track. Yet, even right now, in the midst of Winnie's suffering, KC knew she longed for the thing they'd had from the beginning. Love. Real love, with all its fire and hardships and pain.

KC bit her lip and thought about her mysterious man in the window. She'd never lost control in love the way Winnie had. And maybe she never would.

Finally KC stood up straight and turned off the bathroom light. She tiptoed past sleeping Winnie into the living room, collapsed onto the lumpy couch, and stared up at the apartment's ceiling. She felt tired. She felt lost. She felt sad.

"Winnie and Josh," she whispered to herself. "They're like one long chemical reaction that never seems to fizz out."

She looked up across the courtyard at the apartment, which had suddenly blazed into light. She froze and instinctively reached a hand up to her lips. A figure slipped by the window, then moved into another room.

What? You're not at the masked ball?

KC squinted hard. Was it him, or someone else?

Is it you? You are back in your apartment alone, just like me?

The dim figure moved again, and a light suddenly flooded next to him. KC reached up and bit her knuckle. There was the red vest and the dark hair. The quick, graceful movements. It was definitely him. The guy she'd seen for only a second, but who could move her soul from across a frozen expanse of window and empty air.

The figure stopped, and KC could tell he was looking at her. She could see his arm reaching up to his head, as if he was raking his hair back in frustration.

I'd almost given up on you.

His light switched off, then on again. KC reached up and switched on her own light, then waved sadly into the night. The guy let his shoulders sag, as if he was trying to let her know he was sorry. He held his palms up—a sweet, silent gesture KC immediately understood.

He wants to know if he can help.

Slowly, KC shook her head. As she did, the silent figure placed his hand on his heart.

He's sorry. He cares.

Her eyes brimming with tears, KC nodded back and placed her hand on her heart. She smiled as he nodded back. A wave of peace seemed to wash over KC in the darkness. She lay down on the couch and closed her eyes, somehow comforted by the figure in the window. He was out there, somewhere. She would find him if she looked hard enough. And whoever he was—wherever he was—he cared about her.

Eleven

························

"*I*t was New Year's Day, just after dawn. Crystal Valley lay under a new dusting of powdery snow, and the twinkling streetlamps lining Main Street were just beginning to turn off. Wisps of smoke rose from chimneys, and there was a far-off smell of coffee and bacon. Faith slid quietly ahead on her cross-country skis, her face against the icy air, her heart full of love.

Tears glimmered in her eyes. Seven hours ago, Davis Mattingly had stopped her in the middle of a crowded dance floor, kissed her, and turned her life upside down.

My life will never be the same again, Davis, Faith thought as she stared up into the brightening sky. Suddenly, every dream she'd ever had, every hope, every desire—everything was tied up with Davis now. There was no turning back.

She smiled as she pumped her skis forward past the darkened ski chalet, then crossed the street toward the Bavarian Bakery. She and Davis had stayed at the ball, talking and dancing, until three o'clock in the morning, when the cleanup crews arrived. After that, she'd run back to the apartment to check on Winnie and sleep. But after two hours, she awoke, dressed, and slipped out of the apartment.

Now the morning couldn't wait, Faith thought happily, planting her poles eagerly ahead. Davis had the whole day off, and they were spending it together.

She hurried forward, her skis bumping over the snowy tire tracks. Heading away from the boardwalk, she slipped across the soft snow covering the Red Apple Groceries parking lot until she was on the noisy motel strip. She smiled. Just ahead, she could see the small, cinder-block motel next to the Swifty Gas Station that Davis had described. A blinking, broken neon sign read Tip-Top Motel.

After taking off her skis, she checked a slip of paper where Davis had scribbled his room number. Then she rushed up the motel's open staircase and knocked on the door. She watched breathlessly as it opened and Davis's sleepy face appeared. A lock of sandy hair had fallen out of his short ponytail, and his red, peeling nose made his eyes look greener than ever.

"Hi," he said quietly. He took her skis out of her gloved hand, stepped back into the tiny room, and leaned them carefully against the wall. Wearing baggy jeans and a shredded thermal top, he looked as if he'd just tumbled out of bed. "You're early."

Faith gulped as he turned back to take her hand and pull her gently inside. She and Davis had only been apart for a few hours, but it felt like the most romantic reunion of her life.

"Uh-huh," she murmured back, reaching her arms up around his neck and kissing him on the mouth.

Davis kicked the door shut with his toe as the kiss lingered. Then, a few moments later, he wriggled softly away and flattened her hands between his two bigger, brown ones. He blew on them. "Your fingers are cold."

"Mmmm." Faith sighed. Actually, she wasn't aware of her cold fingers. Or the early hour. For a minute, she wasn't quite sure of where she was or what her name was. All that mattered was that she was close to Davis again.

"Last night was great," Davis murmured, kissing her forehead. She could feel his strong arms wrapping around her. She stared happily at the tiny mole on his browned neck. The white scar beneath his eye. She touched his face, almost in disbelief. It was just her and Davis. And she felt certain it would always be that way. She loved him.

There was the sound of the bathroom door opening, and then Davis pulled away. "Hey, Josh," he said quietly. "Faith's here."

Faith pulled away too. She turned and glanced at Josh, who had dropped to his knees in the corner of the cramped room and was rolling up a nylon tent. A large pack was leaning up against the wall. A can of propane and a few packets of dehydrated food were scattered next to it on the worn rug. Faith slipped her hands into her pockets. A wave of guilt washed over her. She didn't know what to say.

"Hi, Josh," Faith said simply.

"Yeah—hi, Faith," Josh said quickly, barely looking over his shoulder. With the flat of his hand, he quickly smoothed another section of tent. His face looked pale, and there were dark circles under his eyes, as if he'd barely slept. Davis stepped away and began tucking in his shirt, embarrassed.

"I'm sorry, Josh," Faith finally said.

"Yeah. Uh-huh."

Faith felt helpless. "I'm sorrier than you can know," she stumbled, feeling tears come on as Josh looked down at the tent.

"Okay," Josh mumbled, rolling the tent.

"I . . . I just thought there was a chance . . . that you and Win . . ."

"Forget it," Josh said quickly, cramming the roll into a bag.

Faith stopped as Josh finally looked up at her, his deep-set eyes burning, his mouth taut. Davis stepped toward her and placed his hand on her shoulder. Faith drew in her breath.

Josh gave both of them an impatient look. "Look," he said, quickly stuffing the tent and supplies into the pack. Faith saw that he was clearly uncomfortable with the chemistry between her and Davis. Hoisting the pack on his back, he grabbed a pair of cross-country skis from the wall and opened the door. "I'm taking off. I'll be on the Cougar Ridge Trail today. Probably camp tonight—about five miles in."

Davis walked toward him, his palms up. "Look, buddy, come on back tonight before dark. We're checking out the Cascade Hot Springs. Why don't you come on by?"

Josh yanked the door open and headed out with a tense, bitter look. "Sorry. See you tomorrow."

Faith's heart dropped as the door shut. Her face lifted up to Davis's and stayed there. "I feel . . . so bad about all this," she said weakly. "I'm worried."

Davis moved closer and stroked Faith's cheek with the knuckle of his index finger. He smiled sadly down at her.

Faith melted as she stared back at him. Davis's face was so free and joyful, even when he was sad. She could have stood there all day, just looking at his sea-green eyes and his peeling, sunburned face.

"Ready for some cross-country?" Davis nudged her, pulling a hat out of his jacket and grinning. "I've done it exactly once before in my life. You'll have to lead the way."

Faith's heart leapt. She gathered her things and headed out with Davis to the snowy street. A bright sun had broken through, and the air felt clean and new. "Just glide forward and kick back," she explained. "There's a great trail leading from the lodge that runs along Elk River. I thought we could take it."

"Great." Davis smiled. He was already clamping his

boots into their toeclips and patting his small pack. "I brought a snow picnic."

Faith's heart sailed as they glided down the strip toward the lodge. The air was icy cold, and she could feel her hair whipping behind her in the breeze. Her legs and arms worked together in unison, and before long she and Davis were warm enough to stuff their jackets in their packs.

Once they reached the lodge, they followed the ski trail around its busy southern deck, past the hot tubs, glassed-in pool, and skating rink. Near the Crystal Valley Arts Center, the trail angled away from the downhill slopes and headed for a line of bare cottonwoods that marked the Elk River. Soon they came across a group of wooden signs directing them over an old-fashioned bridge onto the River Run Trail.

"It's so peaceful," Faith called out at Davis's back. She pushed her sunglasses up on her sweaty nose.

"Great," Davis called back. His knees bobbed up and down as he kicked and glided along the white snow.

The trail steepened, and Faith could feel her leg muscles straining and a trickle of sweat inching down the side of her face. Soon they were completely alone. The snowy trail hugged the side of a steep hill covered thickly with firs and lodgepole pines. Down below, to the left, she could see the Elk River's snow-covered boulders and the overhanging branches of cottonwoods, snow clinging to every available surface. Her skis seemed to fall into a rhythm that pumped her forward along the path in time with Davis. It almost seemed to Faith that they had the same breath—the same beating heart.

"Ernest Hemingway used to fish out here," Faith called out, her breath coming quick and strong. "I guess a lot of writers have come here for inspiration."

Davis looked solemnly ahead, his arms and legs driving forward up a slight incline. "Maybe they just wanted to get a little peace."

Faith tilted her face up toward the warm sun, which glittered and bounced off every branch and snow-covered rock. "The snow reminds me of a play. Everything all quiet and white and still."

"Uh-huh."

Davis stopped, spotting a wooden bench that had been erected on a ledge overlooking the rushing stream below. Together they hiked across an untouched stretch of powder, then scraped the snow off the bench with their gloves. With a flourish, Davis removed a shiny space blanket from his pack and laid it on the wet boards. Faith unhooked her boots from their bindings and stood her skis on end in the deep snow.

"I like the mountains—more than I ever thought I could," Davis said, sitting down and stretching his arms out. Faith sat down and leaned her neck against his forearm. "Maybe it's the beauty—or maybe it's the danger that goes along with it."

Faith looked at him. Surrounded for miles by nothing but snowy wilderness, Davis suddenly seemed very near. "Danger?"

Davis nodded, staring quietly over the view of rushing water and snow. "It's almost like Hawaii, really.

Beautiful—yet dangerous. You never know quite what to expect. You have to be ready to be surprised." Davis suddenly broke into a smile and took Faith's chin in his glove.

"I know what you mean," Faith said. "The waves look so beautiful and tempting. The volcanoes look so sleepy, as if they could never make another sound."

"The snow lying on the side of the mountain," Davis went on. "Beautiful, but deadly, too, if you're not ready. Frostbite—avalanches—"

Faith felt a lump in her throat. For a moment, she was unable to say a word.

Davis reached for his pack, then caught her glance. His eyes contracted with concern. "What. What, Faith? What's wrong?"

Faith felt his arms around her. She felt so safe with Davis. Free, but safe and whole. Bravely, she fought back tears and looked straight into his eyes. "I don't want to lose you again, Davis," Faith said, her words steady. "After Hawaii . . . it . . . just took me a long time to figure out what to do without you in my life and . . . and now . . . what are we going to do when I have to go back—and you have to . . ."

Davis's eyes narrowed, as if he were in pain. He leaned back against the bench and let his hand stroke her neck with a lazy ease. "We can do it," he said with quiet determination, looking out into space. Then he turned and looked at her. "I'm planning on working my way into Dolphin Enterprises over the next few months. With any luck, they'll transfer Higgenbothem and give me the sales rep job for the western states."

His eyes glowed with energy. "I could visit you all the time at the U of S, Faith."

Faith's eyes clung to his face. "And—college, Davis? You said once you were interested in college."

"Yeah—yeah, sure, Faith," Davis said earnestly, looking down and playing with the hem of his baggy snow pants. "That's what I want more than anything. But it's going to take money. I'm going to have to save."

Faith searched Davis's eyes. Then, as he turned and took her in his arms, everything but the present seemed to fade away. They kissed, urgently and sweetly, as a spray of melting snow flew off a branch suspended over their bench.

"Poor KC," Tory drawled. She slipped a five-dollar bill toward the cashier at the ski chalet and took the pair of snowshoes she handed her.

Winnie paid for her snowshoes, too, watching KC out of the corner of her eye. Last night, at the masked ball, KC had talked to Sean McGlofflin, the owner's son, about her stolen skis. Now KC was optimistic the store might let her work the money off, and she'd just slipped behind the counter with Sean's dad to make her proposal. After all, as KC had pointed out, she worked at an off-campus sporting goods store back in Springfield.

Meanwhile, Winnie and Tory were getting ready for a day of snowshoeing along the Elk River. After seeing Josh last night at the ball, Winnie was too shaky to go downhill skiing. Plus, Tory had actually agreed to go with her.

"KC doesn't run away from her problems," Winnie said proudly, slinging her snowshoes over her shoulder and heading out the front door with Tory. "She'll pay those skis off honestly if it kills her."

Tory rolled her eyes and slammed the chalet door. Together they headed down the snowy steps of its front porch. "What's she going to do?" Tory huffed. "Spend her entire vacation polishing ski boots and sucking up to the McGlofflins?"

Winnie looked at Tory, then away toward the glittering mountains, her eyes raw and weary against the bright sun. She leaned down and strapped on her snowshoes. Tory was definitely a pain. But there was something comforting about being with someone who didn't know every detail of her past with Josh. Luckily, Faith was off cross-country skiing with Davis. And KC had her ski chalet business to take care of.

Tory would do for today.

"Right in the butt!" Tory's shout startled her out of her thoughts. Winnie stood up and watched as Tory headed out into the street on her clumsy snowshoes, yelling at a group of guys on cross-country skis. She watched as Tory bent over, made another snowball, and threw it. *"GOTCHA!"*

"Tory," Winnie protested, clomping ahead into Main Street. Together they headed down the trail to the lodge. "We're snowshoeing, okay? Hiking in the woods. Peace and quiet. You said you wanted to do something different this morning."

Tory snapped her gum, gave Winnie a blank stare, then looked down at her huge, webbed snowshoes.

"Yeah. And here I am looking like a duck, thanks to you."

Winnie bit her lip and adjusted her sunglasses. They cut around the lodge and toward a small footbridge that spanned the rushing Elk River. By this time, Winnie's leg muscles were strong and supple. She liked the slow, quiet rhythm of walking. It gave her time to actually see the trees and snow and mountains surrounding her. It was good to feel her body working again and the blood rushing up into her brain.

After they crossed the wooden footbridge, the trail forked. One snow trail seemed to hug the river, while another shot straight up the mountainside. Winnie looked at a small wooden sign that read Cougar Ridge Trail.

"Come on!" Tory began hiking swiftly along the easier river trail, spotting the same group of rowdy guys she'd snowballed by the chalet.

Winnie tried to choke back her anger. The sparkling, snow-covered trees beckoned her. The last thing she wanted was a fight. "Wait!"

"Come on!" Tory yelled over her shoulder, stopping only to lean over and make a snowball. She turned and threw it at a wiry-haired guy who'd stopped to get something out of his pack.

Furious, Winnie pumped up the trail. Sweat trickled down her back and soaked into her cotton turtleneck, giving her a slightly chilly feeling. A few cross-country skiers streaked by her, followed by a family on snowshoes. The snow-laden trees were quiet and beautiful in the sun. The snow felt light beneath her snowshoes.

She breathed in the sharp, clean smell of pine needles in the sun.

What am I doing? All I wanted was a peaceful morning in the woods. Instead, I'm stuck with an airhead brat who didn't know how to say no to a nose ring.

"Tory—knock it off!" she screamed.

Up ahead, Tory was wrestling in the snow with two beefy-looking guys with crew cuts. A blond-haired guy wearing headphones around his neck stood nearby, laughing. When she heard Winnie's shout, she abruptly stood up, her snow pants encrusted with snow, her hand on her hip. She stalked partway down the trail, then stopped, her eyes blazing. "You know what, Winnie?" she snarled. "You're as dried up and stiff as a prune. I thought you were different than your uptight pals. But you're not."

"Do you know how ridiculous you look?" Winnie yelled back. Her nerves were so raw she was beginning to sob, but she held back.

Tory gave her a nasty look. A wet clump of snow dripped off the tip of her platinum ponytail. "Do you know how ridiculous you are?" Tory stormed back through the clumpy tracks of snow, planting her feet. "You get married when you're eighteen? Then you can't figure out why you're so unhappy?"

Winnie lifted her hand to her frozen face as if she'd just been slapped. Her breath came quickly, as though she'd forgotten how to take in air. A stabbing pain shot through her head. Quickly, she turned and began to head back down the trail. Her snowshoes felt like big lead platters, weighing her down. Peals of laughter echoed through the snowy forest. The frigid river rushed below. She felt lost, alone, and very, very scared.

Finally, Winnie reached the footbridge. She brushed off a wedge of snow from the railing, then leaned her elbows on it, stopping to catch her breath. She stared down at the snow-covered rocks and listened to the deep, calming rumble of the river. In the back of her head, she could hear Tory's crazy, screeching laughter. Lower voices seemed to follow. Winnie could tell they were headed back toward the bridge.

Clenching her fists, Winnie looked away, only to see another guy on cross-country skis approaching from the direction of the lodge. Winnie looked at him. Head lowered and body taut against the weight of a camp pack, the guy's dark-brown hair fell loosely over his eyes.

She looked down again at the frozen riverbed, trying to think.

Josh?

Winnie bit her knuckle. If it was Josh, what was he doing? Was he following her? Was he coming to tell her something important? It was impossible.

She looked over again, her heart pounding. She saw the face clearly this time. The long jaw. The deep-set eyes. She remembered a conversation long ago. Josh had always wanted to go snow camping.

Winnie dropped her head and stared, paralyzed, at the water below. The trail led directly over the bridge where she stood. He would pass. He would see her, just as he had on New Year's Eve.

Winnie felt her heart banging inside of her chest. Would he run away a second time?

Winnie could hear him approaching. Her eyes stinging, she tried to focus on a single snow-covered rock in the stream.

He was behind her now. Could he see her? Would he pass on? Would he say a word?

"Win," she heard his voice behind her shoulder, soft and sad.

Winnie turned around slowly and took in his long, weary face. His nose was red from the cold and his green eyes burned brightly from behind his soft, brown bangs. A quiet, lopsided smile began to form in the corner of his mouth. "Josh," Winnie formed his name on her lips, unable to speak.

"Win . . . I," Josh stammered, taking a step forward on his ski.

Winnie held her breath.

Crack.

Winnie turned wildly around in the direction of the shot that had come from the woods. Then, glancing back at Josh, she saw with horror that he had been hit with something. As he staggered backward, Winnie looked in horror at the drops of red falling into the white snow below him.

"*Aaaaahhhhh, ha, ha, ha, ha.*" Laughter rose up from the trail. Tory and the rowdy guys she'd joined were bounding back down the river trail. As they passed back over the bridge, Winnie watched as Josh touched a finger to the red stain splattered all over his jacket. Then he held it to his nose.

"Paint," he breathed, his face contorted in anger.

"Paint?"

"Yeah, I think so."

"But . . . but," Winnie stammered, her head foggy with confusion and pain, "what's going on?"

"I don't know," Josh said, his mouth taut. "Paint guns are really giving these guys a laugh, I guess. . . ."

"Josh . . . I," Winnie said haltingly, not knowing what to do.

Josh's quiet, sad face had twisted into angry confusion. For a split second, he opened his mouth and tried to say something. Then, tears filling his eyes, he shook his head and pressed his lips together.

Winnie stepped forward, digging into her pocket for a Kleenex. "Here," she said. "Let me help—"

"No," Josh said abruptly.

Winnie drew her breath in as he started to turn away. Then his skis turned, too, and she could see him slipping his pole straps around his wrists in a quick, angry move.

"Josh!" Winnie called out. "Don't—"

Josh began skiing away. She stared helplessly at his back and the rushed movements of his skis as they began to head up the steep Cougar Ridge Trail.

"—leave," Winnie finished her sentence, staring down into the snowy riverbed.

A deep sob pushed up from inside Winnie's chest. Why did she and Josh have to cause each other so much pain? She had a fleeting impulse to throw herself off the bridge or bury herself in the snow. Anything to blot out the terrible pain that was slicing her heart in two.

I know I love you, Josh, Winnie thought with a deep pang in her heart. It may be all over for you. But I'm not giving up until I know for sure.

She stood still for a minute, then turned in the direction of the snowy trail up the ridge. All her wet eyes could focus on now were the tiny drops of red paint that followed Josh's tracks deep into the wilderness.

Twelve

....

"After you wipe down the alpine demos, I want you to take a bottle of SnoSeal to that box of leather cross-country boots near the door," Sean McGlofflin was ordering later that day.

KC blew a shaft of air up into her hot bangs. The McGlofflins had agreed to let her pay for the stolen skis by helping out in the stockroom that day. Plus, for the rest of her stay in Crystal Valley, KC was required to work on inventory early each morning for several hours. Financially, her problems were solved. But her vacation was ruined. Instead of spending her free days skiing and tracking down her mystery man, she was stuck in a dank stockroom with annoying Sean McGlofflin.

She set a splashy pair of downhill skis back in the rack. "Do you want me to polish your shoes, too?"

"Yes."

KC shook out her rag and glanced over at Sean, who was spinning his screwdriver into a shiny steel ski binding. The back of the McGlofflin Ski Chalet was a dark, crowded room with a heavy wooden plank floor that held up huge racks of rental skis, boots, poles, and even summer mountain-climbing equipment. "That's not in the job description," KC shot back.

Moving only his head, Sean grinned widely in her direction. "Sure it is. Did I forget to mention it?"

KC glared briefly over her shoulder at Sean, who was busily pondering a ski-binding mechanism as he snapped it back and forth. Wearing a bleach-stained T-shirt and a pair of jeans with a rag hanging out the back pocket, Sean looked completely removed from the ritzy Crystal Valley scene. Even his freckly skin looked out of place. Just looking at him reminded KC of how much she was missing. She looked longingly through the back door's dusty window. Somewhere out there was her mystery man, KC thought with a lump in her throat. He was probably knifing his way down a steep mountain this very instant. Pondering the vastness of the Sugar Mountain range. Maybe, KC thought—maybe even thinking of her.

"Hey, KC." Sean strode over a few minutes later, rubbing his oily hands off on a rag. His dark, coppery hair tumbled over his forehead, and from the half-smile on his face it was clear he was relishing her bad luck. "Are you okay?"

KC bristled. "Of course I'm okay."

Sean heaved a sigh of exaggerated relief. "Oh, good. I just thought—well—a girl like you isn't used to working such long hours. Need a break?"

KC placed the last pair of skis into the rack, then reached for the can of SnoSeal. To hide the angry, shaking feeling inside her, she immediately grabbed a rag and turned the bottle upside down into it. "I happen to be a person who's used to working very hard."

Sean's jaw dropped and he staggered back a little, feigning surprise. "But—but I had no idea. You seemed so free and easy with your money that day you threw it at me."

KC glared at him, grabbing a boot.

"I—I just naturally thought you were a girl from a very wealthy background. You know. In such a hurry. So impatient with the help around here."

KC sat down on a nearby stool and began rubbing the boot vigorously.

Sean stepped toward her and rested his shoulder against a rough-hewn log column. Then he crossed his arms over his chest and looked thoughtfully up at the wooden rafters. "'Course, most people with bucks will pay the twenty dollars for insurance. Crazy not to."

KC clenched her jaw. "Look, I told you. I'm not wealthy. I'm a student. I'm working my way through college waiting tables and selling outdoor equipment."

"Really?" Sean rocked a little on his heels, his eyes twinkling.

"Yes," KC retorted, picking up another boot and smearing it with SnoSeal. "And maybe—someday—I'll make enough money to be one of those wealthy customers you like to make fun of so much."

Sean's eyebrows lifted. His smile widened. "Gee. Bet you can't wait."

KC bit her lip, instantly regretting her words.

"Tell me," Sean said quietly, leaning over at the waist, his frosty blue eyes bright with fun. His face was close to hers now, and she could see the intense blue of his eyes. "Will you still be in such a hurry? I mean— when you've made all of this money."

KC continued to look down and rub the boot. The strong, oily smell of the room made it seem like she was sitting in the inside of a shoe. She tried to relax. All Sean McGlofflin wanted was to get a rise out of her. She didn't know why she even cared what she said or didn't say. The whole situation was ridiculous. She looked up and smiled sweetly into his eyes. "Well, if I'm as successful in business as I plan to be, Sean, I probably will be in a hurry every once in a while."

Sean threw his head back and let out a small laugh. Then, grabbing a pair of skis off the repair rack, he walked back to his workbench, sat down, and braced one of his long legs against the floor. "Successful businesses always carry insurance, KC. This does not say much for your potential as a big-time businesswoman."

"Look," KC snapped, "how was I supposed to know I was going to get ripped off? It just happened, okay?"

Sean calmly reached for a small wrench hanging from the pegboard over the workbench. Screws, tape, and thin metal strips lay scattered everywhere. "Because resorts like this are always targets for professional thieves."

KC pressed her lips together, bending back down to her work. She reached over and adjusted the work lamp clamped to the wall above her chair.

"There've been lots of thefts this year," Sean explained, flipping over the ski and running his fingers expertly along its metal edge. "In fact, just this morning, a number of thefts were reported. Mostly top-of-the-line skis. But they'll take boots, too. Anything that looks expensive and new."

KC stood up and walked past Sean's workbench and the customer fitting area. She placed two polished boots in the size-eight ladies rack. Then she pulled a rubber band over her thick hair and made a ponytail. "So. How do you know so much?"

"Because I live in a small town, KC," Sean said simply, shrugging his broad shoulders. "My family's home is right in back of this store. Townies who live right off Main Street know everyone and everything that's going on."

"Wow."

Sean shook his head and stood the ski on its end. "You don't get that kind of experience taking classes at college. . . ."

KC reddened, then opened her mouth to protest.

"We have to know everything that's going on," Sean explained. "We go to the Chamber of Commerce meetings and Rotary and Elks. We know the people with money and the people without it. If we don't stay on top of the community, we lose references—contacts, information—everything."

KC's polishing rag suddenly stopped. Something in her mind snapped.

Mystery man. Beautiful apartment with a view. The McGlofflins. They must know him.

"Yeah," KC said, slowly pulling another pair of boots out of the box and unscrewing the cap of the SnoSeal. She saw an opportunity, and she wasn't going to waste it because she was irritated with Sean. "I see what you mean."

"Ha." Sean laughed. "I don't believe it."

"No, really," KC said carefully. "I mean about contacts and everything." She looked down and cleared her throat, trying to act casual. "Take the Sugar Mountain Village, for example. That's where I'm staying."

"Uh-huh," Sean replied, holding a ski in front of him and staring at its binding, as if it were an usual specimen. "Some nice condominiums in there."

KC's heart lifted. "Really?" she said with an innocent look. "You know, I thought the one across from us looked like a permanent residence. Let me see." KC pretended to think. In fact, she'd done some careful research with a map of the complex she'd obtained from the manager. "If we're in Apartment 1029 of Winterfest, the place across from ours must be 1029 Holiday, the building that faces the front parking lot."

"Sure, I know it," Sean said casually, flipping the ski down and grabbing a can of ski wax.

KC thought she was going to faint. She stared hard at the boxes of broken bindings, greasy rags, and tools littering the floor. Sean actually knew the apartment across from hers. That meant he must know the owner. Instead, she faked a casual laugh. "What do you mean—you know?"

Sean leaned a hip against his workbench and flipped the can of wax, catching it in midair. "Holiday 1029." He rolled his eyes. "The owner buys a lot of stuff from us—and we deliver. Last week, we delivered a top-of-the-line snow tent, complete with bag, camp stove, equipment—the works. Threw in four very fine sets of cross-country skis, too, with pricey handmade leather boots. Looks like he's outfitting his entire family."

"Mmmmm," KC said, hanging on every word and barely able to conceal her excitement. She wanted to come right out and ask him who the owner was, but held back. If Sean McGlofflin sensed that she wanted something, he definitely wasn't the type to hand it right over. Instead, she decided to take a different route. "I guess some of the ski teams lodge at Sugar Mountain Village, too."

"Yeah." Sean groaned.

KC put a casual finger to her chin. "Let's see. It seems to me I saw a guy in a red vest that said Briar Ski Team."

Sean whistled softly. "Oh, yeah. We see them all the time. They want top-of-the-line everything—especially service. It's sort of a private ski club for rich preppies on permanent vacation. Fun guys."

KC rolled her eyes. Sean's knee-jerk impressions of people with money were getting on her nerves. She took a breath.

"Hey!" Sean said suddenly, walking around his

workbench and stepping back toward the rental racks. "Hey, there. Can I help you with something?"

KC narrowed her eyebrows and stood up. Someone—or something—was stirring in the dim light. There was a flash of pink, then a headful of platinum blond hair. KC stepped back, slowly registering the familiar figure approaching.

"Tory?"

Sean stepped forward, frowning. "Excuse me, but—"

"This is Tory," KC interrupted, confused.

"Yes, well, hello," Sean replied. "Um. Have you lost your way? I'm afraid our retail section is right behind me."

"Why are you way back here, Tory?" KC burst out. "This is for employees only."

Tory bit her lip, and KC just stood there. "Sorry," she said, looking down. "I . . . I was just looking for—"

"I thought you were snowshoeing with Winnie," KC interrupted, suddenly irritated. "Did you leave her alone on the mountain?"

Tory's empty blue eyes suddenly flashed. Ignoring Sean's gesture that he would escort her back into the store, she planted a hand on her hip. "Winnie? What a bore. I decided to go shopping instead," she said with a flounce of her fluffy hair. "And I obviously walked through the wrong door of this dumpy place."

KC frowned.

"Looks like you're having a lot of fun, KC," Tory snarled, walking past her as Sean led her back into the chalet's main floor. "Way to go."

A few minutes later, Sean returned, his hand

clamped to his forehead. "What a nutcase. Claimed she got lost, but that's crazy. The door is clearly marked Employees Only."

KC nodded. "That was strange."

"I just get a little jumpy sometimes," Sean explained, strolling back to his workbench and picking up a wrench. "With all the thefts."

KC nodded. She leaned back in her chair and breathed in the sharp smell of shoe leather and ski wax. "You think you've got troubles. I have to room with her this week."

Sean chuckled and turned to face her. His freckled face seemed to light up with amusement. "Oh, man. That is trouble. Don't tell me. The reservations network fixed you up with her."

KC laughed. "Exactly. According to reservations, she was Victoria Headly, anthropology major from Cantwell-Jamison College."

Laying a freshly waxed ski against the rack, Sean returned to his workbench and snapped the lid back on the can of wax. "You arrive at your dream vacation and meet The Babe with Big Hair."

KC giggled. "We thought she'd be shy and tweedy with inky fingers and—"

"—short nails," Sean finished.

"Sensible shoes."

"Sensible snowshoes."

Bent over with laughter, KC could barely talk. "She—she showed up with three fifths of vodka in her suitcase. Drunker than a skunk . . ."

"Familiar with every stud at the Iceman Tavern,"

Sean broke in. "I know the whole story."

KC's eyes opened wide. "Yes." She giggled, realizing that Sean knew exactly what she was talking about. She didn't even have to explain. "You're absolutely right. We were in shock."

Sean sat back on his stool and looked at her. "You're expecting a mouse, and you wind up with a blonde with a big appetite for fun. Life's full of surprises."

KC smiled back. Sean was a real smart aleck. But he was definitely smart. "Nothing's what it seems like on the outside."

"I guess it makes life interesting," Sean replied.

"Yeah," KC said with a big smile, looking over at Sean, who was happily juggling three small metal parts from his perch on the stool. Then, in a sudden wave of self-consciousness, KC looked down and pursed her lips. What was she doing jabbering away with Sean McGlofflin—the townie who obviously relished holding her prisoner in his shop while her entire winter vacation slipped away? He'd been teasing her from the moment she arrived in town, and KC didn't like being teased. KC found herself wishing she hadn't said a word to him.

"Of course, what would you know about life— stuck in this tiny business with your mom and dad?" KC suddenly snapped.

For a moment, all she could hear was silence over her shoulder as she grabbed another worn boot and began polishing it furiously. It was about time she told him what she thought—instead of groveling just because she owed his family money. There was a scrape of the stool against the wooden floor, and then she heard Sean set another ski down on his workbench.

"You wouldn't know life if it slapped you in the face," Sean finally said.

"I bet it has slapped you in the face, too," KC said hotly. "The way you carry on."

"Not yet, KC," Sean muttered behind her. "Not yet."

Thirteen

....

A few minutes later, Tory was running tearfully across Main Street, dodging Jeeps and trying not to splash into the deep, slushy ruts. Streetlights flickered on in the fading light. Music boomed from a nearby tavern taking in the après-ski crowd. Couples shouldering skis laughed their way up the hill toward the restaurants.

She'd never felt so alone in her life.

Tory jumped up onto the opposite boardwalk, heading blindly past a row of sportswear shops. She kicked a half-melted chunk of icicle, the image of KC and the McGlofflin guy burning into her brain.

Ever since she'd deserted Winnie on the snowshoe trail that morning, she'd regretted it. In her bulky snowshoes, she hadn't been able to keep up with the rowdy guys and their paint guns. Instead, she'd wandered back to town and had hung out at the lodge, too discouraged to head up the chairlift for afternoon skiing.

"This place is worse than Cantwell-Jamison," Tory muttered under her breath, dodging a happy crowd filing into a pizza restaurant.

In fact, Tory thought bitterly, she'd tried hard not to make the same mistakes here that she'd made at college. She'd made a big effort to get chummy with Faith, KC, and Winnie. And just this morning, she'd even gone along with Winnie's dopey idea to go trudging through the woods on snowshoes. The plan had backfired, but she'd actually tried to find Winnie and KC at the ski chalet, hoping to apologize.

So there I stand behind the rental racks, ready to come clean with KC, Tory thought, zipping her jacket up and down with nervous jerks, and I get scared. All I can think of is—what if she still hates me? All I can do is stand there and listen to the McGlofflin kid about the high-priced equipment in Condo 1029.

Tory sniffed and hurried forward, the frosty air burning her cheeks. "Everything is falling apart," Tory whimpered to herself, her mind sifting angrily through the insults she'd endured since her arrival in Crystal Valley. It clicked and sputtered through the long list: There was the insulting way Davis had pawned Josh off on her at Iceman Tavern. The embarrassment of being ditched by Josh on New Year's Eve, only to discover him kissing Winnie in front of everyone in the room.

The horror of being called a drunk by KC. The terror of being threatened by Faith. And, finally, the hurt of being ditched by Winnie on the river trail when they were snowshoeing.

"What do people have against me, anyway?" Tory asked the empty air. "I'm a person, aren't I?"

When she reached the bottom of Main Street, Tory's eyes were stinging with tears. Instead of turning back, she headed angrily toward the lodge, then down a narrow road that led across the valley and over the Elk River past a directional sign that read Cascade Hot Springs. She hurried ahead down the side of the road, her feet slipping in the ice. Darkness was falling. Cars whizzed by. Cascade Hot Springs. She was vaguely aware that she'd heard of the place before, somewhere.

Her heart pounding, she crunched across a narrow bridge and walked under an arched wooden sign that read Cascade Hot Springs. She didn't care where she was going or what she was doing. All she knew was that she had to do something to get rid of the boiling rage inside her.

Tory rushed past the Springs Restaurant, Booker's Grill, and a group of expensive-looking cabins with a sign in front that read Elk River Bed and Breakfast. Finally, near the end of the road, nestled under a grove of lodgepole pines, she spotted an older, two-story wooden building. Steam rose up from behind the fence surrounding it, and she could hear laughter ringing out in the clear, cold air.

"Cascade Hot Springs Spa," Tory read the sign

aloud, rubbing her gloves together. Her foggy mind began to clear.

Cascade Hot Springs.

Tory remembered now. It had been a few nights back, at the Iceman, when she met brawny Eric Briggs. She found herself moving quickly toward the entrance's rustic front door, remembering Eric's invitation. Inside, the place had a plain cement floor, green wooden chairs, and a big wooden counter, where a blond girl stood, talking on the phone. Tory breathed in the smell of sulfur and chlorine. The air was steamy and warm.

"May I help you?" the girl finally said with a polite smile.

"I'd like to look at the hot pools," Tory explained. "My friends and I are planning a get-together here tomorrow."

"Sure," the girl replied, pointing down a long hall to the right. "If you decide to stay, come on back and we'll get you fixed up with an admission ticket."

"Thanks," Tory said lightly, heading down the wood-plank hallway to a glass door that led to the outdoor pools. At first, Tory couldn't see through the warm, rising steam. But a few minutes later she could make out several round pools set into a tiered deck. Floodlights beamed into the surrounding trees. And laughter rang out through the darkness. Soon Tory felt her smile return. Soaking in a tub just a few yards away was bare-chested Eric Briggs himself, along with the four rowdy guys Tory recognized from the paint-gun incident that morning.

Tory's sense of purpose suddenly returned. Wetting her lips and throwing back her hair, she walked by the tub, then stopped and gave the guys a happy wave. "Hi."

Eric's blue eyes lit up. His muscular chest rose out of the water. "Hey, there, beautiful. You look lonely."

Sitting down delicately at the edge of the tub decking, Tory crossed one leg over the other and gave him a steady smile. "Maybe I am."

Eric waded to the edge of the hot tub and rested his bulky arms on the rim. "Why's that? What's a girl as beautiful as you doing without a crowd of adoring fans? It's what you deserve, you know."

Tory drank in Eric's attention. She leaned over on her elbow until her nose was almost touching Eric's. "Thank you," she whispered.

"Get in your suit," Eric breathed back, his eyes gleaming. Water dripped from his hair down his thick neck.

Tory winked. "Think you can just snap your fingers and I'll jump, huh?"

Eric's brilliant smile didn't falter. Slowly, he nodded his head. "Oh, yeah. I think just this once."

Tory stood up and gave him a sultry look. Then she stood up and stripped down to the tiny pink leotard she wore under her ski clothes. Without a moment's hesitation, she slipped into the steamy water with Eric and his four friends. She felt the hot pool close over her shoulders and all of her cares disappear into the darkness. "I am alone now, actually," Tory admitted, letting Eric slip behind her and slowly massage her back under the water.

"Couldn't get old Davis Mattingly to come 'round, huh?" said Eric, handing her a flask.

Tory rolled her eyes, then took a long, burning sip of straight tequila. "Davis and his friend Josh are scum. My three roommates are even worse. What those people need is a nice big avalanche to come along and bury them all forever."

"Mmmmm." Eric looked around at his friends, only half-visible through the shroud of rising steam. "Avalanche. Davis Mattingly couldn't screw me on another bet if he were under ten feet of snow, that's for sure. Hey. I'm beginning to like this lady very, very much. Have another drink, Tory."

The guys all looked at one another and laughed. Tory winked back. Eric moved away from Tory a little and sat down where he could stare directly into her eyes. Lifting his well-developed arms, Eric slicked his wet hair off his face. Tory took another drink and stared lazily, admiring his brawny frame. Then, suddenly curious, she narrowed her eyes. Running down the side of Eric's upper arm was a long welt of a scar. Tory leaned forward and boldly ran one finger down the length of it. The hot tub bubbled and steamed beneath her. "Must have been a bad gash," Tory teased. Then her face became serious. "Why does it look so familiar?"

Eric's eyes glinted and remained glued to her face.

Tory looked around the tub. All of the guys looked as if they were trying hard not to laugh. She frowned. "What's the joke?" Tory teased. "Some big secret?"

Eric pressed his lips together, suppressing a laugh.

Then something clicked in Tory's mind. "That scar," she said with a mischievous look. She raised her finger into the air, then shook it at him. "You're the guy who streaked past the lodge that afternoon, aren't you, Eric?"

Eric just grinned and shrugged. "Hey, guys. She's not only beautiful. She's very, very smart."

Tory giggled. "One of my bitchy roommates had her skis stolen during that little performance of yours."

"Aw." Eric looked smug. "Too bad. Huh, guys?"

"Yeah, too bad," one of his wiry-haired buddies answered, taking a long drag on a cigarette and shaking his head.

Tory looked around the circle of faces. She recognized them, all right—from that morning's paint-gun party. Two of the other guys were big, like Eric, with flattop crews. The third, a long-faced guy, wore a gold chain around his neck and had headphones lying on the towel behind him. Her face broke out into a grin again. Somehow just thinking about KC's stolen skis and her dull job in the backroom of the chalet made her giggle. KC, Faith, Winnie—and all the rest of the uptight snobs in Crystal Valley—deserved everything they got.

Tory narrowed her eyebrows. These guys were as naughty as they come. And something was definitely going on. "Hey." Tory moved over and nudged Eric in the ribs. "You've got some kind of gig."

Eric looked mysterious. "If we did, why would we tell you, beautiful?"

Tory reached out and took Eric's chin between her

thumb and her forefinger. Eric was up to no good. If she had to guess, she'd say he was playing with fire—and the law. She smiled at him. So what? Who cared about being good in a world filled with back-stabbing cruelty? "Because I want to know."

"Why?" Eric challenged.

Tory took a breath, then half-closed her eyes. All the pain and rejection she'd felt seemed to focus itself in her brain. And in one, wild, crazy moment, she realized what she wanted. She wanted revenge. "Because I want in, Eric."

Eric's eyes darted around the soaking tub, his face serious. The rest of the guys looked uneasy. Then Eric stroked his chin thoughtfully. "Why should we trust you?"

"Because there's no turning back for me," Tory said quickly, suddenly as serious as she'd ever been in her life. She felt a knot in her throat, but her eyes were as dry as a desert. "School. Family. Friends. Nothing's worked out. Everything that was supposed to be good in my life has gone bust."

Eric looked impressed.

"I'm not going home," Tory said firmly, staring into his eyes. "So I'm going to need to make my way—any way I can."

After a short moment, each guy in the soaking tub nodded. Then Eric moved forward, his face earnest. "Look. Here's our gig. Me and my buddies here spend most of the winter season traveling the ski circuit. Aspen. Park City. Tahoe. Skiers have a nasty habit of leaving a lot of expensive equipment lying around when they get good and distracted. That's where we excel."

A few of the guys chuckled. Tory listened intently.

"The streaking skier is our best act," Eric explained. "Everyone's tired at the end of the day. The guy with no clothes distracts those rich college kids with their fancy equipment. They look away, we swoop down, and *bingo*—we take our pick of the best unlocked equipment and stow it neatly away in our handy van."

"Then you sell it," Tory said cheerfully.

"Yeah," Eric said with a laugh. "And the insurance companies are the losers."

"And the red paint-guns . . ." Tory began.

Eric shrugged. "This morning's distraction. No major haul, but a few minor pickings around the springs. Problem is, we pull too many of these stunts, and everyone starts to catch on. The authorities move in. I think we're about done here. But I want to pull off a couple more jobs before blowing out of here." Eric ran his eyes up and down Tory's wet body. "Sure could use a new recruit."

A mean thrill ran up Tory's spine. She racked her brain for an idea—any idea—to prove how serious she was. Then she remembered. "Condo 1029, Holiday," she murmured to herself.

"What?" Eric said.

Tory looked at him, her brain suddenly as clear as ice. "It's a pricey condominium across from the place we're renting at Sugar Mountain Village—on the tenth floor."

"Yeah. I know the place."

Tory took a breath. "I overheard a conversation today, that's all. Turns out the condo is loaded with brand-new equipment from the ski chalet. Four sets of skis and custom-made leather boots. Tents, bags, the works."

"Breaking into a condo is risky," one of the guys said quietly. He grinned. "But very profitable."

Eric smiled, too. Then, reaching his arm out, he pulled Tory's slick body next to his. He nuzzled her ear. "I can see you have a taste for adventure, beautiful. But we'll need your help on this job if we do it. In fact, we'll probably need one other person, too."

"Like I said," Tory said, kissing Eric's lips lightly, "I want in."

Eric's smile broadened. Quickly, he caught Tory's waist just as she pulled away. Then, with a powerful movement of his arm, he pressed her against his chest and kissed her hard on the lips. Tory felt herself giving in. Eric Briggs was exactly what she needed. Her world was slippery and confusing right now. But all of a sudden, Tory realized with a smile, she had something to hang on to.

Fourteen

Pounce, pounce, pounce.

Winnie's bulky snowshoes made her feel like a flat-footed troll.

Hop, hop, hop.

Since morning, she'd been wandering up the Cougar Ridge Trail, vaguely following spots of red paint dribbled in Josh's ski tracks. Hours ago, however, the dribbles had disappeared, and she'd ended up climbing through the frosty woods to the top of Cougar Ridge, just trying to get her bearings. Winnie's strong runner's legs were in great shape for the trek, but when she reached the top, all she could see were miles of forested ridges and ravines. All signs of the cross-country trail markers had disappeared. The only landmarks she'd passed were the Forest Service's ominous avalanche barriers and warning signs.

Winnie's toes were getting cold, and the trees began to cast long shadows on the bluish snow.

"So I'm lost," Winnie said out loud, trying to blot out her panic. "Lost on the inside. Lost on the outside. For once, there's logic in my life."

Winnie plunged ahead, now in deep snow, deciding to head down the ravine and follow the watershed until it reached the big Elk River. She couldn't remember why she'd come this way, except that she'd had a foggy impulse to find Josh and yell at him for running away again.

Just a little habit of ours. Josh runs away. Winnie yells and screams. Josh runs away again. Winnie screams.

Winnie's toes pressed into the tips of her boots as she headed down the increasingly steep terrain. Gray boulders stood out all around. Only a few scraggly firs remained as a cushion between her and the void of rock and snow. She took a deep breath, determined not to panic.

"I don't need you, Josh," Winnie shouted into the freezing air. "And I wasn't meant to find you today. My brain was just on the wrong channel—a really sappy country music channel where all the lost-cause romances work out in the end." Winnie took a few hops down on one foot, spreading her arms wide and freely. "All it took was a turn of the dial," Winnie babbled on. "Da, da, da-da-duh," Winnie screeched, grabbing a tree branch as she continued downward. "I'm on a screaming guitar channel now, Josh. Da, da, da-da, duh. Don't mess with meeee, 'cause I'm freeee."

Plunging down the side of the mountain, Winnie sang loudly, pretending the scene was being filmed for a rock video. In the back of her mind, she knew she was in danger of hypothermia, hiking alone near nightfall in the snowy mountains. But to blot out the fear, she did somersaults, clutched tree trunks like lovers, and imagined she was in a band of wandering gypsies, seeking refuge in the woods from the harsh, humorless world.

When she reached the bottom of the ravine, she could hear the distant rush of a creek buried under snow, but there was still no sign of a marked trail. An icy crust began to form on the snow. By now she was exhausted, and she couldn't fight off the images of Josh's face flashing in her brain. His eyes this morning on the bridge—so full of—what? Love? Fear? Pain? He was so close, she could have taken him in her arms. But then what? Would he have pushed her away? Six months ago, Winnie thought she knew everything about her husband, Josh. Now she realized that she hadn't learned enough. And she was paying the price.

Working her way down the ravine, Winnie shivered in the dimming light. She was wearing all her warmest clothes, but the wild ride down the hill had covered her with snow, which had begun to melt into her snow pants. She stumbled along, her eyelids sagging with fatigue. Then, just as she was about to stop and rest, she spotted a speck of red paint in the snow.

Josh?

Winnie held her head up and looked around. She smelled something cooking. Hurrying forward, she reached a bend in the ravine where the stream-bottom widened, leaving a large open space in the snow. Tears sprang into Winnie's eyes. A small, red snow tent was pitched in the clearing, and a light shone from inside. It looked like a bright, glowing lantern against blue dusk. Spread out on a log near the tent was Josh's paint-spattered jacket.

For a moment, Winnie just stood there, shivering and confused. She tried to think. Josh had seen her twice in Crystal Valley, and both times he'd run away from her. She had to face that their relationsip was over. The last thing she needed was for Josh to think she was following him.

Winnie dug her thumbs into the straps on her backpack and took off. Ignoring her freezing wet boots and blue fingers, she bounded downhill until she heard Josh's voice.

"Win!" he shouted over the sound of her crunching snowshoes. "Win—wait."

Winnie plunged ahead, trying to ignore his voice. But a few moments later, she heard the sound of cross-country skis behind her. A hand touched her arm. She turned and tried to plaster a lighthearted expression on her numb face. "Oh—hi," she said lightly.

Josh just stood there in his thermal shirt and hastily tied boots, staring and shivering. "Win—what are you doing way out here? It's almost dark."

Winnie tried to control the deep shaking in her chest. She clenched her teeth to keep them from chattering. "Snowshoeing," she replied with what started out as a happy smile. Her numb lips twisted awkwardly in the cold. "It's great. You should try it sometime."

Josh looked at her as if she'd just sprouted horns.

"Bye," Winnie croaked, turning away and starting to leave.

"Stop!" Josh called out.

A moment passed while Winnie paused in the snow. She looked down, suddenly praying that he would say something. "What?"

"Look."

"What?" Winnie insisted, looking up cautiously. His face looked stiff. Confused. The darkness around them began to press in. Winnie's toes felt like blocks of ice.

"You're cold."

"Uh-huh." Winnie stood there, staring down at the chunks of ice covering her pants.

Josh hesitated. "Just warm yourself by the stove a little while. Okay?"

Slowly, Winnie turned around. Inside, she felt weak with happiness and relief. "Oh," she said casually, "okay. Just to warm up a little."

"Yeah. Just to get warm."

Winnie lifted her chin up. "But I have to get back to town tonight. I have a date."

Josh gave her a funny look. For a moment, he just stood there staring. The wind blew through the trees across the ravine. Winnie held her breath. Would he react? Would he order her to stay away from other men? Would he wrap her in his arms and tell her he loved her?

"You're going to have to shake the snow off your clothes before you get in the tent," Josh said instead, turning and gesturing for her to follow. When they got back to the tent, he helped her unfasten her snow-shoes. Then he cleared his throat, unzipped a small flap in the tent, and crawled inside.

Winnie bent her knees and squeezed through the small opening. Then she rolled onto her bottom and kicked the snow off her feet before zipping the flap closed. Inside, the tent was warm and close. Josh had already set up a small, aluminum camp-stove, which vented to the outside, where a pot of water bubbled warmly. Spread out in front of it was Josh's puffy down bag. Winnie took off her boots, crawled forward, and sat down cross-legged. Josh moved carefully to one side and flopped on his stomach. Then he pulled a tin cup out of his pack and poured a packet of something into it before adding the hot water.

"Win," Josh said, looking away into the tiny fire.

Winnie felt her heart climbing up into her throat. "Yes?"

"Hot chocolate." As he passed her the cup his hand shook, nearly spilling the drink.

"Oh." Winnie's heart sank back down again as she took it, holding it carefully with her frozen hands. The tent roof pressed into her damp hair, forcing her to huddle down on her stomach next to Josh. Together they almost completely filled up the small triangular space, and their combined body warmth seemed to heat the tent. Winnie felt her heart expanding and contracting like a giant accordion. Without even realizing it, she found herself taking in the nearness of Josh's rumpled hair—the quickness of his long hands as he filled the tiny camp pot again with his water bottle—the clean smell of his cotton shirt next to hers. Winnie's throat tightened. Everything was coming back to her in a rush of clarity. Everything they'd had. Everything they'd lost.

"Too hot?" Josh asked.

"No—no, good."

"Warming up?"

"Yeah, great," Winnie stammered, unable to think. The nearness of Josh was overwhelming her, but she refused to let him see it. "Handy I ran into you."

There was a pause. Winnie stopped in mid-sip. Would Josh protest? Would he realize in a flash that their meeting in the middle of the frozen wilderness was more than handy? Would he come right out and say it? Would he say that it was fate?

"Yeah—handy."

Winnie closed her eyes.

"Cold out there." Josh reached into the tent's side pocket for a small spoon.

Winnie had a sudden urge to scream. "Got painted by some punks today, huh?" Winnie said instead, quickly glancing over at Josh's face. Tears began to form in her eyes, and she blinked them away.

Josh grimaced. "Neanderthals."

"Lowlifes," Winnie agreed, biting her lip. She had an impulse to grab Josh's shoulders and pull him close, but she fought it. The idea of Josh rejecting her again was too painful. She could bear his stiff politeness more than she could bear that.

"Uh-huh," Josh mumbled, looking into his cup.

Winnie took a deep breath. Summoning all of her strength, she set her cup down and began to reach for her snowshoeing boots at the foot of the tent. "Gotta take off."

"What—what, Win—you're not serious." Josh sounded a little desperate, lifting Winnie's spirits a bit. "It's past sundown, and you're not prepared. Anything could happen."

"I'll be okay."

"I can't let you."

Winnie paused.

Well? Are you going to tell me why you can't let me? Are you going to tell me you care? Or that you can't live without me?

Winnie slipped on her boots, bolstered by Josh's slight show of concern. It reminded her of so many other times when he'd tried to protect her and comfort her. All at once, she realized that she'd never let him. Even when she'd lost the baby. Even when she was suffering more than she thought possible. It was always Winnie doing it her own way. Winnie blaming. Winnie shutting Josh out. And now it was too late. It was too late to change. "I have to get back."

Desperate, Josh grabbed his flashlight from a side pocket in the tent. "At least take this. Please."

Winnie slowed down, then reached out for the flashlight. For a split second, their eyes met. Winnie looked down, then tried to click it on and off. She sighed. "It doesn't work, Josh. And I'm going anyway."

Josh seemed to shrink back in the tent, obviously upset and confused. He buried his face in his hands and shook his head. "Don't do it, Win. We're off the marked trail. Your clothes are wet. You won't be able to see. If you get back at all—it will be hours past your—your date."

Finally Winnie flopped back down on the tent blanket. She knew Josh was right. She'd just needed him to make the argument. "Okay," she said quietly. "But I want you to know that I'm staying only because I'd be risking my life going back now. That's what you're saying, right, Josh?"

"Right."

"And I'll sleep right here on the tent blanket," Winnie went on carefully, "on this side."

"No, you take the sleeping bag," Josh said firmly. "I'll take the blanket. And I'll stay on this side of the tent."

Davis whistled as he pulled on his swim trunks in the locker room of the Cascade Hot Springs Spa. His faced burned from an entire day of cross-country skiing with Faith, which was followed by a candlelit dinner at a hole-in-the-wall Italian restaurant. He smiled to himself, smoothing back his loose hair. Then he locked his things and pocketed the key. Everything about the day had been right. The blue sky and the high, hot sun. The trail that hugged the Elk River until a huge, icy waterfall was in view. It was like Hawaii all

over again. And Faith—what more could he possibly
want from life?

Outside it was dark, but the floodlights lit the
clouds of steam hovering over the hot tubs. Slowly, he
made his way across the decks, looking for an empty
tub. Faith, who had run back to her condo to grab her
swimsuit, was due back any minute. High-pitched,
drunken laughter rose from a nearby tub.

"Hey, look who we have here," a male voice called
out through the foggy air. "Davish Mattingly," the
voice slurred. Davis paused, tensing at the menacing
tone. The steam was so thick, he couldn't see the bodies jamming the tub. But from their long, slobbery
laughs, he could hear that they were smashed. A dark
head suddenly emerged from the fog, and Davis immediately recognized the broad, sarcastic smile. It was
Eric Briggs.

"Hey, Davis, my man," Eric drawled, looking
around at his buddies. "Hey, guys. This is the low-life
scum who screwed up my bet on the snowboarding exhibition."

Davis's lip curled in disgust.

"Couldn't do it, could you—you heap of dung,"
Eric spit. "You just had to show off on that last turn."
Davis stepped back a little as Eric lunged drunkenly
across the tub toward him. "I lost five hundred bucks
on that lousy turn of yours, Mattingly. And you're
going to pay."

"Back off, Briggs," Davis said in a low voice.
"You'd placed the bets before you ran into me at the
top of the run. Forget it. I changed my mind."

"Oh, yeah?" Eric came back with a crazy look in his eyes, flexing his forearms against the side of the tub. "Is that so?"

"Yeah, it is," Davis said curtly. "Now get out of my life, Briggs. People like you are trying to ruin the sport."

Eric's heavy brow scowled. He pointed at Davis's face as he took a swig from his flask. "You owe me five hundred bucks, Mattingly." He gave the group around him a smarmy look. "Either that or a little help with a business gig I've got going in the valley."

Davis frowned.

"Hey, it's okay." Briggs smiled. "I've already recruited blondie. You know her, don't you?" He looked around and shrugged. "Must be out powdering her nose."

"I don't know who you're talking about," Davis snapped.

"And if you don't help me—or pay up, Mattingly," Eric threatened, "I'm going to that little Romeo of a boss you've got. Higgenbothem. And I'm going to let him in on our little deal at the top of the run that day. Do you think he'd like to hear that his golden boy is dealing on the side for extra cash?"

Davis's throat suddenly tightened. "What?"

Briggs smiled broadly, nodding. "What's the matter? Didn't think I knew who your big bad boss was?"

Davis started to lunge for him, then stopped. "I didn't do what you wanted, Briggs," he said slowly and distinctly. "There was no deal. Get it?"

"There you are," Faith's cheerful voice interrupted.

Davis froze. Slowly, he looked around. The last thing he wanted was for Faith to know about Briggs. She smiled at him, slipped her hand in his, then looked over at Briggs and his cronies as if she thought she was about to be introduced.

"Davis?" Faith repeated. She looked at his face with concern.

He shook himself, then tugged her away. "Come on. There's an empty tub right there."

"I'll be sheeing you, Mattingly," Eric called out, his voice slurred and drunken.

Faith pulled him away lightly, dropping her towel, revealing her slim body and sleek bathing suit. "Whoo. Nice guys, huh? Who are they?"

Davis squeezed Faith's hand. Until then, he hadn't realized that he was clenching his jaw and a knot had begun to form in his stomach. All he needed right now was an Eric Briggs in his life. Just when things were beginning to look up. "I don't know, Faith." Davis tried to sound nonchalant. "Bunch of screwballs who didn't like me winning the exhibition, I guess."

Faith laughed, hurrying into the tub. "Come on," she called out with a happy laugh, swinging her legs into the steamy water. "It's freezing out there. And this is just what we need for our sore muscles. That was an eight-mile run today."

Davis smiled weakly.

Faith snuggled up, a mysterious look on her face.

Davis looked at her. "What?"

Faith slipped down lower in the tub, grinning. Her

long hair floated in strands on the surface of the water. "Just something."

Davis cleared his throat, trying not to let Faith see that anything was wrong. He settled into the hot, bubbling water, letting the heat sink into his bones. "What?"

Faith's eyes sparkled. "I just got off the phone with my friend, Lauren Turnbell-Smythe at the U of S."

Davis touched the side of her face and smiled. "Homesick already, huh?"

"No, silly." Faith giggled. Her face was radiant from the sun. "Lauren's staying on campus over winter break to work on an investigative piece for the paper."

Davis made a face.

"Anyway," Faith said, taking a deep breath, "I could barely hear her over the terrible phone connection in our condo. . . ."

Davis sank deeper into the water, trying to pay attention to Faith. But Eric Briggs's threat kept creeping back into his thoughts. What if he did talk to his boss? Higgenbothem would probably jump at the chance to throw him out on the street. His future with Dolphin Enterprises would end. He'd have to return to Hawaii. And his dreams of being near Faith would vanish.

Faith's eyes were merry with laughter. She tickled him in the side. "Anyway, I was able to tell Lauren all about how much you wanted to get into U of S so that you could get your degree and we could be together."

Davis looked at her. "You did?"

"Yeah." Faith's eyes opened wide as if she

couldn't understand why he wasn't jumping up and down for joy.

Davis swallowed.

"And," Faith continued, "tomorrow Lauren's going down to Admissions to check out any loans or work-study programs you might be eligible for." Faith swam toward him and wrapped her arms around his neck, ecstatic. "Isn't that wonderful?"

Davis gulped. In a few short minutes, his life was getting to be more complicated than it had been in nineteen years. Faith. She had so much hope for him. So much love. Did he deserve it? "Um. Yeah, Faith," he mumbled.

Faith looked shocked. "Davis? What's wrong? This is what we want. Isn't it?"

Davis bit the inside of his lip and forced a smile. He felt a sudden pang of guilt. All day he'd been so upbeat and happy to be with Faith, he'd neglected to tell her about the downside of his life. And now, just as Briggs was making his life more complicated than ever, she really needed to know the truth. Only, it was just too hard to talk about right now. "It's—it's just that everything's happening too fast."

Faith shook her head. Water streamed off her hair onto her shiny shoulders. "I'm sorry."

Davis moved closer to her. Then he wrapped his arms around Faith's slippery waist and planted a fierce kiss on her lips. "Yes," he whispered, trying to breathe. "It's what we want. The hot water's just getting to me. And . . . and just being near you, Faith . . . I guess I just love you so much, I . . . I'm having a hard time thinking straight."

Fifteen

KC kicked a chunk of dirty snow, then headed down the path that led from downtown Crystal Valley to the Sugar Mountain Village. It was past dark, and the fence along the path was already glittering with its hundreds of tiny lights.

"Sean McGlofflin," she muttered with disgust.

Zipping her ski jacket up to the neck, she thrust her hands into her pockets and crunched quickly through the snow. A pair of cross-country skiers flew by on her right. Moments later, a group of five guys hoisting snowboards hurried in the opposite direction, toward the night-skiing runs.

KC let out a long breath that almost sounded like

a growl. After eight hours stuck in the chalet stock-room with Sean, she felt like a wild animal that had just been let out of its cage. She was sure she'd wiped down at least a couple of hundred pairs of returned skis. Completely polished twenty-five pairs of cross-country ski boots. Swept the floors. Dusted the climbing gear. And then, after all that, Sean actually had made her wax and rewax the chalet's entire stock of snowboards.

You wouldn't know life if it slapped you in the face.

KC gritted her teeth. How dare he say that to her? She frowned to herself. And what exactly did he mean? KC lifted her chin up into the freezing breeze. Darkness was falling, and she could see the first bright stars appearing in the dark-blue sky. The problem with Sean McGlofflin, KC thought with irritation, is that he got off on trying to confuse people with his crazy, meaningless phrases. She hated his wise-guy jokes about the local tourist scene—and about her, personally.

KC ran her ski glove along the fence, then made a snowball and threw it hard at a passing snowmobile. She'd rather break her leg than spend another moment with that guy. But the worst thing about Sean McGlofflin's smart remarks, KC thought, was that she couldn't wait to top them with her own.

Crunch, crunch, crunch.

Thinking about the maddening Sean had made her walk faster than she'd realized. Soon the path swung close to the road, and the lights of the Sugar Mountain Village loomed ahead in the bluish dark.

"And you, Mr. Mystery Man," KC whispered to

herself, gazing at the yellow lights on the tenth floor, "couldn't be more different than Sean McGlofflin." She'd barely exchanged words with her wonderful, gentle friend in the window, but she knew instinctively who he was and what he stood for.

For one, he's intelligent, KC thought, feeling a tiny stab in her heart. He's romantic. Thoughtful. Kind. I can tell by the way he stands and the way he moves. I can tell by the way he looks at me from so far away.

KC sighed. When the manager had let her see the the condo registry, there had been no name next to Holiday 1029. For a while, she'd considered knocking on his door. But something held her back. Maybe, for once in her life, she wanted happiness to chase her down, instead of the other way around.

Darkness had settled in when KC finally reached the complex's huge parking lot. Black, icy ruts criss-crossed the ground. KC's fingertips burned with cold. Exhausted, she found herself thinking back over Sean's massive collection of clever put-downs, all of which had been directed at her that day.

"You don't get that kind of experience taking classes at college," KC mimicked Sean out loud. Stopping in front of the deserted main entrance, KC turned and planted her hands on her hips. "I'm not going to college to prepare myself for life as a small-town ski chalet owner, Sean," KC argued into thin air. "I'm planning to run a large, multinational corporation after I—" KC suddenly broke off when her eye caught a flash of red out of the corner of her eye.

Her heart froze. She stared in disbelief. There, only

fifty yards away from her, was her mystery man, heading quickly toward the condo entrance, shouldering a pair of downhill skis and poles. KC felt something inside burn, but her feet remained on the parking lot like two large blocks of ice.

"It's you," KC whispered to herself, watching him bend his head down as if he were lost in thought. He looked even taller than the first time she saw him. A few floodlights lit the glass doors at the condo entrance. And as he reached out to pull one of them open, he turned and paused briefly to look over his shoulder.

When he saw KC, the guy stopped and stared at her for a brief moment. Every nerve in her body raced. She opened her mouth to speak, but no words came out. All she could do was watch helplessly as his look turned into a grin and a short wave. He touched the top of his ski hat in a quick salute. And the next moment, he was bounding inside the lobby, where KC could see him rushing into the elevator bound for the Holiday condos.

He's hurrying away, KC thought in desperation. She suddenly sprang forward, realizing what her mystery man was doing. He'd recognized her, yes. But he wasn't ready to talk face-to-face. He was signaling that he was returning to his apartment. For now, they would communicate through their windows.

She dashed across the icy lot, then rushed through the glass doors and out again through the inner quad. Then she ran across to the Winterfest building and entered her own lobby. This time, however, she shoved

open the metal door to the stairs—too anxious to wait
for the elevator. Her legs burned as she took the steps
two at a time to the tenth floor.

"Go, go, go, go," KC whispered to herself as she
jogged down the hallway and slipped her key into the
door. To her relief, the apartment was deserted. KC
didn't stop until all the lights in the living room were
blazing and the drapes were thrown open. Then, her
heart racing like an alarm clock, she stared into the
darkness, waiting.

A moment later, the lights in Holiday 1029 flicked
on, and KC thought her heart was going to split open
with joy. There he stood in his red vest, directly in
front of his window, staring at her over the distance of
darkness and space. He waved.

"Yes," KC cried softly, waving back. "It was you.
Yes, I'm the girl you just saw."

Then KC watched in amazement as he picked up a
phone near where he was standing. He pointed at it,
punched a number, and a splitsecond later KC heard
her own phone ringing.

"Hello?" KC stammered into the receiver, looking
across at the distant apartment window. She bit her lip,
overwhelmed with nervousness. But when she listened
for a reply, all she could hear was a far-off voice, nearly
drowned out by the ocean of static on the line. The
phone line was terrible.

"Hello!" she heard the distant male voice. There
was a wave of crackling, followed by the end of a sentence, ". . . don't mind me calling. I had to talk to
you. . . ."

"It's okay," KC shouted back, "I wanted to talk, too."

There was laughter, then a pause on the other end of the line. "Look," the voice said in a faraway voice, "are you okay now?"

"Yes. I'm okay now," KC breathed, remembering the last time they'd communicated. She'd been desolate over Winnie and Josh after the New Year's Eve party, and he'd noticed, even from this distance.

Another wave of static cut in. ". . . just wanted to tell you that I can't stop thinking about you."

KC felt faint. She watched as his distant figure dropped onto a chair in front of the window. "I can't stop thinking about *you* either," KC blurted. She wanted to scream and shout. She wanted to tell him to rush right over. She wanted his name. But something told her to slow down. Something told her that her sensitive, distant friend was serious and needed more time.

"I feel—this connection to you. . . ." he said, his voice trailing off into a rush of static. "Does that seem strange?"

KC shook her head. "No," she shouted, tears spilling down her face, "I don't know what it is, but—"

The line screeched into KC's ear, and she pulled it away for a moment. ". . . usually hard for me to just come right out and say this to a girl," the guy went on, as if he couldn't hear her answer. "I . . . beat around the bush too much . . . afraid of being turned down, I guess. . . ."

KC's head was spinning. An incredibly handsome man like that? Shy about approaching a girl? He was almost too good to be true. "It's okay," she replied.

There was a long pause, and KC saw her knuckles whiten around the phone receiver.

"It's beautiful here, isn't it?" he asked her. "Do you like it?"

"Yes," KC said eagerly. "I wish I could stay here forever, but I have to go back to school."

". . . me, too," his voice answered from the end of a long sound tunnel. "I'm a freshman—majoring in economics."

KC gasped. "I'm in college, too," she stammered, "majoring in business." She wanted to joke—laugh—cry. But his voice was so thoughtful that she held back. There was another pause, and KC began to worry that they'd lose their connection. What if they were cut off before they could exchange names? "What are you going to do with your major?" KC shouted, desperate to keep talking. "I mean, are you interested in business—or teaching—or research?"

KC strained but couldn't make out his garbled answer. She bit her lip and struggled to think of a reply. "That's great. I'm sure you'll do well at whatever you try."

". . . have to go," the faraway voice called out. "Look . . . like to meet?"

"Yes!" KC practically screamed into the receiver. She looked up, laughed, and nodded into the window. In the distance, she could see him bend over, as if he was sharing her laughter.

". . . good place downtown called Michael's," he said. ". . . at seven tomorrow night?"

"Yes, yes," KC replied, her voice trembling. She

froze, wondering if he'd recognize her. Did he actually know she was the girl he'd bumped into in the lobby that first day? Did he know that he'd seen her only moments ago in the parking lot? "I'll be there. You'll—you'll know me because—because I'll take a white rose with me."

A wave of static overwhelmed the line and for a second KC thought she'd lost him. But a few moments later there was quiet, and she could hear his faint reply. ". . . can't wait to meet you."

KC dropped down on the sofa and waved to the distant figure in the window. "I can't wait either," she whispered to herself, a balloon of happiness rising inside her and lifting her off the ground. "I'll be counting the minutes."

Sean turned off the living room light and whistled as he headed back into the kitchen. Suddenly, the Holiday 1029 condo in Sugar Mountain Village was the most beautiful spot on the face of the earth. He felt so light and happy he could barely feel his feet on the floor.

"I talked to her," he said to himself with a grin, making a victorious fist. "I did it."

Still whistling, Sean's mind turned over and over again the conversation he'd had with the faraway girl in the window. She'd been smart. She'd been gracious—even sweet. She'd been everything he'd hoped for in the past few days of watching her and agonizing over who she was.

"I can never see your face," Sean whispered, "but I

can't stop imagining it. Every moment of the day."

Sean grabbed a small watering can and headed for the potted philodendrons. For the past week and a half, since returning home from the university on break, he'd been acting as the wealthy condo owner's daily caretaker. Every night after working for his parents at the ski chalet, he came here to water the plants, feed the fancy tropical fish, and generally keep an eye on the place. He could see why, too. The condo was literally stuffed with expensive equipment. Ski equipment. Television sets, VCRs, and stereo gear. Antique Austrian armoires. The owner was definitely into the bucks and wanted his stuff protected.

Sean shivered and zipped his red vest up a few inches. Funny about the rich, he thought to himself. They were swimming in money, but still too cheap to let him turn on the heat. Each night when he came in, Sean had to borrow a Briar Ski Team vest from their closet just to keep from freezing.

"I'm not complaining," Sean muttered to himself, smiling out the window toward a faraway square of yellow light across the quad. "Not complaining at all."

Sean stopped, put down the watering can, and raked his fingers through his hair. Tomorrow night. Tomorrow night he would meet her at last. His stomach churned. He hadn't been on a date since the senior graduation dance. The first semester of college had been tough. He'd been carrying a heavy course load and literally had no time to meet anyone. Yet somehow he knew his meeting with this mysterious, lovely girl had to go right.

"There was something sweet about her," he whispered to himself, gazing out the window. "Smart, but caring, too."

Sean suddenly rolled his eyes, thinking back to his turbulent day with snotty, insufferable KC Angeletti. If KC had an exact opposite in the universe, his mystery girl would be it. KC was controlling, self-centered, and way too smart for someone so heartless. His beautiful girl in the window had a generous sort of intelligence. She was kind—gentle.

"You've been first-rate entertainment, though, KC, don't get me wrong," Sean said, tossing a can of fish food in the air and catching it again. "All I have to do is pretend I'm a high school dropout stuck in the small-town chalet rental racks. Then I can just sit back with sheer amazement and watch Miss Superiority Complex. Nothing funnier this side of the Rocky Mountains."

Sean gave the condo one last check. His head was spinning. His fantasy girl suddenly had become real flesh and blood. He was actually going to meet her in one day.

It was late. Inside the tent Josh lay propped on one elbow, staring at the tiny yellow flame that flickered in his candle lantern. The inside of the tent glowed red-orange. Outside, he could hear the distant roar of the snow-buried river, the occasional falling crack of a frozen branch, the wild, rushing sound of the wind high in the trees.

He turned and looked down again at Winnie's

sleeping face on the bunched-up jacket beneath her cheek. A slight smile was on her lips. Her eyelashes formed two feathery half-circles, and spiky bangs framed a high, smooth forehead. Josh dug his fingers into his scalp, just watching and remembering. He knew every line and curve of that face. He knew every feeling it could ignite. Happiness. Pain. Hope.

"Why do you scare me so much, Win?" Josh whispered, his eyes clinging to her face.

Winnie stirred softly in the down bag. There was a soft groan and a sigh. Her slim, bare arm stretched out from beneath the covers. Josh stared at the soft, downy hair near her elbow. The tapered fingers. His throat swelled with feeling. Once he thought he knew everything about Winnie. Now he realized how much he didn't know.

"You were so angry, Win," Josh said softly, feeling tears gather behind his eyes. Memories began to float back. Winnie chattering about her latest caller on the Crisis Hot Line. Winnie cramming for exams. Winnie behind him on his motorcycle, roaring down the mountain highway.

Josh lay on his back and stared up at the candlelight flickering against the tent ceiling. Marriage had been hard, but Winnie's pregnancy and miscarriage had made it impossible. Both were accidents, but she'd blamed him for both. Tears spilled down Josh's face. Being blamed for every bad thing that happened in Winnie's life wasn't what he'd counted on. And yet, he loved her. Winnie wasn't just about pain. She was about joy and adventure, too. They connected in a way he never had with his parents or his friends. Winnie's crazy energy somehow brought everything together for him.

"Mmmmmm," he heard Winnie stirring again. Sleepy and disoriented, she lifted her head and looked at Josh. Then her brown eyes widened and seemed to melt. "Josh."

Josh's chest tightened. In the smoky glow of the candle, Winnie was more beautiful than he'd ever seen her. She rose up on one elbow, and the top of the sleeping bag tumbled a little off her bare, smooth shoulder.

Winnie's eyes glistened. Her lower lip trembled. In her eyes he could see fear, but also love. "Josh, I . . ." Winnie started to whisper before she shut her lips tight, looked down, and shook her head. A tear slid down her cheek, and Josh reached out instinctively to catch it with the palm of his hand.

"Don't . . ." Josh blurted softly. Winnie caught his hand in hers and brought it up to her lips. He felt a surge of love flood through him. "Don't cry, Win."

Winnie's face was soft and damp. She kissed his hand, then she kissed the warm crook of his elbow. In the darkness, he could feel her moving toward him until her lips met his. Josh reached out and pulled her close. His arms encircled her and held her tightly as he kissed her back. He breathed in, not thinking, not remembering—just taking in the unfolding moment as if there were no tomorrows, no regrets, and no pain.

Outside, he could hear the river rushing by. There

was a distant squawk of an owl. Then, next to him, the sound of Winnie carefully pulling down the zipper of her sleeping bag. Filled with longing, Josh slipped in next to her tiny, familiar body.

Sixteen

"Good morning," KC chirped, pushing open the door of the ski chalet's stockroom the next morning. "Cold enough for you?"

"Colder than a witch's nose," Sean replied. He was sitting in his usual place behind the repair bench, stirring a mug of coffee. He looked sleepy in his rumpled flannel shirt and faded blue jeans, but KC noticed something bright in his blue eyes that was different. And it was only seven o'clock in the morning.

"Colder than frost on an ice pick," KC replied, sailing into the room as she pulled the gloves off her frozen fingers. She imagined that she looked different, too. How could she possibly look the same? How could she even function today? Her mystery man had actually called her the night before. She'd barely slept last night after she'd talked to him.

Actually, it was a miracle she'd made it into work today at all. Hot sunshine the day before had softened much of Crystal Valley's snow cover. But last night, the temperatures had dropped way below zero. Now everything in the valley was covered with hard, glassy ice. KC's walk into town had been long and treacherous, but her heart was light. Tonight was the night she would meet her mystery man.

"Colder than a sailor's shower," Sean replied.

KC grinned up at the ceiling and thought. Even irritating Sean McGlofflin couldn't get her today. Anger and worry were behind her. From now on, everything would be smooth sailing. She unzipped her ski jacket, hung it up, then slowly turned around. "Colder than a dead man's eyes," she finally said.

Sean turned the sides of his mouth downward and nodded with appreciation, gulping his coffee. "Not bad. You win."

KC pulled off her woolen hat and bowed. "Of course I won. Now what do you want me to do, Master McGlofflin?"

"Bad hair day, huh?" Sean deadpanned.

KC touched her ugly, hat-flattened ponytail and gave him a bright smile. "For your information, I don't care what I look like in your dark, dank stockroom. And let's not beat around the bush, okay? According to your parents, I am your inventory slave for two hours and two hours only. Then I go my way, and you go yours."

Sean smiled back steadily. "I'll be counting the minutes."

KC rolled her eyes as Sean poured her a cup of hot coffee and handed it to her. The stockroom's wood stove was roaring, and she walked over to stand by it. Now that she didn't care about Sean's teasing and wisecracks anymore, it made her wonder about him. She felt a tiny, generous pang. Was this his life? Did he actually spend all of his time stuck in his parents' shop in this tiny resort town?

KC sneaked a glance over at Sean, who was shuffling for something on a big metal desk. She looked away as he picked up two clipboards and gave her one. KC quickly scanned it. "Ugh. Athletic socks to Zebraskinwear. I had no idea you had this much merchandise in the store."

Sean gave her a good-humored look. "Surprise."

Together they marched out to the store's deserted floor and went right to work. The ski chalet's sound system was cranked up, and Sean switched on the local oldies FM station. KC's job was to inventory the downhill skis, boots, and poles while Sean worked on cross-country touring equipment.

KC hummed along with the music. Her fingers swiftly counted stacks of ski-boot boxes. Since last night's phone call, a light had gone on in her life that blotted out everything else. Now even the corny Christmas tune on the radio filled her with happiness. She'd completely forgotten how much she detested working off her stolen skis at the ski chalet. And Sean McGlofflin—well, even Sean McGlofflin seemed okay this morning.

"Oh, the weather outside is frightful," KC sang along with the radio. She grabbed a rung of the stock ladder and headed up to the size-ten boots on the top shelf.

". . . but the fire is so dee—lightful," Sean finished, looking up and laughing. He was sitting cross-legged on the floor with his clipboard, his freckled face flushed and grinning.

KC looked at him and half-frowned. Sean looked pretty happy himself this morning. Every other occasion she'd had to spend time with him, he'd been funny. But it was a hard, sarcastic funny. Now he looked as if he'd just swallowed a canary. He was actually beaming.

"Hey," KC said, her gaze shifting to the window facing the street. A long row of ice-blue icicles hung over the chalet's front porch like daggers. "Look at the ice."

Sean leaned back on his elbows, smiling. "Oh, yeah. It's icicle weather. Mom and Dad are always worried about icicles falling on their customers when the front door slams."

KC giggled. "I worked at my mom and dad's business, too. Except they were always worrying about their customers eating enough organically grown vegetables."

Sean laughed again and jumped to his feet. "Actually, we're more into blood and mayhem. Hey. I'll show you what the McGlofflin kids always did with these torturous instruments of death."

KC's mouth opened as Sean rushed out the front

door, then returned a moment later holding a giant icicle in each hand. He slammed the door shut with his foot, then pounced toward KC's ladder next to the ladies' active-wear racks. *"En garde,"* he shouted, his mouth taut with mock seriousness. He steadied one of the icicles, then suddenly threw it, spinning upward, right toward her.

KC gasped, then reached out her hand to catch it. Amazingly, the slippery icicle landed in her grip. Laughing, she bent her knees and pointed it down at Sean. "Prepare—to die," she shouted, slowly climbing down the ladder. She giggled. Her hand burned with cold.

"You will pay," Sean retorted, hopping forward on both feet and taking a quick stab at KC's leg.

"Die." KC jumped off the ladder, dropping her clipboard but hanging on to her weapon.

Together they crossed icicle swords and circled the children's ski rack. His mouth sputtering with suppressed laughter, Sean stepped back and KC lunged at him, swiping at his sword and shattering it in two.

"No!" Sean shouted, falling down and crawling away on his back. He shielded his face dramatically while KC placed her boot on his stomach. Pretending to struggle, he grabbed her leg and shook his head back and forth.

"Prepare to meet your maker," KC said with a forceful shout, pushing her foot down a little. She pointed her still-intact but dripping icicle at Sean's stomach and poked his flannel shirt.

"No!"

KC circled him playfully, giving in to his strangely

funny mood. "Or the devil himself. Which is it, Mr. McGlofflin?"

"The devil! The devil!" Sean yelled back crazily as KC started to poke him.

KC saw his hand lunge for her ankle, and the next second she was lying sprawled on the floor beneath the ski-goggle display case. Sean immediately grabbed for her wrists, but KC tucked and rolled away onto her knees. She was too late, though. Suddenly Sean's muscular arm was wrapped around her waist, and he was dragging her back toward his broken icicle sword. His bare forearm rippled with the exertion, and KC could smell the clean cotton of his turtleneck.

"Please spare me, oh master," KC shrieked, "for I must live!"

Convulsed with laughter, Sean finally let go of her waist and collapsed on the floor, gasping for breath. KC was laughing and gasping, too. She rolled over on her knees and pounded his back with her fists. Then she tousled his coppery hair and fell back, exhausted, under a sportswear rack. Purple and pink ladies' ski bibs hung in her face. Tears of laughter streamed down her cheeks.

"And why must you live, KC?" Sean asked between breaths. He was still chuckling, lying on his back next to the cash register. Bracing himself with one foot, he scooted across the floor until he was lying on his back next to her. He laced his fingers under his neck and looked over at her.

KC smiled up at the ski-binding poster dangling from the ceiling. All she could think of was the face of her mystery man and the wonderful talk they'd had last night. The spell had been cast. "Because life is good, Sean," KC finally said with a grin. She reached over and patted him on the head.

"Yeah." Sean sighed, his smile far-off and wide. He crossed one leg over his knee and gave her a look of happiness. "It sure is. Sometimes when you least expect it."

Seventeen

Davis zipped up his baggy windbreaker and tucked in his shirt. The Crystal Valley Lodge's lobby was a lush, wood-paneled affair, complete with rustic willow furniture, soaring beamed ceilings, and picture windows facing the mountains. Bellhops in gold-braided jackets scurried. Skiers lounged in front of the huge stone fireplaces.

Clearing his throat, Davis approached the front desk. "Ron Higgenbothem's room number, please?"

He smiled and rocked on the balls of his feet as the clerk turned away and checked the registry. He'd made the appointment the night before. Today was the day Dolphin Enterprises was going to find out just who Davis Mattingly was. And how he intended to make something of his future with the company.

"Suite 56. Fifth floor," the clerk behind the desk replied.

Davis moved away, trying to hide his reaction.

Suite 56? Higgenbothem's staying in a suite, but he can't come up with my paycheck?

Pausing in front of the lodge's tasteful glass-case display of Rocky Mountain birds of prey, Davis tried to collect himself. Higgenbothem was a lowlife, true. But he was also his boss. And Davis was determined to use him for his own purposes.

Taking a breath, Davis headed for the glass-lined elevator, where he ran a comb through his damp hair. Last night he'd done a lot of thinking. If Faith was going to stay in his life, he was going to have to start making plans for the future. It was time for him to start taking his life seriously. And now he knew what his next step would be. Higgenbothem was returning to Dolphin Enterprises' Los Angeles headquarters at the end of the month to become its new vice-president for marketing.

And when Higgenbothem was gone, Davis was going to get his job. His life was on the brink of success.

The elevator slid open at the fifth floor and Davis headed down the carpeted hall, trying to screw up his courage. With Higgenbothem's recommendation, Dolphin Enterprises would take him seriously. Faith was right. He wasn't cut out to demo equipment for the rest of his life. He had brains. Drive. An understanding of the product. Companies like Dolphin were always on the lookout for ambitious people like him.

You just had to get in there and show your stuff.

"Bye, darling," a fortyish woman in a fur jacket was whispering in front of Suite 56. She blew a kiss inside, then closed the door, fluffing her dyed hair as she passed Davis in the hall.

Davis checked his watch and waited a few minutes. His appointment with Higgenbothem was at nine-thirty.

"Hello, Mattingly," Higgenbothem said with a curt look after Davis finally knocked. He waved Davis inside and pointed to a chair near the window. Then he smoothed the sides of his gray hair in the mirror before sitting down at the table between them.

There was a long silence. Higgenbothem was giving him a hard stare.

Davis cleared his throat nervously. He wasn't used to asking for favors. Plus, Higgenbothem's thin mouth looked even more tense than usual. His gray eyebrows bristled over his stare like two storm clouds. "I've been doing some serious thinking," Davis began, folding his hands earnestly in front of him. He suddenly wished he'd never reminded Higgenbothem about his late paycheck.

Higgenbothem's eyes seemed to radiate contempt. He recrossed his legs on the silky, upholstered chair, and took a sip from his coffee mug. "Serious thinking, hmm?"

Davis frowned and shifted. Higgenbothem had a sarcastic sense of humor, but he'd never seemed so hostile. Davis tried to shake off his fear. He was going to ask for Higgenbothem's help. There was no turning back now. "Your position as western sales rep will be open when you go back to L.A.," Davis began carefully.

Higgenbothem's face tilted. He let out a sarcastic chuckle and leaned back in his chair. Then he crossed his arms over his chest and rocked a little. "Yes it will be, Davis."

Davis coughed, then looked Higgenbothem in the eye and tried to remember what he wanted to say. "I wanted you to know that I'm interested in that position, Ron. Dolphin Enterprises is a great company, and I think I have a lot to offer."

"You do, do you?" Higgenbothem said with an icy stare.

Davis was starting to get seriously nervous. Something was going on. "I've got valuable experience with the equipment," he continued, feeling the sweat begin to break out on his back. "I'm personally acquainted with all the largest dealers in the western states. And I think I have the aptitude for the sales end of the business. . . ."

Higgenbothem's eyes were beginning to burn. Slowly he leaned forward and pointed a finger at Davis's chest. "You're trying to tell me you want advancement in this company?" he growled.

Davis's jaw dropped. "Yes."

"Let me tell you something," Higgenbothem began to yell. "Punks like you make me sick!"

Davis fell back in his chair.

"Thought you could make a little money on the side, did you?" Higgenbothem ranted, slapping both palms down on the table in front of him.

Davis's heart sank. Eric Briggs. Eric Briggs had actually talked to him.

Higgenbothem stood up and began pacing the room. "Make a few bets on the side. Rig the exhibition so that you fall and make yourself look like an ass on the SnoPro board."

Davis stood up, too, his fists clenched at his side. "But I didn't fall, did I, Ron?"

"Aw, you changed your mind to suit your fat head," Ron shouted back. "The point is you hang out with punks like this Eric Briggs. Yeah, yeah. He talked to me. And I'm glad he did—"

"I didn't do it, Ron," Davis said with a steady stare. "He approached me on the slope. But I didn't go for his scheme."

Higgenbothem leaned forward until he was almost touching Davis's nose. "Get out of here. You're fired."

Davis froze. "Fired?"

"How dare you tell me you want to get ahead in this fine company when you make deals with scum like that!" Higgenbothem shouted. Marching toward the suite's entry-closet door, Higgenbothem yanked out a snowboard and thrust it at Davis. "Here. Here's your severance pay. Don't ever come near me again. You've got no job, Davis. And you've got no reputation with this company—or any other, if I can help it."

Davis's head was spinning. Quickly, he grabbed the snowboard out of his boss's hands and pulled open the door to the hallway. Anger had nearly swelled his throat shut. He turned and gave Higgenbothem a piercing look. "You're wrong, Ron. You're way out of line. And you can take your job and stuff it."

Throwing the board on his shoulder, Davis stalked down the hall and down the fire escape until he was outside. Blinded with rage, Davis stomped through the ice-crusted snow until he was far from the lodge and well into town. Everything in sight glittered in the bright sunlight. The freezing air burned his lungs as he climbed up the lodge trail toward Main Street.

He passed the ski chalet, then blindly marched forward up the icy boardwalk past the tiny town square, Bailey's Drugs, and the Iceman Tavern. Davis had no idea where he was going or why, but his blazing anger wouldn't let him rest. Finally, at the top of Main Street, Davis stopped in front of a large bed-and-breakfast house, turned and looked down at the street, which twisted down the hill toward the smooth valley bottom. In the distance, he could hear the city's noisy orange sand-trucks approaching. Before long, the streets would be covered with brown sand to give the vehicles traction. For the moment, however, a beautiful blue glaze coated the surface of the road. It almost looked like a river seeking the ocean. Or a long blue wave spilling down onto the flat beach.

Davis's chest felt as if he just fallen face-first off a cliff. Being with Faith had made him want to make something of his life. In two short days, she'd filled him with hope and energy. But in a few brief minutes, he'd lost everything. His job. His future. And Faith—maybe even Faith.

The thought of her made his heart sink even further. She had so much hope for him. Davis's eyes grew hot as he leaned against the inn's picket fence and looked at the beautiful view. Faith was knocking herself out trying to get him information about the University of Springfield. Admissions requirements. Loans. Work-study grants. What Faith didn't know, Davis thought bitterly, is that he'd already spent a disastrous semester at Honolulu State. His high school years had been spent goofing around the beach, learning how to surf. So by the time he got to college, he realized he barely knew how to study. In fact, he barely knew anything at all, except surfing.

"I flunked out, Faith," Davis whispered into space. "I couldn't hack it."

He closed his eyes, fighting back the pain. It was incredible. He'd actually made a breakfast date with Faith so he could tell her the good news about Dolphin Enterprises. Why had he been so confident they would want him? Davis clutched the snowboard, sick at heart. He was supposed to be meeting Faith right now, in fact, at the Blue Ridge Café.

Instead of moving, however, he just stood there at the top of the hill, thinking of a faraway blue ocean. Air that smelled of flowers. Wind so warm it could rock him to sleep.

Davis suddenly opened his eyes and stared at the smooth, glassy street that meandered like a gentle blue swell through town. From here, it looked like the perfect wave. He could almost hear the far-off cheers from the beach. He could almost smell the sun and the salt on his skin and feel the surfing trophy in his wet hand. In his mind, a huge ocean swell lifted him. He looked at the course ahead of him. The wave broke. The crowds and the cheering and the glory were all waiting for him below.

"Josh," Winnie mumbled, turning over in the down bag. For a moment, she forgot where she was. She blinked and stared at the red nylon tent-flap inches from her face. And then she remembered.

Josh. Together with Josh. Last night . . .

Her body suddenly felt light and free. Her eyes flew open and she sat up, bunching the fluffy sleeping bag around her neck and grinning. The sound of Josh's early-morning puttering behind her was like beautiful, familiar music. Slow, precise, careful Josh getting ready in the morning . . .

"Are you up?" She heard a sharp voice—was it Josh's?

Winnie turned around, expecting to feel his arms circle her waist in the old way. "Good morn—"

"Look," she heard the distant Josh-voice again. She stared at him. His lips were two hard edges. His green eyes were cool as stone. Without looking at her, he folded the camp stove and unhooked its propane bottle.

"I'd like to break camp within the next few minutes," Josh said quickly. "Why don't you get your things on?" Winnie looked away as her face went numb. She felt Josh crawling behind her toward the tent flap.

"I'll wait outside while you dress," he added.

Something went dead inside of Winnie. With trembling hands, she felt for her face. Was she still there?

Had last night been a dream? Had Josh been the man who had slept next to her and kissed her like no other man could?

Or was he just a ghost from the past?

She closed her eyes and saw the nightmare again. Josh walking toward her, arms outstretched. Josh turning away. Josh approaching. Josh leaving. And leaving. And leaving.

What's wrong with me?

Winnie tried to calm her mind. Had Josh definitely decided to end the relationship? Maybe he'd realized something in the night and was about to give her a chilly speech about how he'd made a mistake getting close to her again. Then again, maybe Josh was just as confused as she was. Maybe he was just paralyzed.

Then something began to occur to Winnie. She wiped her wet face with her palms and sniffed. Was she as confused as Josh? She didn't feel confused. In fact, from the moment she saw Josh at the New Year's Eve masked ball, she knew she was still in love with him. Winnie slowly relaxed her muscles and fell onto her back in the bag.

I'm not the old, crazy, perpetually undecided Winnie, she thought in amazement. I'm not confused at all. I know exactly what I want. And what I want is Josh.

Outside, she could hear Josh's boots crunching back toward the tent. "The old Winnie would tell Josh off, then run for the nearest male body back in Crystal Valley," she whispered. "But I'm not the old Winnie anymore, am I?"

A fresh flood of tears poured down her face, but

inside, Winnie felt as strong and settled as she'd ever been in her life. She reached over and untied the nylon flap covering the tiny mesh window next to her bag. The brilliant morning blazed into her eyes. She squinted, staring at a sheet of glittering snow sloping up from the riverbank. High up on the ridge, she could see a grove of bare, white aspen shaking in the morning breeze. Winnie bit her lip. They looked so beautiful against the blue sky.

Winnie turned and zipped herself out of her bag. Then she pulled on her boots and jacket. Strapping her fanny pack around her waist, she emerged from the tent and spotted her snowshoes propped up against a tree trunk a few feet away. She looked behind her. Josh was already pulling the tent stakes up, his face ashen and tense.

"I love you, Josh," Winnie said abruptly, feeling the old strength rising up inside her. Her voice seemed tiny against the huge mountain landscape. She breathed in the alpine air like a tonic and planted her feet. "But I'm not going to let you hurt me anymore."

Josh looked down and yanked another tent stake out of the snow.

Winnie stood up taller and faced him squarely. "If you're trying to reach out to me, Josh," she called out, "then you're just going to have to do it. I can't do anything if you keep running away. It hurts too much."

Josh gave her an angry glance, reaching into the collapsed tent and grabbing the down bag. Yanking the end up, he began shoving it into his pack.

"I want to get back together," Winnie finally said, her heart clear and calm. "And I don't want a divorce."

For a moment, Josh didn't move. He just stood there next to the crumpled tent, staring at a faraway spot in the distance.

"If you don't want what I want, then fine, I'll be okay," Winnie said bravely. "But if your heart says you want to give this another try, you can't keep running away."

Josh turned and stared at her, his lips shut tightly and his eyes hard with pain.

Winnie took a breath, then bent down to put on her snowshoes. "Figure out what you want, Josh," she continued, suddenly exhilarated by the feeling of strength within her. When she stood up again, she straightened her pack and gave Josh one last look. "I'm heading back now, Josh. You know where to find me. Good-bye."

Winnie's legs felt like iron. She plunged ahead down the riverbed, crunching through the icy layer on the top of the snow. Though she was still on an unmarked trail, she was sure she would rendezvous with the main cross-country runs as she neared the Elk River somewhere below.

She followed along the bottom of the river embankment, her breath coming out in white puffs against the freezing air. Up ahead, the riverbed took a sudden, steep drop. She stopped and stared at the situation. To the right, her snowy trail appeared to plunge into a ravine. To the left, it was possible to continue straight along the side of a forested hill, then perhaps find an easier way down to the bottom.

Winnie put away her snack and frowned. She walked carefully forward toward the ravine, then stopped when she neared the edge. She stared at the bottom and smiled. Below, she could see the well-worn cross-country trail she'd taken up the day before. Civilization. Maneuvering down the steep incline through the snow didn't look that difficult, and it would save her hours of hiking time.

A flash of orange caught her eye, and Winnie walked ahead a few feet to get a better view. Up ahead, along the top of the ravine was the Forest Service's familiar orange netting along a cliff of snow that sagged menacingly over the trail. She squinted and read the small signs. Keep Out. Avalanche Danger.

Winnie smiled and shook her head at the signs. "Avalanches," she muttered to herself. "Nothing's going to move in this cold." She shivered. The busy trail below beckoned her. Already, she could see a few skiers. Once she reached it, it was probably only an hour's walk back to the condo.

Taking one last look at the freezing, blue sky, Winnie stepped forward and headed down the steep drifts banking one side of the ravine. She was strong. She was tough. She was never going to let anything hurt her again in her life.

Eighteen

"K C?" Faith was yelling, knocking furiously on the ski chalet's front door. "KC?"

Faith knocked on the paned window, rubbing the frosty glass to get a better look inside. Faith knew that KC had slipped out early that morning to do inventory for the McGlofflins. But she suspected KC hadn't gone into the back bedroom, where she would have seen that Winnie and Tory's beds were empty. A scribbled note had been left on Winnie's pillow, saying they'd planned a snowshoeing trip on the River Run Trail.

But neither one came home last night.

Faith felt sick. The last time she'd seen Winnie was the morning after the disastrous New Year's Eve ball— almost twenty-four hours ago.

"KC!" Faith called out again, continuing to bang on the red door of the chalet.

Faith leaned against the door and rubbed her cold hands together. She tried to think back. Winnie, Tory, and KC had been in bed, asleep, when Faith left yesterday morning to go cross-country skiing and hot-tubbing with Davis. When Faith returned last night at eleven, KC was back, sound asleep on the couch, but Tory and Winnie were still out. Still, Faith just figured Winnie was partying like crazy with Tory at one of Main Street's hot spots.

I should have done something last night, Faith thought desperately. Anything could have happened to her.

"KC!" Faith shouted a final time, banging on the door. She could hear loud music coming from a radio inside. Finally, the door flew open, and KC and Sean McGlofflin appeared, flushed and giggling.

"KC," Faith panted, stumbling inside and shutting the door. She collapsed on the wooden bench next to the cash register. Her face was almost too frozen to speak. "Winnie never came home last night."

KC's happy face fell. "What?" she breathed, setting her clipboard down on a nearby counter. "But she and Tory—"

"Right," Faith said quickly, hugging her arms around her chest. The tips of her leather gloves were soaked and her cross-country ski gaiters were dripping all over the wood floor. She rocked forward a little and sobbed. "She and Tory went snowshoeing yesterday morning. You know."

KC paled.

Tears sprang to Faith's eyes. "Anything could have happened, KC. There are a million avalanche warnings up around Elk River. One of them could have broken a leg too far away to seek help. There's hypothermia to think of. . . ."

KC covered her face in horror.

"I should have gone looking for her last night." Faith began to sob. "I . . . I guess I was just super-tired. . . ."

KC stepped forward. "Faith. I went to bed, too. I just thought Win was probably partying her head off with Tory. She does that when she gets upset. It's her release valve."

"It's all my fault," Faith wailed, bending over at the waist and crying into the palms of her hands. "I never should have played matchmaker. All I did was make her pain worse. And now she's gone running off. . . . I should have invited her along with me and Davis yesterday. We were going up there, too. . . ."

Sean knelt down in front of Faith, his brow furrowed with concern. "Look, did they tell you where they went snowshoeing?"

"Um—Faith," KC interrupted, her face wet with tears. "This is—uh—Sean McGlofflin."

Faith and KC looked at one another with wild eyes. "Yes. Winnie said they were going to the River Run Trail. That's where Davis and I went yesterday morning," Faith sputtered, trying to think. "But we never saw them. I suppose they could have gone up the Cougar Ridge Trail that branches off it. That's where Josh Gaffey told us he was going."

Sean stroked his chin, concerned. "Cougar Ridge is steep terrain. No place for beginners."

"I know," Faith wailed, covering her face with her hands. If only she and Davis had invited Winnie along with them. If they hadn't been so lost in their private little world, this never would have happened. "And on top of everything else," Faith moaned, "I don't know where Davis is. He was supposed to meet me at the Blue Ridge Café for breakfast a half hour ago. But he never showed up. The town's covered over with a sheet of ice. There've been two car accidents this morning on the main drag alone . . ." Faith choked, unable to continue.

KC sat down next to Faith and slipped her arm around her shoulders. She gave her a long, sideways hug, then pulled her around and looked at her in the eyes. "You know how Winnie gets when she's upset," KC said quietly. "She takes off."

Faith sniffed and nodded, but the stabbing pain in her heart wouldn't go away.

"And as for Tory . . ." KC sighed. "Winnie probably couldn't stand Tory for more than ten minutes. They probably went their separate ways on the trail. Tory probably found a hunky guy and . . ."

"Yes, but what about Winnie?" Faith cried, her lips shaking with fear and cold.

"Winnie always takes care of herself," KC insisted, though Faith could see the fear in her eyes, too. A small tear gathered in the corner of KC's eye, and she blinked it back. "Well, she does, Faith. And she's run away before."

Faith tried to think. Winnie wasn't the type to stay out all night with a guy she didn't know. And if she'd run away, why were her bags still at the apartment? Winnie could be flighty and emotional, sure. But she would never worry her friends like this. Something had to be really wrong, and KC knew it.

KC was frowning. "What's that, Sean?"

Sean shrugged and stood up, peering out the window. "Sand trucks heading this way. They'll be dumping the stuff all over Main Street in a few minutes."

Faith heard it, too. It was a far-off sound, like a roar or a cheer. Sean opened the door when a group of cars started honking out on the street. Then, in a rush, he threw on his jacket and bolted outside with KC at his heels. Faith stood up and walked outside into the freezing air. As she looked up the hill from the chalet's front porch, Faith could see spectators bunched at street corners and storefronts, all staring at a point high on Main Street. Curious, Faith walked out to the icy street and shaded her eyes.

"Never seen anything like this," Sean was muttering. "And I've lived here all my life."

"What?" Faith moved closer and tried to see what they were staring at.

"Can you see him now, Faith?" KC was pointing up the hill, way above the little town-square park, near the German bakery. "It's a guy on a snowboard."

Faith frowned. "In the street?"

"Illegal as hell," Sean muttered. "Police are always trying to crack down on the skateboarders in the summer who come down there. They don't want this idea to catch on. But—hey—maybe he'll get away with it. He's good."

Faith didn't want to think about guys pulling stunts. She wanted to think about Winnie and where she was. Still, when she finally spotted the distant snowboarder, it was difficult to keep her eyes off him. He was actually trying to make his way downhill through the morning traffic, dodging cars, lampposts, and landscaped meridians. She watched, transfixed, as the lone snowboarder twisted, jumped, and meandered his way down the ice like a bird gliding in a breeze.

Something made Faith stiffen. Maybe it was the baggy orange windbreaker. Maybe it was the shock of pale-blond hair flying above the broad shoulders. He ducked between two cars, then jumped up and executed a 360-degree twist, landing gracefully on bent knees.

"Davis?" Faith whispered.

KC nudged her. "Is that Davis?"

"Davis Mattingly?" Sean piped in. "That's Davis Mattingly—the SnoPro guy?"

Faith gulped as the snowboarder twisted closer and closer down the hill. It looked like him. But what could he possibly be doing? He was acting like a crazy man. And he was supposed to be with her at the Blue Ridge Café. "Um. I'm not sure."

"Sure it is," KC suddenly cried out. "Yeah. That's Davis all right."

Faith's heart sank. KC was right. But all Faith could do was just stand there on the street, paralyzed.

What's he doing? It couldn't be a SnoPro promotion. Sean just said it was illegal. And it looked as illegal as anything she'd ever seen. Davis jumped curbs and sailed down the icy sidewalks, dodging pedestrians and pretending to tip his hat as he did. He swooped in front of cars and did a giant nosegrab as he vaulted off a loading ramp, finally landing inches from the hood of an idling pickup.

Faith felt sick. There was something in Davis's eyes that she didn't like. He careened across the street, jumped into the town's tiny main square, then vaulted onto the handrail of the staircase leading down to its lower level. After riding the rail, Davis plunged back into the now-stopped traffic, barely missing an idling van. There was the sudden pierce of a police siren, and Faith watched in horror as a city police car swerved in front of Davis to stop him.

Suddenly, Faith couldn't hold back another minute. "Davis!" she shouted, running out into the street and waving her hands over her head as the police got out of their squad car. "Davis," she cried out, "what are you doing?"

"Faith—KC!" another male voice called loudly from behind. "Faith!"

Faith turned around, confused. She look frantically at the crowd behind her, then back up to Davis again.

"Faith!" the voice called out again, hoarse and desperate.

Faith felt like screaming. "What? KC—who is that?"

"Oh, no," she heard KC cry, turning and running.

Faith turned and saw a guy with a wild look on his

ragged, frozen face. At first she was too upset and confused to wonder who he was. But when she saw KC run down and grab his worn-out down jacket, she realized who the guy with the desperate look was.

It was Josh.

Faith hurried toward him, dread beginning to fill her mind. She knew Josh had gone cross-country skiing near the Elk River. Had he run into Winnie? Had something happened?

"Faith—Faith." Josh began to stammer uncontrollably, his eyes darting into the distance like a wild man on a hunt. "You've got to . . . you've got to help. . . ."

Slipping her arms around Josh's waist, Faith struggled to calm him down. A nervous sweat broke out all over her body. Something was wrong. Terribly wrong. "Slow down, Josh," Faith murmured, her voice cracking with worry.

Sean stepped forward and gripped Josh's forearm. "It's okay, man," he said with a steady look. "Tell us how we can help."

Josh's lips were trembling. Shaking his head wordlessly, he took a deep breath, then paused. "It's Winnie."

Faith and KC exchanged panicked looks.

"She . . . she . . . I ran into her somewhere off Cougar Ridge yesterday at sundown," Josh went on. "Then I made her stay the night in the tent to warm up. She . . . she was so cold. . . ."

Faith watched in horror as Josh broke down again, clawing at his head with his wet gloves.

"She . . . she left this morning before me," Josh cried. "I followed her tracks . . . and . . . saw that she went right into an avalanche area."

Faith and KC gasped.

"I followed her tracks down into the ravine," Josh stammered. "But they stopped." He looked up at them, his eyes filled with tears. "A lot of snow had just fallen down off the side of the ravine. There had been an avalanche."

Faith felt her legs buckle.

Sean flinched and turned to run back to the chalet. "I'm calling Search and Rescue."

Josh, KC, and Faith hurried down the hill in his wake. "I spent about an hour digging through the snow," Josh went on. "I used long branches to locate . . . you know . . . locate something under the snow. . . ."

Faith grabbed his elbow as Josh began to fall. KC's face was contorted with fear. And Faith felt her heart begin to split in two.

When they finally reached the ski chalet, the front door was open and Sean was rushing out. "Search and Rescue's meeting us at the lodge in five minutes," Sean yelled, before stopping and glancing across the street, where he could see shopkeepers running out their front doors and shouting.

"I've been robbed!" yelled the owner of Sandra's Ski Togs.

"Police! There's been a theft!" the cashier at European Leathers screamed.

Faith watched as Sean slowly turned around to look inside the chalet. He stepped inside as Faith, Josh, and KC followed.

"What's wrong?" KC wanted to know.

Sean turned around and gave everyone a desperate look. "Look what happened while we were watching Davis pull that stunt. The ski and boot racks. Cleaned out. Robbed. It looks like the whole town was distracted. Because everyone else was robbed, too."

"Yeah, we have a possible single avalanche-injury," Josh could hear the far-off sound of a scratchy Search and Rescue radio in the thin air.

"Over here," Josh yelled, his voice hoarse and raw. He stabbed the thin search rod into the pile of ice and snow. "Please."

The two red-jacketed guys he'd met at the ski chalet gave each other grim looks and lifted their own rods out of the snow. Then they walked slowly toward him.

Josh searched their faces, sick with grief and fear. "What?" he shouted.

"Hey—hey, pal," one of the guys said with a sad look, his hands hanging limply at his sides. "We've completely searched this site. . . ."

Josh's body began to convulse with sobs. "No, no, no, no," he wailed. "You don't understand. You see, she ran off . . . after . . . we had . . . had an argument. And . . . and I'll never forgive myself if . . ." Josh struggled to continue before falling on his side in the snow and completely breaking down.

". . . two miles southwest of Deer Run. Ski Patrol requests assistance . . ." the Search and Rescue radio squawked into the thin air.

"Look, pal," one of the guys said quietly, kneeling

by his side. "This was not a major avalanche here. And we've searched it for the past thirty minutes with heat sensors and rods. All state-of-the-art equipment. There's no way anyone's buried under here."

Josh made a fist and began pounding it into the snow, barely aware of their presence. All he could think of was Winnie's calm, proud voice that morning as she left him.

Good-bye, Josh.

Why was he so afraid of her? She'd always loved him as much as he'd loved her. But she needed him, too. Maybe that was the thing that put such terror in his heart. She'd needed him so much.

"She needed me to care for her," Josh wailed as the two Search and Rescue guys lifted him up under the arms. He looked into one face, then the other. "Do you understand how much that scared me?"

"Sure, fella," one of the guys said, nodding quietly. "Sure I do."

Josh stumbled a little, trying to walk in the chunks of fallen snow. "It was just . . . just that I wanted her to take care of me. Don't you see? I kept waiting for her to take care of me."

The two guys dragged him to a nearby log and sat him down. "Look," one of the guys said, rubbing his forehead. "Imagine for a moment that your girlfriend . . ."

"My *wife!*" Josh shouted. "She's my *WIFE. THE WOMAN I LOVE.*"

The guy held his hands up. "Okay, okay. Let's just think this through. If, for some reason, your wife is not buried here in this snowfield, where do you think she'd be? The lodge?"

Josh bit his lip, his eyes darting around wildly. "Uh. What did she say? The . . . uh . . . Sugar Mountain Village. Yeah. Or the lodge."

Quickly, one of the Search and Rescue guys radioed his headquarters and gave them the information. A few minutes later, the radio crackled to life again. The dispatcher on duty had checked out both locations. There was no Winnie Gottlieb at her apartment in the condo complex. And she did not reply to a page at the lodge.

"Okay, then," the first guy spoke up. "Why don't we take you back to police headquarters in town? They can take it from there. Meanwhile, we've got a compound fracture on one of the alpine runs and two missing skiers just north of here."

Josh felt his mind breaking into a million pieces. "We've got to look for her again. We've got to. I've got to tell her I love her. . . ."

He felt two strong hands placed on his shoulders. The muscles in his body sagged. Josh heaved a huge sigh, suddenly realizing how foolish he looked. And what a complete mess he'd made of his life and Winnie's.

"We know you want your wife," the stranger's voice was saying into his ear.

Josh opened his eyes and stared across at the snow-laden trees clinging to the side of the ravine. The rays of a brilliant morning sun were just beginning to catch the lip of the ravine. All around him the snow began to glitter and flash.

"We'll take you back into town in the Sno-Cat,"

the voice said. "And you can look for your wife there. All we know for sure is that she's not here."

"You'll find her in town," a different voice joined in as Josh felt another wave of regret surge through his heart. "A month from now, you two will be laughing about this whole thing."

"Yeah," Josh whispered into the frozen air. "If it's not too late."

Nineteen

Meanwhile, Davis sat in the Crystal Valley Police Station, feeling his life slip away like a perfect wave that had trailed off into a rocky and unexpected reef.

"Watch your step, son," Officer John Brightly was lecturing. His bright face bulged over the tight collar of his uniform and his closely cropped hair made him resemble a marine sergeant. "I could charge you with reckless endangerment—pulling a stunt like that in heavy traffic."

Davis's chest tightened. What had happened to make him sink this far in life? A few months ago, he was Hawaii's number-one amateur surfer, cheered on by thousands. Now he was two steps from a jail cell.

The officer stood up and jerked his thumb backward. "Keep the snowboard on the side of that big mountain up there, pal, and off my beat. Call me crazy—but I'm going to give you another chance."

Davis was the one who felt crazy. At that very moment, in fact, it seemed as if the station's cubical walls were slowly inching toward him, waiting to squeeze him to a horrible death. Back home, the local cops would have laughed and shaken their heads over a friendly stunt like that. Compared to his tiny Hawaiian island home, the trendy resort of Crystal Valley was a police state.

"Thanks," Davis managed to mumble, shaking the grim-faced officer's hand. "Don't know what got into me." He stood up and turned. Then he grabbed his snowboard and walked numbly out of the dreary cinder-block building. Outside, the bright sunshine nearly blinded him.

Davis stomped down the sidewalk, then headed across the icy main street, toward the lodge. *First he gets involved with Eric Briggs's lousy betting. Then he lies to Faith about being college material. Finally, he makes the huge mistake of thinking Higgenbothem would give him an ounce of help with his career.*

You're just a big loser with the wrong impulses, the wrong timing, and the worst judgment in the world, Davis thought bitterly. *The sooner you go crawling back to Hawaii, big guy, the better.*

Davis hurried ahead, too distraught to know where he was going or why. Since walking into Ron Higgenbothem's hotel suite three hours ago, his life had gone from what seemed like a golden beginning to an endless black pit. One minute, success was right around the corner: He was the western sales rep for Dolphin Enterprises, saving big money for college and meeting Faith every weekend at the U of S. The next minute, everything was switched around: He was just another stupid punk sitting in a police station. Unemployed. Blacklisted by his former boss. And, with his current luck, dumped by Faith. There were no safe places for him anymore.

Davis kicked a lump of yellowish ice and stared down the hill toward the bustling lodge, swarming with skiers and sunbathers. A few downhillers heading for the half-day ticket lines crowded past him.

And why shouldn't Faith say good-bye? Davis thought bitterly. I'm a loser. What could I possibly offer a girl like her?

Davis stared up at the craggy mountains soaring above Crystal Valley. The air was bitter cold, and even the smells of distant baking didn't make him feel any better. He stopped, lost in his own miserable world, unaware of the passing skiers and snowmobiles. Then, slowly, he began to think about Faith. He hadn't been straight with her over the last few days. Since their reunion, things had seemed too good to spoil with a lot of blunt talk about failure and worry.

Davis's eyes burned. She was so radiant and hopeful. How would she react to the fact that he'd flunked out of Honolulu State? Would she still want to drag him back with her to the U of S? Would she still want to hang out with the beach bum from Hawaii while the rest of her friends were pursuing careers in computer technology, business, and theater?

Shifting the weight of the snowboard on his shoulder, Davis began to step forward along the trail.

Then again, maybe the truth is what Faith really wants. After all, I wouldn't be so crazy about her if she weren't as honest and good as she is. Why can't I have as much trust in her as she has in me?

Davis turned and hurried back into town, suddenly desperate to find her. He'd tell her about losing his job. He'd tell her about flunking out. He'd tell her everything. It was the only way she'd ever know who he really was. And if the universe could grant him just one crummy little wish, it would be that she would forgive him.

Once he was back on Main Street, Davis checked into the ski chalet, then stopped at a pay phone outside to call her condo. When he couldn't reach her, Davis decided to head down to the lodge, where he could wait by the fire. His boots crunched through the chunks of ice littering the street. But the high, whiny sound of a snowmobile barreling down the city street distracted him from his thoughts.

Davis looked over his shoulder. The snowmobile was a fancy one, sleek and black and very fast. And hovering over the machine's handles was a ruddy face framed by a head of slick black hair. Davis turned away and started to cross the street, intent on getting down to the lodge.

"Hey," he heard a voice calling him over the whine of the snowmobile. "Hey—Mattingly."

Davis turned around, then stopped at the edge of the street, stunned. He stared at the big, smarmy smile and the creepy space between the two front teeth. The slicked-back hair. The confident, dead eyes. It looked like Eric Briggs. But after the phone call to Higgenbothem—and what he'd done to his career—Davis couldn't quite believe Eric Briggs would have the nerve to approach him.

Davis just stared, his jaw clenched like an iron spring.

"Hey, buddy," Eric called out, slowing next to the sidewalk and holding his hand up for a jovial high-five. Wearing fluorescent orange ski bibs and metallic sunglasses, Eric had a sickening grin on his face that made Davis want to inflict serious harm on his jaw. Instead, Davis just gave him a curt look and walked ahead, ignoring his hand. *The guy had just ruined his life. Now he has the guts to call him buddy?*

"Hey, hey, hey, hey," Eric called out with a laugh. His snowmobile engine purred quietly behind Davis. "Come on, Mattingly. You didn't think I'd forget you, did you, man? I just wanted to say thanks."

Davis stopped and turned around in disgust. "What are you talking about, Briggs?"

The muscles in Eric's thick neck bulged a little as laughter began to bubble up out of his beefy chest. "I'm talking about you, man," he chortled, reaching over and nudging Davis in the shoulder. "Welcome to the business."

Davis bristled with hate. "Get lost, Briggs," he muttered, before turning away and heading across the street toward the lodge trail. The sound of the idling snowmobile picked up as Briggs continued to follow close behind. Davis felt something at his side. Something being slid into his pocket.

Davis jerked around and stared hard into Eric's eyes. "I told you, Briggs. Get away from me." Annoyed, he dug into his pocket and pulled out what felt like a hard roll of paper. He looked down and clenched his teeth. Eric Briggs had just slipped a thick roll of bills in his pocket.

"That's just your starting salary," Eric drawled. "Sorry it couldn't have been more. But you look hungry enough."

Davis gripped the roll of bills and threw it into the street. "What's going on, Briggs?"

Reaching over the side of his snowmobile, Eric delicately picked up the money, grinned, and rolled it back and forth on the open palm of his hand. "Come on, Mattingly. The boarding stunt this morning in beautiful downtown Crystal Valley. It was outrageous. The perfect distraction." Eric put a knuckle to his chin, looking thoughtful. "With all those shopkeepers out watching you instead of their businesses, I'd say we were able to come away with, say, eight thousand dollars' worth of merchandise." He snapped his fingers. "Just—like—that."

Davis's throat was choked with anger. Slowly, he turned around and stared at Eric's broad, taunting expression. "It was a stunt, Briggs. A stunt. Get it? It didn't have a purpose. I'm not interested in your sleazy gigs and never have been."

Eric's blue eyes went cold. "Cops won't look at it that way."

"Yeah, well, I don't have anything to hide," Davis snapped back, walking away.

The snowmobile crept behind him. "I have another job for you tomorrow night, Mattingly."

Davis stopped in his tracks and wheeled around with an angry stare. "You're not getting it, are you, Briggs?" he exploded. "I'm not interested."

"But you will be interested if the cops get an anonymous tip connecting you to all those thefts this morning," Eric taunted.

Davis's eyes widened. "What?"

Eric chuckled. He sat back on his snowmobile seat and crossed his arms over his chest, smiling. "The idea kinda grabs you, doesn't it?"

Davis felt nauseous.

"Well." Eric put his hands out in front of him, palms up. "It was a pretty incredible coincidence, wouldn't you say? You have a little fun on Main Street, and we clean up."

Panic began to clutch at Davis's throat. Eric Briggs's schemes were beginning to wrap around his life like a vise. No matter how hard he tried, Briggs wouldn't let go. Suddenly, Davis couldn't think or move. He just stood there in a muddy patch of ice as the traffic crunched by and the unforgiving sun glared into his eyes.

"Hey, look who's here," Eric suddenly cried. "One of the Crystal Valley Police Department's finest."

Davis turned in horror, just as Eric hopped off his

snowmobile and grabbed his elbow. Davis felt Eric pulling him into a kind of sideways hug, just as a familiar black-and-white patrol car slowed down next to them. Eric leaned into Davis's ear. "I'll call you tomorrow at your motel and give you instructions for your next job."

But before Davis could pull away from his powerful grip, he realized that Eric was lifting one arm and waving to the officer inside the car. A split second later, Davis saw the big red face and the marine haircut.

It was Officer John Brightly.

> Dear KC and Faith:
>   I'm checking out early. It was fun while it lasted, but it didn't last, did it? You know what the French say: C'est la vie. By the time you read this, I'll be on the train back to Jacksonville. Surprise, Mom!
>   Love, Winnie
> P.S. Bring the rest of my stuff home with you, okay?

Winnie set the pencil down on the condo's kitchen counter and put her key on the note. Then she picked up her overnight bag and headed for the door. Something told her she should be raw with grief. She almost wanted to feel her eyes bugging out with crazy thoughts—her nerves galloping away like wild horses in her demented brain. After all, she'd reunited with Josh last night, only to lose him again this morning. Everything was gone now. No hope. No future.

But Winnie hadn't shed a tear. All she knew was what her heart told her, and what no one—not even Josh—could take away. She loved Josh Gaffey. She wanted to be with him for the rest of her life.

Hiking her overnight bag on her shoulder, Winnie headed out the door into the bare hallway, went down in the elevator and then out the glass doors into the bright, icy morning. She straightened her sunglasses and headed carefully across the Sugar Mountain Village parking lot toward the main road, where she turned left and began her walk into town. The Crystal Valley Train Station was located just to the north of the Main Street junction.

Home. Home's where you start all over again.

Four-wheel-drive trucks and big tourist buses with chains on their tires rumbled by. Winnie moved bravely forward, her head bent against the freezing blasts of air. Slowly, her thoughts drifted back to her hike that morning off the Cougar Ridge Trail. A tired smile formed on her lips.

"At least I made one good decision," Winnie muttered to herself, zipping her jacket higher. She felt deep exhaustion taking over her body. "Taking the steep ravine down to the main trail saved me hours of hiking time." She rubbed her bottom. Though she had fallen several times on the way down, at least she hadn't broken a leg. The fluffy snow had cushioned her. What's more, she'd ended up only a few hundred yards away from the Elk River Bridge, saving herself more hiking time.

"It may have been avalanche country," Winnie sang

out, uncapping a tube of Chap Stick and smearing it all over her lips, "but at least the avalanche decided to wait until I got to the bottom."

Winnie tramped ahead, past the riding stables, the Crystal Valley Center, and the Elk River Cabins. Strangely, she felt disconnected from all the pain she and Josh had been through. It was almost like being an old woman remembering a lost love. So beautiful, but so distant.

She sighed and hiked her bag up higher on her shoulder. A pickup truck passed her with a honk. The road began to widen, and up ahead she could see the upper end of Main Street, with its quaint shingled roofs and smoking chimneys.

Love. Winnie shook her head. She knew what it was, and she knew the dark path that led away from it. Picking up a long stick, Winnie bumped it along the split-rail fence that bordered the path. Somehow her thoughts about Josh had made her think of KC.

You have no idea, KC.

All through high school and college, KC had had her share of romances. But something told Winnie that KC always trailed a lifeline behind her before she jumped in—at least until this week.

"Mr. Mystery Man," Winnie said with a wistful look at a cross-country skiing couple that passed her on the path. "She sees his face for one minute, and it turns her life around." She wished KC would hurry up and figure it out. Love wasn't about falling for a face. It was about losing yourself to someone else, then hoping you didn't lose yourself along the way. It was about pain and longing and compromise. She understood that now, and she was ready to make the sacrifice.

Can't you see that, Josh?

Winnie crossed the road and turned right at the junction, heading up the road past a large motel and gas station until she spotted the sign for the Crystal Valley train station. A long staircase dropped from the road onto a quaint platform. There was a brick ticket-office, old-fashioned benches, lampposts, and holiday wreaths hanging from the wrought-iron railings.

She grabbed the railing and headed down to the ticket office, exhausted and sad, but still resolved to make a clean break from Josh. She would go home. She would return to the U of S. She would start her life all over again. And if Josh wanted her back, she would go to him.

"Excuse me," Winnie said to the middle-aged woman behind the ticket window. "I need a one-way ticket to Jacksonville, Oregon—via the Twin Rivers connection."

The woman looked at her. "It just left, darling." She checked her watch. "Ten minutes ago."

Winnie stepped back, confused. "What?"

"Bad luck." The woman looked sympathetic.

Tears sprang to Winnie's eyes. She hadn't counted on being stranded in Crystal Valley. Her heart was already home. "But . . . but, I need that . . . train. I'm going home and . . ."

The woman slid a train schedule across the counter and gave it a quick look. "You can catch the seven-thirty tomorrow tonight, hon."

"Not until tomorrow night?"

"The schedule is a little erratic this time of year," the woman explained. "With the snow and all."

Winnie stepped back from the window and gave the station waiting-room a desperate look. Winnie hiked back up the staircase, feeling her body give in to raw nerves and the lack of sleep. She couldn't stay. She couldn't face Josh again. Not in a million years. If he wanted her—he'd have to come after her. When she reached the top of the stairs, she gulped a lungful of mountain air and rubbed her groggy eyes. Down the street, toward town, she could see a large chain-motel with a sign boasting bargain rates and in-room Jacuzzis. Feeling for her mom's "emergencies-only" credit card in her bag, Winnie marched forward toward the entrance. Her life as a crazed romantic was over. She would stop here. She would rest. And then she would go home and start over.

Twenty

S ean McGlofflin took a deep, nervous breath.

He was locked in his knotty-pine bathroom, just off the garage, near the tiny back bedroom his parents had walled off for him when he was a junior at Crystal Valley High. Now it was choked with shower steam. He finally opened the door and tried to let some air in by swinging it back and forth several times. But the effort only made him break into another nervous sweat.

"Great," Sean muttered to himself, knotting a towel around his waist. Desperately, he tried to rub a clear spot in the mirror. He reached for a can of shaving cream. In exactly one-half hour, he was due to meet the beautiful, mysterious girl in the window. The thought of it made his blood rush into his face.

"Hey, Sean," he could hear his father bellowing down the hall.

There was a bang at the door, and his dad's pudgy face appeared through the steam. "Hey—big date, huh, Seanie? A bit of advice. Take it easy on the after-shave, pal."

Sean slammed the door and gripped his head, staring at his half-shaven face in the mirror. His coppery hair stood out all over his head. "Why didn't I get a haircut? Why am I doing this?" he moaned to himself, his thoughts popping inside his head like nervous machine-gun fire.

Dinner at Michael's? He didn't even know the girl. Her face was a blur. Her voice—mere static on the end of a telephone wire. All he had to go on was the strangely sweet way she stood there, watching him through the darkness. The girlish tilt of her head. The gentleness of her words.

"But Michael's?" Sean said to himself, taking a towel and wiping off the remaining bits of shaving cream. He stared at his square-jawed, freckled face. A good Irish face, his mother always said. The hair. Wild. Needed a haircut, but no time. What was the use? What was he thinking? He had to raid his savings for this event. What if they had nothing to say to one another?

"Okay, okay, okay," Sean finally stopped himself. "Just stick your neck out for once in your life, McGlof-flin. You don't always have to be right."

He hurried, pulling on his pants, shirt, and sweater, trying not to think too much. Minutes later, he was climbing up Main Street, pulling gloves onto his cold hands. The freezing, milky blue air was so cold it made his eyes water. His heart pounded. But after he passed the tiny town-square and Bailey's Drugs, he could actually see the restaurant, and he knew there was no turning back.

Tucked into the hillside at the top of the main drag, Michael's was an Austrian chalet-style building surrounded by tall firs. During the holiday season, the trees were always decorated with tiny white Christmas lights. Yellow candlelight blazed through the windows out into the freezing, bluish night.

Sean lifted the collar on his jacket. A cold wind had begun blowing down from the northwest early that afternoon. A front of high, gray-clotted clouds had followed. From the looks of things, a major snowstorm was headed their way. In the meantime, however, the dropping temperatures had frozen everything from slush to puddles into a hard, black glaze.

It was a local joke that Michael Schott, owner of the restaurant, insisted that his customers be hungry when they came to eat. For that reason, he had kept the long, stone staircase that wound up from the road to the front door. It was the only way in and the only way out. Thankfully, small floodlights had been installed along the way to help the guests. But tonight, the going was treacherous.

Gripping the staircase railing, Sean had to struggle to keep his footing on the icy steps. When he reached the quaint deck at the top, he stared at the restaurant's cheerful red door and the wide expanse of old-fashioned paned windows. He stopped to catch his breath and steady his nerves. Then, on impulse, he ducked over to the window, hoping to catch a glimpse of his lovely mystery girl. The girl with the tilting face and the single white rose in her hand.

Sean peered inside. Though the light was dim, he could see the faces in the crowded room. His heart pounding, he scanned the room until his gaze stopped at a small table in the corner. There, a dark-haired girl sat alone, gazing into her candle. A single white rose lay on her plate.

"It's her," he breathed, staring at the tumble of dark curls flowing down the back of her pink sweater. Her back—straight and slim in a strangely familiar way. Her neck—long and white. Her ears—wearing a single white pearl, just like . . .

Sean frowned and shifted. His breath made a steamy cloud on the pane, which he quickly rubbed away with his fist. He stared harder at the girl as she stirred in her seat, then reached one long white arm down to the purse at her side. She lifted it, and then, in a single swift movement, turned her head slightly toward the window.

The yellow candlelight illuminated her beautiful face. Sean stepped back and closed his eyes. He'd seen the face, yes. But he couldn't believe what he'd seen.

"Okay, let's try again, McGlofflin," Sean muttered to himself, stepping back up to the window. The problem with him was, he'd been spending too much time with KC Angeletti. He was starting to see things.

Sean peered through the window again. An embarrassed flush crept up his neck and began to flood his face. His knees felt weak with disappointment. There was the same long neck. The same beautiful jawline and soft, lovely lips.

"No," Sean whispered, biting his lip until it bled. "It can't be."

He tried to absorb what he'd seen. How could this be happening? He'd spent days dreaming about the beautiful, mysterious girl in the window, only to find out that she wasn't a mystery at all. Anger began to rise up in his chest.

That girl was only KC Angeletti?

Stepping away from the window, Sean pressed his back up against the side of the building, shocked. He could barely breathe. KC? The lovely, sensitive girl in the window was the abrupt, sharp-tongued, self-centered KC Angeletti? KC with the grubby ponytail and stockroom apron? KC was like a troublesome kid sister. A brat.

"How could I have been so stupid?" Sean cried softly, gripping his head and flattening his back against the wall once again as a blast of freezing air nearly knocked him over. "And how could she do this to me?"

Sean felt sick to his stomach, as if he'd just been punched with a fistful of reality. He shook his head as the wind began to howl. What had made him so sure of himself? He'd always done just fine playing it safe as the class clown. Now he was finally doing something sincere and real. But it was backfiring on him worse than he could ever have imagined.

Sean stepped across the deck, leaned over the railing, and stared at the valley. Had this been a trick? Had KC known all along it was him? Had she lured him here to Michael's as a practical joke so that she could laugh in his face in front of the entire restaurant?

Sean made two fists and wanted to howl back at the wind blowing up from the valley.

He knew KC Angeletti. Even if it wasn't a joke, she would overturn the table at his feet when she found out her mystery man was only Sean McGlofflin. She'd throw her water goblet at him. Insult him. Humiliate him.

She'd do it, too. Beautiful, clever girls like KC Angeletti do it to saps like me all the time. It's a form of recreation with them.

Turning away, Sean hugged his chest against the cold. The wind blew bitterly against his face. A huge piece of his heart had suddenly been ripped away. But all he could do was walk numbly down the steps into the dark night.

"Would you like to look at the menu while you wait, miss?" the waiter was asking.

KC looked down and shook her head. Tears flickered in her eyes. She could feel the curious stares boring into her back.

"Very well," she heard his chilly reply.

She took a long, shaky breath, then checked her watch and listened to the wind rattling the restaurant's paned windows. Blood rushed into her face, and she jammed a knuckle between her teeth to keep from screaming. It was seven-twenty. Their date had been for seven. Her heart was slowly ripping in two.

"Ten more minutes," KC told herself, glancing out at the whirling snowflakes dotting the black night. "Maybe the weather held him up."

She bit her lip, trying not to look at the bustle of happy couples sitting and chattering at the nearby tables. Soft classical music filtered through the room. Glasses clinked. And a cheerful fire burned in the hearth at the end of the room. Slowly, she took one finger and trailed it along the soft outer wax of her candle. The weather hadn't held her up.

Seven twenty-five.

A part of KC wanted to search for a logical explanation. Maybe his car stalled. Maybe he was in a serious skiing accident. Maybe—KC dug her nails into her forearm and checked her watch again.

Seven twenty-eight.

"He would have called," KC whispered to herself, looking down at her plate as her hair tumbled over her cheeks. Tears spilled. Falling in love with a guy she didn't know was one of the craziest things she'd ever done. And look where it got her.

Seven-thirty.

KC felt a sharp pang go right through her heart. There was no question now that she'd been stood up. The date had been a joke. Tears flooded her eyes. Or maybe the date was real, and her mystery man had changed his mind when he saw her. She glanced at the window to her left and nodded to herself. Sick at heart, she knew the only thing left to do was to leave as gracefully as possible. Slowly and carefully, KC reached behind her for her coat and readied her hand for her purse. Then, the moment the waiter left for the kitchen, she stood up and left swiftly through the front door.

A freezing blast of air hit her face as soon as she stepped outside. Since she'd arrived a half hour ago, the temperature had dropped at least ten degrees and the wind had doubled. Tucking her head, she wrapped her coat collar close around her neck and made her way across the restaurant's slippery wooden deck. Though tiny lights cascaded down the staircase, it was darker than ever and KC could barely see through the thickening snow. Trembling with cold and anger, she slipped her gloves on and began her descent.

"I'm . . . I'm just as crazy . . . as Winnie," KC cried out, fumbling for the rail. A terrible moan rose out of her chest. Sobbing and bent at the waist, she had to stop just to get her balance on the railing. For a moment, she had to hang on with both hands as a violent gust blew by. Now her nose was dripping and tears had completely flooded her face, mixing with the freezing snow.

KC plunged forward down the steps, feeling the anger surging inside her. What was she thinking of? She'd never exposed herself like that, even with guys she knew and had loved. Some part of her always kept a face-saving route in the back of her heart.

I didn't get to where I am by acting out crazy fantasies like this. I'm KC Angeletti: most likely to succeed, president of future business leaders, and university business major in the exclusive Tri Beta sorority. I don't fall in love with strangers. I don't let myself fall apart.

"I am in control!" KC heard herself sob into the snowy night.

A gust of wind whipped up from the street below, and KC fell against the railing. The icy staircase beneath her boots barely had enough snow on them yet to give her traction. She heard a sickening crack and watched as a huge, snow-laden branch snapped off a pine and fell into the street below, barely missing a van. She gritted her teeth and moved ahead. The snow blew into her eyes like tiny shards of glass, making them water. She shivered, her thoughts wandering back to Winnie.

In high school, KC remembered, Winnie was always falling in love. With her English teacher. With a guy on a motorcycle she'd glimpsed for a moment. Once even with an older guy who played in the band at their senior prom. KC couldn't remember how many times she'd lectured Winnie to be more careful.

"Even Josh," KC muttered tearfully. "Even Josh was a virtual stranger when she fell for him. And she'd only known him a few months when she married him."

When KC finally reached the bottom of the restaurant's staircase, she made her way through the driving snow toward the top of Main Street, where the boardwalk began. From there, she planned to head down toward the ski chalet, and take the Sugar Mountain Village path back to the apartment.

"Made it," KC whispered to herself. Four-wheel drives moved slowly by in the blinding snow, their windshield wipers barely able to keep up. A few straggling groups of après-skiers hurried into the Iceman. As the snowfall thickened, her visibility was dropping, but she stomped forward with confidence now, casting furious looks at the now-dark shopfronts. The Crystal Works. Bob's Cobbler's Bench. The Schussing Sandwich. Everything about Crystal Valley suddenly seemed like a silly waste of time. She shouldn't have come at all. She should have stayed back in the dorms, studying.

The boardwalk flattened out, and KC prepared herself to cross the street toward the ski chalet. Her whole body was trembling with cold by now, and her gloves were so stiff it was impossible to grip onto anything for balance. Still, KC tramped forward, warmed by her mounting anger and swirling, dark thoughts. There was a momentary lull in the wind, and she hurried ahead, thankful that a sheltered area of the boardwalk was just ahead, right in front of the ski chalet.

"Sean McGlofflin," KC snarled to herself, glancing at the chalet's dark windows and the brightly lit ones in the McGlofflin home behind it. "You'd think this was very funny, wouldn't you? You'd love to laugh at me. You'd love to mock the fact that I let down my guard for an instant."

KC's breath was coming quickly now. Just thinking about Sean's infuriating smile was making her angrier than ever. Her boots stomped against the bare wooden boards, which appeared to have been shoveled free of snow and ice earlier in the day.

Sean McGlofflin—you make me sick.

KC felt her boots wiggle, and she was suddenly aware that the bare boardwalk was actually a sheet of glassy ice. Without the snow for traction, KC realized she was without a surface to dig her boots into. She'd been walking way too fast.

"Oh, no," KC cried, as she slid on one foot and tried to stop with the other. Instead, she felt her whole body go out of kilter. The fierce wind picked up again, this time with even greater force. Desperately, she flailed her arms, trying to regain her balance. But before she could react, both legs flew out to her side, one foot twisted horribly to the left, and her body smashed down against the icy wooden boardwalk.

In the long, terrible moment it took to fall, KC heard an agonizing crack. "H-help," KC gasped, trying to regain the wind that had been knocked out of her. Snow swirled into her eyes. She moved slightly on the icy boards, trying to get up. But sickening pain shot through her left leg. She opened her mouth to call out, then reached her glove to her lips. A wave of nausea swept through her.

"Oh, dear." KC was aware of a faraway voice. "Fred—park the car." An arm slipped under her head, and KC opened her eyes. A silver-haired woman's kindly face appeared. "Looks like you've had a bad fall!" KC could hear her shouting over the storm.

KC was suddenly convulsed with bitter sobs. "My left leg," she wailed. "It's broken. I know it's . . . it's . . . just like before. I—"

A warm hand stroked her cheek. "Now you just rest here, hon," the voice called out. "My husband's

calling for help right now. Don't want to move you."
The woman turned away. "Bring the blanket before
you make the call, Fred."

KC stared up into the purplish black gloom of the
night, feeling the pain grip her leg and travel upward
through her whole body until her head hurt.

Sean McGlofflin, KC thought, her thoughts flaring
and stumbling over one another. She thought of his
face—suddenly ghastly. She grabbed the woman's arm.
"Sean McGlofflin made me fall," she cried. "I . . . I
just think about him and . . . I . . ."

"I know, dear." The woman patted her. "Try to
stay quiet now until help comes."

KC gripped her arm harder. "But you don't understand," she rambled, only halfway aware of what was
happening now. She could barely see through her
tears. "Sean McGlofflin just thinks he can get inside of
me and make me give up my dignity. But don't you
see? He made me break my leg—but he can't get the
rest of me."

Twenty-one

"**S**he left a message on my machine yesterday morning, Josh," Francine Gottlieb was saying over the phone, her voice urgent. "She said she was planning to take the next train home to Jacksonville."

Yesterday morning. Winnie called her mother yesterday morning. "Is everything okay, Josh?"

Then she must have gotten back to town safely. The avalanche—it didn't get her—*she's okay.*

"Yeah. Um. Yeah, Francine. Fine."

Josh blinked away tears. He'd spent the entire night not knowing whether Winnie was dead or alive. And now he knew for sure. She was okay. Slumping into the motel's couch, he looked over at

Davis and gave him the thumbs-up sign.

"Josh?" Winnie's mother was saying. "Josh—are you still there?"

He cleared his throat and with his free hand grabbed on to a clump of hair dangling over his forehead. "Uh . . . yes, Francine. Sorry. I . . . uh . . . just ran into Winnie this week in Crystal Valley."

"You did?" Francine's voice was tense.

"Yes," Josh struggled to explain, "and I guess we got our wires crossed. Didn't realize she was leaving so soon."

There was an anxious pause on the other end of the line. "Well, you know Winnie. She didn't actually tell me when that next train was supposed to leave. For all I know, she might still be up there in the mountains."

Josh bit his lip. If Winnie wasn't home, where was she?

"Don't worry, Josh," Francine said, just as another gust of wind shook the building. "Winnie's fine. She's always been able to take care of herself."

Josh bristled. "Thank you, Francine," he replied between clenched teeth, before finally hanging up.

Winnie takes care of Winnie, and Josh takes care of Josh. No wonder our marriage broke up. What was the point?

Josh stared down at Davis, who was sitting on the floor of the room, rubbing wax into the bottom of his snowboard. Though his hair hung limply over his face, Josh detected a faint muscle-twitch under one of his dark-circled eyes. Since yesterday, Davis had been strangely quiet. And he looked terrible.

"Winnie's okay. She called her mom," Josh said.

Davis coughed, not looking up. "Good."

Josh stood up and headed across the room. "Yeah. Guess she got off the mountain okay after all."

There was a long silence as Davis rubbed the wax, his knuckles white from the effort.

Josh frowned and looked away. He stuffed his hands in his pockets to keep them from trembling. Then he looked out the window. Through the sheet of diagonally blowing snow, he could see that a tractor-trailer had jackknifed on the busy road right in front of the motel. Whirling red police lights blinked through the storm.

Josh shifted his weight and listened to the wind howling against the motel's cheap aluminum-frame window. Since last night, the storm had dropped a foot of snow on the valley. Cars were buried. Utility poles were down. And most of the ski runs were closed. But all Josh could think about was Winnie. There was a clutch at his throat as another rush of emotion threatened his cool exterior.

"Winnie is okay," Josh mouthed the words. She wasn't out there in the wild mountain storm. She was safe. Josh squeezed his eyes shut, remembering how tiny and vulnerable Winnie had looked against the snowy mountainside when she'd wandered into his campsite. Sure, Winnie was tough and independent, but maybe there was a part of her that needed someone. That needed him.

Josh braced his long arms against the window and stared down at his feet.

"What's eating you?"

Josh's head snapped up at Davis's question. He looked at his friend. "Winnie doesn't want a divorce."

Davis seemed to jump at his statement. For a moment, he just looked at Josh with his red-rimmed eyes. Then he looked quickly down again, staring at a container of wax that he was turning over and over with his hands.

Josh felt stupid for bringing up the subject. He could tell something was going on with Davis. But he had a sudden, crazy need to know what Davis thought. "Look . . . Davis," Josh stammered. "You gotta help me out here. I mean, you and Faith . . . I mean, it's pretty clear that you two are serious."

Davis's head dropped abruptly.

"And that you click."

Josh walked closer to Davis, his arms wrapped tightly over his chest. He looked down. "Come on. You've been with plenty of girls. How do you know when you've found the right one? I mean—the one you love."

Davis didn't look up. There was a long silence.

Josh looked wildly out the window. "Then how do you know when to stick it out?"

The room was completely still. And when Josh looked back at Davis, his friend was staring at the carpet, shaking his head.

"Davis?"

Abruptly, Davis stood up. "I don't know."

Josh frowned. Davis's green eyes were empty and

nervous as he hurried over to the ripped sofa and grabbed his orange jacket.

"Guess you just do what you gotta do, Josh." Davis checked his watch.

"Yeah, but—"

"And you're the only one who knows the answer to that."

Davis plunged down the ice-encrusted motel staircase and headed through the storm away from town toward the Highway 26 junction. The swirling snow stung his eyelids like a cloud of furious needles. Breaking through the fresh drifts was nearly impossible in his boots. But he knew he couldn't stop now.

Wasted and heartbroken, Davis rubbed the foggy face of his watch. Ten more minutes.

As promised, scuzzy Eric Briggs had called his motel room the night before, ordering Davis to meet him at the Flying Peak Truck Stop that morning at ten o'clock. The choice, as Eric put it to him, was clear. Help him with a major condo robbery that night and Briggs would back off permanently. Refuse, and he would tip off the police—connecting Davis's snowboarding stunt to yesterday's string of downtown robberies.

"Advice," Davis muttered to himself. "Josh Gaffey wants advice from me about women. What a joke."

Davis's muscles tensed against the freezing wind. Tire chains rumbled by, and a snowplow's slowly rotating yellow light broke into the darkness. He plodded forward, through the clogged traffic and buried parking lots. He finally reached the truck stop's parking lot, which was sprawled next to a chain motel and a brightly lit coffee shop. Following Eric's instructions, he looked for a late-model black van parked next to the coffee shop's back Dumpster. His head and feet aching with cold, he finally spotted the vehicle. For a moment he just stood there as the snowstorm pounded his ears and his boots sunk deeper into the powder.

I could turn around right now. I could leave town tomorrow. Davis grimaced. He could leave town tomorrow maybe, but not tonight. Eric would have plenty of time to make that call to the police.

I'm trapped. Briggs has got me.

His hand rose and finally knocked on the van's side door. The door slid open, and a cloud of smoke emerged. The volume on the van's stereo system was cranked up full blast, and Davis could barely see inside. Suddenly Eric's face appeared and a hand extended to pull him inside. Davis fell back into one of the van's backseats, trying to make out the faces in the dim light.

"Shut that music up!" Eric shouted over his shoulder, sitting down opposite Davis and crossing his legs. Eric Briggs's smarmy smile had disappeared, and in its place was a completely cold, businesslike exterior.

"Okay!" Davis heard a female voice. An instant later, the music had died and a familiar pretty blond head popped up from behind the front passenger seat. Davis recognized her at once as Tory Headly—the girl he'd set up with Josh for New Year's Eve. Winking,

Tory wiggled four fingers at him, then flounced back into her seat, out of view. Davis looked away and scanned the four guys seated in the back with Eric. Two were beefy, weight-lifting types wearing crew cuts. The third guy was a wiry, dark-haired chain-smoker who peered through the van's curtain every moment or so. Way in the back, a fourth guy dozed on his back, a pair of headphones attached to his head.

"I'm going to make this very quick," Eric continued in a smooth voice. "We're hitting a luxury condo in the Sugar Mountain Village right after dark tonight. That's at six-thirty, folks. We've spent the last twenty-four hours casing the place," Eric continued. "There is no alarm system, and the security is practically nonexistent." He motioned toward the windows and let a toothy grin spread across his face. "And the weather's cooperating, isn't it? All those cops are gonna be helpin' old ladies with stuck cars tonight, boys."

Eric went on in his efficient monotone. "The number of the condo is Holiday 1029. And we have good information on its contents. It's a very large haul—ski equipment, stereo stuff, the works—so we've gotta move fast."

The wiry guy next to the window shot a worried look at Eric. "What about that house-sitter? That—uh—oh yeah, Sean McGlofflin . . ."

Davis's stomach tightened. He recognized that name. McGlofflin—of the ski chalet, where he and Higgenbothem had been earlier to promote their snowboards.

Eric turned and gave Davis an all-business look.

"That's where you come in, pal. A dope named Sean McGlofflin comes into 1029 about seven-thirty every night to check on the place. We should be done by then, but there's no guarantee he won't show up early."

Davis felt the blood draining out of his face. "Yeah, I'd recognize the guy."

Eric grinned and punched Davis in the shoulder. "All right. If our friend Sean comes early, you gotta make him stay away. Okay?"

Davis nodded and closed his eyes.

"Six-thirty, pal." Eric shook his hand, motioning for one of the crew cuts to open the door. "Take it easy."

Davis stepped out of the van, numb with regret and fear. He stumbled back through the snow, deciding to avoid his motel room and Josh. His shame was so deep, he knew he could never look anyone straight in the eye again.

By this time, the snowstorm had reached blizzard proportions, and the highway into Main Street was littered with stalled cars. Davis trudged back past the truck stop toward Main Street, where he headed diagonally across the Red Apple grocery store parking-lot toward the Iceman Tavern. Through the wind and blowing storm, he heard a voice calling him.

"Daaaaaaaaaaviiiiiiis."

Davis turned his head, recognizing Faith's voice. She was hurrying across the parking lot, clutching a brown paper bag to her chest, her ski hat encrusted with snow and ice.

"Daaaaaaviiis, stop!" she yelled louder.

Something made Davis want to just walk on, as if the sound of the storm had drowned out her call. He wanted to run from her open, honest face. He couldn't bear to look into her blue eyes.

"Davis!" Faith finally caught up with him at the edge of the lot, grabbing his arm.

Slowly, he turned around and stared into her glowing face.

"Whew," she cried, yelling over the snow. "I'm glad I caught you. Hey. Are you okay? We missed our breakfast together and then I saw you snowboarding in the street and the police car—"

"Yeah," Davis interrupted her. Anger began to boil up inside him. He couldn't bear to see her beautiful, trusting face.

Faith's eyes dimmed a little. She let go of his sleeve and seemed to search his eyes. "KC broke her leg and I . . ." Faith gripped her bag harder and looked down. "And I was just getting her a few things. . . ."

Davis stiffened. What could he say to her? She was too beautiful and good for him. How could he even think about dragging her life down with his? He opened his mouth to speak, but a gust of wind rushed by, nearly knocking them over.

Faith's eyes look worried. Her teeth began to chatter with cold, and Davis had a sudden urge to take her in his arms. But he couldn't. Things were different now. Faith couldn't be a part of his lousy life.

"It's just that I haven't seen you," she struggled, "and . . . so can you come by and talk?"

Davis just stared at her.

A tear began to form in her eye. "Lauren called back," she said, as if she was desperate for him to speak. "It turns out that the U of S has one of the best work-study programs in the country—"

"Stop it!" Davis heard himself shout over the wind. "Just forget it, Faith. These are your plans, not mine. I never said I wanted to go to the U of S."

Faith's expression went dark.

"I'm not the person you think I am," Davis cried, turning away as his throat grew too tight to say another word.

"Davis!" Faith called out through the howling wind.

But by the time her cry reached him, he had reached the other side of the lot and was fleeing for the safety of the storm.

Twenty-two

"That feels awfully tight," the middle-aged woman in the pink ski bibs was complaining. "I'm just a beginner. I don't want my boot stuck in the binding when I fall."

Sean closed his eyes briefly. It was nearly closing time at the ski chalet, but several customers were still lined up, waiting for rental fittings. "Mrs. Brennen," he attempted a smile as he sprung the release and helped her step off the fitting block, "these are state-of-the-art bindings with multidirectional release. They're especially made for the lighter or less aggressive skier. And I've adjusted them carefully for your weight and ability."

The woman pressed her lips together, then shook

her finger at him and smiled. "If you didn't have such a twinkle in your eye, I'd complain. I'll give them a try."

Sean's head pounded as he guided the woman through the swinging wooden door, where his mother was positioned to take her money.

"Thanks," he managed to say, his stomach as tight as a hard piece of rubber. He raked his fingers through his hair and ducked once again to peer outside through the shop's front windows. Since discovering the truth about KC Angeletti the night before, he couldn't sleep. He couldn't eat. And his heart wouldn't stop pounding in his chest. His mouth was as dry as cotton.

After he had returned home from Michael's the night before, he'd stared at his bedroom ceiling for hours, listening to the roar of the storm. Discovering the true identity of the girl in the window had made him angrier than he'd been in a long time.

KC Angeletti—of all people!

But as the hours passed, he began to remember every detail of KC's face in the restaurant candlelight. The unfamiliar, sweet expression on her face. The eagerness and hope. She'd been so beautiful. She'd been so different from the KC he'd known in the shop.

I should have turned back. I should have told her it was me.

A terrible ache filled Sean. Even when he closed his eyes, he could still see the curve of her cheek. The beautiful soft mouth. The steady gray eyes as they looked expectantly toward the restaurant window.

Sean sat down on a bench behind the counter and

pressed his fingers into his brow, miserable and confused. He'd recognized something in her eyes in that split second he'd seen her through the foggy windowpane. They were two of a kind, he and KC. Their hearts bruised easily, so their shells were thicker than most. As thick as ice.

He bit his lip and listened to the wind howling through the firs behind the shop. KC hadn't shown up for inventory that morning, and it was pretty clear what had happened. KC wasn't the kind of girl to blow off work like that. She must have discovered his identity.

"Please come this way," he instructed a family of four renting the all-inclusive weekly package. Their feet clomped against the bare wooden floors, and the wild snowstorm outside pelted the windows. All Sean could do was go through the motions of his job, sick at heart. KC Angeletti. The more he thought about her, the more he realized how stupid he'd been to walk away. He'd lost her now.

Sean selected a pair of alpine rentals and placed them on the fitting bench. "Okay, Dad," he said with a curt smile. "Your turn."

He clenched his jaw in anger. Why had he been so afraid? He should have just walked into Michael's, sat down at her table, and told her the truth. Why was it so hard for him to let down his lousy, self-assured, cocky front? Why couldn't he be honest and take the consequences for once, like a man? So what if he'd been humiliated. Wasn't KC worth taking a chance on?

Sean stayed at work until the last customer had been fitted and the cash register had been emptied and locked. He flipped the Open sign to Closed, then stared out into the dark blizzard. The snow was falling so thickly he could barely see the streetlight in front of the shop.

He slipped on his coat, hat, and gloves and readied himself for his nightly trip over to the Sugar Mountain Village. The owners of Condo 1029 in the Holiday building had been specific about his house-sitting duties. The rare fish needed feeding every evening. And the plants would quickly wither in the dry heat if he didn't water them on a regular basis. Most important, the owners did not want the place to seem a vacant target for burglers.

He turned off all the chalet lights and locked the cash register. Usually, he headed out for an hour or two of night skiing before going to the apartment. But tonight was different. It was way too stormy to ski.

"The lifts probably aren't even running," Sean muttered to himself, pacing back through the store until he finally stopped in the middle of the shop's retail section. He stared at the ladies' wear and the high boxes of ski boots KC had been inventorying yesterday morning.

Oh, the weather outside is fright—ning. . . .

Sean felt a pain in his chest. Thinking about KC and her beautiful, happy face was impossible.

"I could just go over there and see her," he whispered to himself, his heart beginning to beat in his ears. KC's apartment, after all, was just across from where he was headed anyway.

If she doesn't know the truth about me now, I'll

tell her. And if I never learn what it's like to be honest with someone I care about, I may as well throw myself into the Elk River.

Luckily, the McGlofflins' four-wheel-drive Jeep was available, and Sean managed enough traction to make it up Main Street, then east to the Sugar Mountain Village. Since it was only about six-thirty, he planned to meet with KC first, then head over to Holiday 1029 for his nightly chores. The storm raged bitterly against his windshield wipers. And by the time he bumped into the snow-clogged village parking lot, he could barely distinguish between parked cars and the snowed-over piles of plowed ice.

"Hi, KC," Sean practiced saying into thin air as he tramped toward the huge apartment building. "KC . . ." Sean took a deep breath and started over, trying to ignore the icy crystals blowing into his eyes. "KC—I'm afraid there's been a mix-up. You see, I'm the guy you were supposed to meet . . ."

Sean stopped next to the building's brightly lit entrance, suddenly terrified.

KC. You may think this is strange coming from me. But I'm glad that was you in the restaurant.

He breathed in and straightened, then felt his knees buckle beneath him.

KC. Was that supposed to be some kind of joke? You knew that was me in the window of 1029— didn't you?

Sean squeezed his eyes shut, paralyzed. The wind howled in his ears. There was no way he could talk to KC now. Maybe another time when—when he was more in control of himself. Seeing her now would be too humiliating.

So Sean simply rushed ahead and flung open the glass doors to the condo lobby and hurried to the elevator. He punched the button for Holiday 1029 and shoved his hands into his pockets, waiting.

"Sean?" he heard a gruff voice to his left.

Sean swung around and saw a guy in an orange ski jacket and jeans walking casually toward him. Though his head was bent down and his hands were stuffed in his pockets, he recognized the pale-blond ponytail and tanned face at once. It was Davis Mattingly, the guy from the snowboarding demo tour—the guy who turned Main Street into a half-pipe yesterday morning and blew everyone away.

Davis cleared his throat, as if he was slightly nervous. "You're Sean, aren't you?"

Sean extended his hand, glad to have someone distract him from his thoughts of KC. "Hey—Mattingly. Way to go on Main Street yesterday," he replied. He punched him in the shoulder. "Just catching a little air in the name of good public relations, huh?"

Davis tugged his cap down on his head. "Sure," he mumbled, jamming his hands deeper in his jacket and looking over his shoulder.

Sean frowned. "Hey, pal. Police didn't give you much trouble over that, did they? Look—I've been reading about you for years in the surfing magazines. If you need a little local help with those guys . . ."

The elevator suddenly clanged and Davis's eyes leapt

in the direction of the door. Sean stared at his agitated face. "You going up?"

Davis rocked on his feet, as if he wanted to walk away. "Uh—no. Look, Sean. You can't . . ."

Sean watched as Davis closed his mouth. It was as if something deep inside was telling him not to go on. Davis's dark-circled eyes lifted upward for a split second. Then his lips shut tight.

"Anything wrong?" Sean asked.

Davis suddenly looked him in the eye. "No," he said, his voice serious and low. "Not anymore."

Sean stood there and watched, confused, as Davis turned and hurried toward the door to the complex's inner courtyard. The last thing he saw was Davis jogging across the snowy expanse toward the student housing in the opposite building.

"Okay," Faith soothed, "just six more steps forward and you're in your comfy couch."

KC gripped Faith's waist and hobbled through the door into the apartment. She'd spent a lonely, painful night in the hospital, and now Faith was returning her to the apartment couch.

KC dropped into the worn velveteen cushions, biting back tears. "Here's where my problems started, right here on this couch." She pointed her thumb toward the view of the opposite apartment. "And here's where they end."

Faith's lower lip trembled as she looked down. "I'm so sorry, KC, that this had to happen to you." She dropped down to the floor and leaned her back against the couch, pressing her trembling fingers into her forehead. "I bought cocoa—and croissants at the grocery store," Faith said, her sentence ending a tearful squeak.

KC stared at Faith's pale face and tense mouth. "I'm the one with the leg fracture, Faith."

Faith gave KC a long, sad stare.

Tears began to spill down KC's cheeks. "And I'm the one who didn't even have the guts to call in to work."

Faith cleared her throat. "Why didn't you, KC?" she asked softly.

"Because," KC cried, "if I told Sean McGlofflin I broke my leg, he would ask me how. And I'd have to say I was walking through town. And he's just the kind of guy to find out that I was stood up at Michael's restaurant."

"Wouldn't he understand?" Faith asked, pulling a Kleenex out of her pocket and blowing her nose.

"NO," KC wailed, clenching her fists. "Don't you understand, Faith? He would tease me and ridicule me. And and I just can't take that right now. Okay?"

A gust of wind knocked violently against the apartment window, causing Faith and KC to jump. The snow was so hard it sounded like sand being blown into the glass. KC watched as Faith abruptly stood up. "The nurse said you could have your pain pills when you got back."

KC felt a wave of pain rise up her leg and into her back, but Faith's faraway look and red-rimmed eyes were starting to alarm her. Just looking at her friend's misery made her want to forget her own. And she felt sure that Faith was going through something serious, something KC suspected had to do with Davis. KC looked down at her lap. "What happened, Faith?"

There was a tiny sob from the kitchen as Faith opened the refrigerator door.

"Come on. You're my best friend," KC insisted. "Who else can you spill to?"

Faith walked back with a pill and a glass of juice, a tear sliding down her cheek. "It's Davis."

KC bit her lip. She knew it.

Faith slid down onto the floor and rested her back against the sofa, staring out at the wild snowstorm. Through the window, they could see apartment floodlights flickering on and off. Gusts of wind banged the shaky windows so loudly they could barely talk. "Everything was going so well," Faith began. "When we met on New Year's Eve, it was like a dream, KC. We both realized that we wanted to be together."

KC stared, heartbroken, as Faith rolled over on her side, pressing her fingers into her wet eyes. They'd been best friends since the eighth grade, and KC had never seen her like this. Faith was deeply in love with Davis, that was clear.

"I saw him on my way to the hospital to pick you up," Faith cried. "He said . . . he didn't want to apply to the U of S. That he wasn't the person I thought he was."

KC frowned. "Just like that?"

"There's something wrong with me, KC," Faith cried. "He's probably just another flaky surfer. . . ."

"Faith . . ."

"I never should have pinned my hopes on him. Never."

For a long while, KC just lay there on the couch, stroking Faith's hair and listening to her cry. Outside, there was a huge crash, like a falling tree, then the sounds of shouts below. KC felt the pain pills take effect. Her leg felt better, and her head seemed to float on the pillow. "Maybe we just let ourselves get carried away," KC finally said, "by the mountains and the air and all the beauty. Maybe we wanted everything to be too good to be true."

Faith sniffed and nodded. "Like Josh and Winnie getting back together," she said with a bitter laugh. "Yeah—right. Good one, Faith."

KC's eyelids felt heavy. "When I saw that guy on the stairs. I just wanted him to be the one for me, Faith," she whispered. "It didn't have anything to do with reality. That's what romance is, isn't it? Imagination."

"Pure fantasy," Faith agreed.

"I guess the rendezvous at Michael's was some kind of a funny prank for him," KC said, staring at the ceiling.

"It's okay, KC," Faith comforted her, just as another gust of arctic wind slammed against the building, nearly shattering the windows.

Faith let out a tiny scream as the apartment suddenly went black.

"A blackout!" KC cried.

"Don't move, KC," Faith ordered through the inky darkness. KC could feel Faith bracing herself on the sofa as she stood up. "I'm going to look for a flashlight."

KC let her head fall back and closed her eyes against the pitch black. The wind continued to scream, and she could hear the snow swishing against the glass window. There was the sound of cabinets opening, drawers banging, and, finally, a crash.

"Tory's liquor supply," Faith called out through the velvety darkness. "Great—uh—okay. No. All I can feel is Winnie's fruit-flavored gummie bears. I don't remember ever seeing a flashlight in here, do you? Candles?"

"No," KC replied, spooked by the heavy darkness. It was so dark she couldn't even see the hands in front of her face.

"Look, KC," Faith insisted, groping back to the couch. "I'm going to run back to that grocery store and get some flashlights and candles."

KC could hear the rustle of Faith's jacket. She stiffened. The last thing she wanted was to lie alone in horrible darkness.

"Will you be okay?"

"Yeah, I will be, Faith," KC replied, biting her lip and closing her eyes. Outside, she heard the sounds of breaking glass, scuttling garbage, and groaning tree branches. She tried to ignore it. All she wanted now was to sleep and forget everything. Her lost love, her throbbing leg, and especially the irritating Sean McGlofflin.

Twenty-three

A cold sweat broke out on Tory's face as she followed Eric Briggs down the tenth-floor hallway, headed for Holiday 1029, the luxury Sugar Mountain Village condo they'd been planning to rip off for the past two days. Her hands trembled with fear, staring at Eric's broad back. To her left, two of Eric's partners slid silently past the row of numbered doors, listening carefully for movements inside. Behind her, the other two accomplices dragged a sleek utility cart with a sign that read Acme Moving and Rental.

Tory froze when they reached the condo door. For the first time since she'd been entangled in Eric Briggs's life, she felt scared. There was a sudden whoosh and a bang, and Tory jumped. Outside, the storm raged on, shaking the building and rattling her nerves worse than ever.

"Okay, get your butts in gear," Eric was saying in a low, threatening voice. "We've got exactly five minutes. The storm's getting worse, and that means accidents and mayhem, folks. Cops always come running."

Eric turned away, and with his muscular arm planted against the door he placed a high-tech device over the dead-bolt lock. Seconds later the door jerked open, and Eric peered inside. Then he nodded to Tory and the rest of the group, waving them silently through.

Tory felt sick with terror. What was she doing there? This wasn't a game anymore. It was the real thing.

"Move," Eric hissed as the lights flicked on and Tory stumbled inside. Plush carpeting covered the big entry, then spilled into the huge living room, studded with antiques, oil paintings, and expensive rugs. A vaulted ceiling soared above them, and large picture windows stared out into the dark. Meanwhile, a big cabinet held a wealth of stereo and video equipment. To the left, there was a European-style kitchen and a hallway leading down to the bedrooms.

"Eric," Tory suddenly whimpered, beginning to cry softly as the utility cart rolled behind her toward the living room. She looked over at him for reassurance. What was she going to do? Her hands were shaking too violently to do anything.

The door shut quietly, and Eric's four buddies

moved quickly ahead. Tory suddenly felt Eric's powerful hand grip her upper arm. Squeezing it as hard as he could, he shoved her against a closet door and stared into her face. "Now." He moved closer, breathing into Tory's ear. "No matter what happens, I don't want to hear a peep out of your big mouth. Got that?"

Tory gulped and nodded, horrified. Only yesterday, she and Eric had been having a great time bumming around Crystal Valley, getting toasted and spending lots of money. They were almost a couple by now. It wasn't until this very minute that she realized what it all really meant. This was serious. She could get into a ton of trouble. Besides, Eric was turning into a real creep.

"Okay, then," Eric continued, looking over his shoulder at the others, panic rising in his eyes as the wind shook the building. "I want you to take the back bedrooms. Go through the dresser drawers. Jewelry, watches . . . anything that looks like it has a big price tag on it."

Eric squeezed harder on her arm, and Tory muffled a scream. "Okay," she cried. "Okay, just don't break my arm."

"Fall apart and I'll kick your ass," Eric spit before releasing her and flinging her against the wall. Tory's head banged. Her hands continued to shake with terror. Over his broad shoulder, she could see Eric's four accomplices, stone-faced and swift, ripping stereo components from the shelving.

Tory sucked her breath in. It was clear that this condo robbery was sheer, cold-blooded routine to these guys. They were so ruthless. So totally scary.

Tory stepped forward toward the bedrooms, then stopped, pressing her back against the wall and sneaking a look into the living room.

"Let Maxwell do it, lard-butt," Eric was snarling into the face of one of the bigger guys while the storm raged against the big windows. "Find the ski equipment—like I said."

"Sure—sure Eric." The guy stepped back and held up his hands. "Sorry. I just forgot."

Tory gasped as Eric pulled a switchblade out of his back pocket and flicked it open. Then, in one swift moment, he grabbed the guy's arm and pulled it behind his back. Tory's head began to spin. Eric was actually pointing the tip of the blade at the guy's neck. "You screw up, Taylor, and you're dead. Do you hear me? You're in the grave, buddy. This is our last job here, and nothing's gonna come down, you hear me?"

"Oh, man . . ." the guy moaned before Eric abruptly released him. Tory froze as he turned around and pointed the knife in her direction. "Don't think I don't see you. Get your little butt in there, Tory," he screamed.

Tory gasped and ran down the hall. She stared in a blind panic at the plush master bedroom.

Get me out of here, Tory thought desperately.

Suddenly, the storm outside seemed to become even worse until Tory was convinced the roof of the apartment was about to fly off. The wind sounded like the scream of a wild animal.

"What am I doing?" Tory whispered to herself,

touching a hand to her neck. This wasn't fun. This wasn't adventure.

Outside, she heard an earsplitting crash and the sound of a million electric wires buzzing and popping all at once. There was a flash in the sky, then a loud clicking noise.

Click.

Tory gasped, "The lights are out!"

She turned, her eyes groping for a sliver of light— anywhere—just to help her get her bearings. She looked toward the window. She could still hear the batting of snow against the glass, but she could see nothing. The bank of lights from the opposite build- ing had disappeared, too. There were shouts from below and from the condo next door. The room was absolutely pitch black. Tory swayed, her knees buck- ling in sheer terror. Weak with fear, she headed back down the pitch-black hall, her hands grasping the wall for balance.

When she reached the living room, all she could see were two tiny beads of light. Two of the guys were holding up cigarette lighters while Eric and the two others frantically emptied an antique armoire filled with brand-new ski and camping equipment.

"Go, go, go, go," one of the guys was whispering in a panic, throwing an armful of skis on the cart, banging them against a large television set. "We're screwed. We're never gonna make it out of here. Cops will be everywhere."

"Shut up, Taylor," Eric growled, shoving a small table away with his foot and overturning it. "Shut up, all of you, and keep your damn mouths shut."

There was a scuffle and a bang.

"Eric—what . . ."

"Shut up," Eric hissed. She could barely make out the boxes of new downhill ski boots that were being dumped onto the cart. "We need a damn flashlight, Tory, okay? Does that register in your tiny brain?"

Tory was trembling all over. She tried not to think about the switchblade in Eric's pocket. "Eric." She made an effort to sound sweet as she clung to the wall, searching to make out the outline of his head in the heavy darkness. "Look, Eric. I don't think I'm cut out for this line of work." She let out a nervous giggle. "Didn't work out, okay? So if you don't mind . . ." Tory began to move ahead, groping for the opposite wall and hoping to find her way to the front door.

She could vaguely see Eric's head move with a jerk. A second later she could see that he'd grabbed one of the cigarette lighters. He held it in front of him so that she could see the angry shadows on his dark face. His eyes were glittering and fixed on hers. Slowly, he rose from his crouched position and walked toward her, holding out the lighter, a cruel smile on his lips.

"No, Tory," he whispered, reaching for the knife in his pocket. "Can't do it."

Tory stared, horrified, at the hand in his pocket. "No!" She tried to stifle her scream.

Eric snapped out the knife, extinguished the light, then grabbed her around the chest. She could feel the edge of the cold blade being held to her neck.

"Just can't let you blow right now, Tory. In fact,

there's somethin' real important I want from you."

Tory could barely speak. Her whole body convulsed with terror. She tried to see the door through the blackness. The wind roared menacingly outside the window.

"Huh?" Eric held her closer and flicked the edge of the knife with his thumb.

"Y—yes," Tory stammered.

"Good," Eric replied in an eerie, singsong voice. "Now I want you to get your butt over to your condo across the way and find us some flashlights. Okay? Think you can manage that? The power's out, so the elevators probably don't work. You're gonna have to use the stairs for once in your life, monkeybrain."

Tory nodded crazily as Eric flicked on his lighter, dragged her to the door, and looked down the dark hallway. Then, in one rough motion, he grabbed her jaw with his fingers and twisted her head around to face him. His mouth stretched into a weird grin. "You gotta come back, Tory. Okay?"

"O—kay," Tory sobbed softly.

"And if you don't"—Eric squeezed harder—"I'm gonna come after you. This is my last job here in the valley, and it's big money. I won't hesitate to cut down anyone who tries to screw it up for me. I don't care how pretty they are. Understand?"

"Yes," Tory moaned before he let go of her jaw and flung her roughly in the direction of the dark, windy staircase.

*   *   *

The stairwell–fire escape of Sugar Mountain Village was completely dark. Faith clutched the steel railing as she stepped down through the blackness. The arctic storm howled through the cement and metal-grate vents, sweeping the steps with icy grains of snow. From here, the wind sounded like a screaming cat. Or a woman calling for help. Shivers rose up her spine.

She'd left five minutes ago to buy flashlights in town, but in the darkness, the staircase was slow going. Terrified of falling down the metal staircase, she clung to the icy cold railing.

Clank, clank, clank, Faith's boots pounded against the metal stairs.

"Four more floors and I'm there," Faith told herself, her eyes searching for a hint of light. "I think." She suddenly wished she'd stayed back in the condo and just waited for the power to return.

There was a long, wild gust of wind. The entire staircase was enveloped in a huge, echoing howl. Faith could barely breathe. The darkness was so thick she couldn't see her hand in front of her. Her head was spinning, as if her mind needed to know which way was up and which way was down. What if she lost her way? Her fingers were already burning with cold. A night alone here . . . she would freeze to death.

Faith's heart stopped. For an awful second she thought she was going to scream. Someone else was in the staircase, and getting closer. She told herself to remain calm. After all, the complex was filled with people like her who were without power and needed to get supplies. Still, there was something heavy and slow in those steps, Faith thought desperately. Something heavy and disturbing.

The footsteps drew closer. Faith opened her mouth to say something, but all that escaped was a whisper, quickly drowned out by the roar of the wind. Something banged against the building, and Faith was immediately paralyzed with fear. She heard the footsteps and the rustle of clothing only inches away from her in the inky darkness.

She gasped, then heard the footsteps stop next to her. A hand grabbed her arm.

"Aaaagghhhhhhhh!" Faith screamed. Who was it?

"Faith?" she heard a male voice next to her.

Faith froze. The voice sounded familiar. "Yes?" She groped for the railing.

"Faith—it's me," the voice called out over the blowing storm. "It's Davis."

She pressed her lips together, the memory of his words in the parking lot burning into her brain. *These are your plans, not mine. I never said I wanted to go to the U of S. I'm not the person you think I am.* Tears spilled down Faith face. She was glad that she couldn't see his face and that he couldn't see hers. "I don't want to talk to you."

"Faith," Davis said urgently.

Faith exploded. "What are you . . . doing?" she sputtered, gripping the railing and continuing down the stairs. "First you avoid me. Then you tell me to get out of your life. Then you frighten me to death."

She felt Davis behind her. "Faith. Please. I was just headed up to your place. . . ."

"Well, you can just turn around, Davis Mattingly," Faith cried into the dark, howling stairwell, "because you've hurt me enough. Go away."

There was another sudden gust of wind. This time it shook the building so hard that Faith thought it was going to collapse on their heads. The wind screamed through her ears, and she instinctively gripped Davis's arm.

"Faith—please listen!" Davis had to shout to be heard.

Faith's free hand tore at the darkness. The dank walls seemed to be closing in on her. Sobs rose out of her chest. She sat down, gripped Davis's arm harder, and leaned against him, desperate for something—anything—to hang on to. His slippery jacket felt good against her cheek. She took a breath and thought of all the other moments she'd spent with Davis. She remembered them so clearly, and they were beginning to wash over her with an overpowering force. The sunsets over the ocean. The long hours staring at the fire in the lodge. The bright green of his eyes against his sunburned face. Faith knew she'd never be able to forget him, ever. . . .

"There are things about my life," Davis began as the wind died down a little, "that I've avoided telling you, Faith."

Faith frowned. "What things?"

Davis sighed. "Look. You have this idea that I'll go to the U of S with you, and everything will be great."

Faith remained silent.

"But what I didn't tell you," Davis went on, "is

that I did give college a try. A year ago. At Honolulu State. I flunked out, Faith," Davis said quietly. "Okay? I went home after one semester."

Faith went numb all over. "And . . . you were too ashamed—"

"Yes," Davis interrupted. "Don't you understand how it makes me feel hanging out with you and KC and Winnie and Josh? You're all in college—getting your degrees and talking about your careers as if it was the most normal thing in the world. You talk about Hemingway and writers I've never read. You talk about directing in the theater." Davis broke off, taking a shaky breath. "Faith . . . I haven't been to a play since I was a kid in school. And I'm . . . I'm just hanging . . ."

"You have a job," Faith cried, trying to take in everything Davis was trying to say. The wind blew through, and she shivered.

"No, I don't, Faith," Davis muttered. "A guy named Eric Briggs had a major-league betting gig on last week's demo. He wanted me to fall on the last turn. . . ."

"He was trying to fix the bets?" Faith breathed, shocked, her teeth chattering in the dark. "Did you go along with him?"

"No . . . not in the end," Davis explained. "But Briggs was ticked and tipped off Higgenbothem. So I got fired. Then Briggs and his buddies ripped off a bunch of Main Street shops that morning I was boarding down the street."

"The McGlofflin Ski Chalet," Faith gasped.

"Briggs is promising to pin the burglaries on me," Davis went on, "unless I help him tonight with a job he's doing on the other side of the complex."

Faith turned and touched Davis's dark face with her fingertips. "Right now?"

"Yes," Davis said in a sick, whispery voice. Faith heard his breathing turn into a cracked sob.

Faith gripped his arm. "What are you going to do?"

Another gust of wind shook the building, and Faith slipped her arms around Davis's waist.

"I . . . don't . . . know," Davis cried, pulling her close. "I could kill myself for buckling under to an animal like Briggs. But I panicked. I wanted to be rid of him, but now it looks like I'm headed for jail. Sean McGlofflin recognized me in the lobby—I've got to do something, Faith. Help me. I've got to do the right thing."

Sean had been staring at the blackness for what seemed like hours when he finally reached the tenth-floor landing. His fingers were bruised and probably bleeding. His feet were freezing, and his shirt was soaked with sweat.

He'd been trying to get up to the tenth floor for his nightly house-sitting duties in Holiday 1029. But just before his elevator reached the tenth floor, the power apparently went out. He'd spent the past twenty minutes stuck alone in the elevator, listening to the storm beating against the building. It had taken him forever to find the lever that would let him open the doors manually. Even then, they'd been nearly impossible to slide apart. At one point, his fingers had been jammed when the doors snapped back. Finally, he'd been able to wedge his hip into the opening, but the elevator had stopped somewhere between floors.

Running his hand down the wall for balance, Sean headed for Condo 1029 and searched his jacket pocket for the keys. He sighed with relief. At least I'll be able to kick around here for a while in peace, Sean thought to himself. And if the lights go back on, maybe I'll catch another glimpse of beautiful KC.

Twenty-four

KC's mind was dangling on the edge of sleep. The painkillers had dulled everything: the pain, the terrible memory of her faithless mystery man—even the sting of Sean McGlofflin's teasing remarks all week. Right now, all she could register was the wild roar of the storm outside. The snow sweeping against the glass. She closed her eyes, almost enjoying her solitude and the pitch-blackness of the condo. There was no moonlight. No light from the apartment across the way. Nothing except velvety black.

Bang.

KC's head jerked up at the sound of the door slamming. "Faith? You back?"

There was a sniff, then a tiny sound that sounded like weeping. It drew closer in the dark. She heard a long sob, then the bump of someone against the table.

"Winnie?"

From the kitchen, she heard another soft cry, then a dull voice. "It's me . . . Tory."

KC gasped. "Where have you been? You didn't come home last night."

Drawers opened, and KC could hear the shuffling of silverwear and utensils. "Flashlights," Tory was mumbling.

"Faith just went out to buy some flashlights," KC called out, rubbing her eyes. "We couldn't find any."

"No!" Tory shouted, her voice shrill and on the brink of hysteria. A drawer slammed. "No, no, no, no, no, no, no!"

KC blinked and let out a short chuckle of disbelief. "Relax, Tory. She'll be back in a minute."

"Uh-uh." Tory was sobbing. KC could hear the clink of a bottle, silence, then the sound of Tory gasping, as if she'd just taken a long drink. KC frowned. Something was definitely wrong with Tory.

"Aaaahhhhh!" Tory cried out. KC could hear her yanking open cabinets and kicking the walls. "I've got to find a flashlight or I'm dead." There was the sound of more gulping and sobbing.

"Stop screaming, Tory!" KC yelled, trying to sit up at the end of the couch. She drew her blanket up around her chin. "My leg is broken. I can't help you!"

"I've . . . I've got to get back to 1029," Tory was gasping, "or he'll come after me with that knife."

"Knife?" KC shouted back, feeling the pain in her head and leg beginning to creep back. "What knife? And what do you mean ten twenty-nine—?" KC broke off before she finished the question. At first, she thought Tory was talking about the time. But then, in a flash, she realized it was an apartment number. An apartment number she definitely recognized.

". . . crazy in there . . . they don't kill him, too . . ." Tory was mumbling. KC could tell that she was still guzzling from the bottle as she staggered around the room. There was a bump, then the sound of Tory stumbling onto the floor.

"Kill who?" KC said quietly, a strange fear beginning to curl around her in the darkness. She heard the swish of a bottle being upturned, then Tory gulping it down and finishing with a gasp. "Kill who, Tory?" KC asked again, digging her nails into her forearm, feeling the blood begin to pound in her ears.

". . . guy who takes care of the place," Tory mumbled. "Eric and his guys are . . . taking a lot of stuff . . . out of Condo 1029. You know. . . ."

KC trembled. "I know?"

Tory slipped into a long crying jag before she could speak again. ". . . cute guy with the red hair at . . . you know, that guy who rents the stuff at the ski . . . shop where you . . . work. Sean something . . . comes every . . . night to . . . house sit. . . ."

KC stopped breathing. "What?" she stammered.

"Eric'sssssuchalousy . . . creep," Tory mumbled before she became perfectly silent and began to snore. KC shook with frustration. Tory had passed out cold.

Meanwhile, KC's heart was banging inside of her chest. Was Sean McGlofflin the mystery man in the window of 1029? How could he be? KC thought wildly. She covered her face with her hands, trying to steady her swirling thoughts. What had happened to her tanned mystery man with the dazzling smile and the coal-black hair? Had he been a dream? It was crazy. It was impossible. It couldn't be true.

"Sean McGlofflin has a job there?" KC cried softly. She thought back. She remembered the way he knew the apartment. He'd told about the ski chalet deliveries. It made sense. And yet, how could it be true? Sean was sarcastic and mean. He wasn't the same guy in the window. He wasn't the tender voice on the other end of the line.

KC's eyes misted over. Maybe he was. Maybe he was someone just like her. Someone hard and prickly on the outside, but longing for love on the inside. Of course Sean didn't approach her at Michael's. He'd probably seen her first, then run away. KC knew how bitchy and impossible she'd been all week in the shop. Sean was probably horrified to discover she was his mystery girl. Sean McGlofflin probably hated her guts.

"Yet . . ." KC whispered, turning her head to the darkened window across the complex. She remembered the last morning they'd worked together, joking, singing, and icicle fencing. Even then she'd sensed a different Sean beneath his wise-guy exterior. And something better inside of herself when she was with him. "Something tells me, Sean McGlofflin, that the real you was right there in the window all along."

KC bolted upright on the couch and pressed a hand over her mouth. Tory's ramblings had suddenly taken on new meaning. *"Sean!"* she cried out, just as the power began to flicker back on. Turning her head quickly toward the opposite apartment, KC saw that it, too, suddenly had power. *"Sean!"* she screamed again as she rapidly took in the view.

The huge picture windows were now flooded with light, and KC quickly saw Sean's tall figure through the flying snow. She blinked as she realized that he was not alone. Instead, to her horror, she saw that he was surrounded by several large guys.

"Sean!" she cried out again, staring urgently at the window. She tried to get up, then collapsed back on the couch. The wind howled through the courtyard. She kept her eyes focused on the faraway window. The blurry figures approached him—then one of them was throwing Sean against the wall. KC watched helplessly as his body hit, then crumpled to the floor.

"Sean!" KC screamed into the wild night. Her eyes strained to see, but the lights in the condo across the way began to flicker again, then die out.

"Oh, no," KC began to moan. "Oh, no." Her stomach tightened, and her hands grew cold. An instant later, her apartment went dark, too. She thought of screaming or breaking the window to get attention. Right now nothing in the world was as important as saving Sean. Forcing herself to stay calm, she heaved herself off the couch until she was lying on her side. Then, dragging her cast along the carpet, she headed in the darkness toward the phone.

KC's mind began to work quickly. From what she could gather, Tory had hooked up with a bunch of goons who were robbing the condo Sean went to every night. And now they were ready to kill him. She realized right then that she was probably Sean's only hope.

Panting with exhaustion, KC pulled herself over to the kitchen counter, where the phone loomed above her head. Using her left leg to pull herself up, she somehow managed to grab the phone before she dropped back down again. Nearly passing out from pain, KC finally punched 9-1-1.

She held the phone to her ear, then dropped it. The phone was dead.

KC knew she had to think. Tory was unconscious. Faith was gone. The phone was dead. The only thing left to do was to somehow get into the hallway and start yelling.

"Come onnnnn," KC breathed, as she struggled valiantly to pull herself up. But the next moment her leg collapsed beneath her. Her body fell back to the floor. And she could feel herself slipping gradually into helpless semiconsciousness.

Whoooooooooooooooooooo!

Josh's head snapped up. His boots, resting on the train station's electric baseboard-heater, were burning. His ears were freezing. He opened his eyes. The light—strangely dim . . .

"Winnie's train," he stammered, grabbing his jacket and running for the door out to the train platform. It

was impossible that the train could be leaving right
now. He'd spent most of the day at the station drinking stale coffee and pacing, waiting for the moment
when Winnie might descend the stairs and walk toward
him. But when the lights went out an hour or so ago,
he'd apparently fallen asleep.

Now he was pushing his way out the door, but the
platform was crowded with departing skiers. Standing
on tiptoe, he could see the silver train with its long
row of windows. Clumps of snow were melting and
sliding down its sides, and beyond the platform's
cover, he could see the winter snowstorm raging,
wilder than ever.

"*All aboard!*" a voice screeched from the loudspeaker.

"Winnie!" Josh pushed his way past a woman wearing a fur hat and several station employees hoisting ski
equipment into the train's baggage compartment. A
freezing wind drove down the length of the platform,
stinging his eyes.

"Train Number 503 departing for Jacksonville via
Twin Rivers will be leaving platform two in approxi-
mately two minutes."

Josh bounced up and down, searching desperately
for a glimpse of Winnie among the ski tips, fuzzy hats,
and towering backpacks. His knees bumped against a
bench, and Josh immediately jumped on it. The
throng swirled around his feet. His gaze moved frantically over the chaotic scene. But it wasn't until he
looked toward the far end of the platform that he saw
something small and familiar. It was a bright-purple

cap. It had fuzzy earflaps. It had a big yellow brim shaped like a duck's bill. It was crazy. It was outrageous. And it was Winnie's.

"Winnie!" Josh screamed, jumping up and down and waving his arms over his head.

Whooooooooooooooooo!

"Winnie!" Josh shrieked at the top of his lungs as the hat disappeared into the train. A space appeared in front of the bench and Josh leapt down, pushing his way up the platform until he was nearly before the front passenger car's brightly lit window. The wind howled. The train whistle blew. And, slowly, the train began to move.

"You've got to hear me, Winnie," Josh yelled, planting his gloved hand onto the side of the vibrating train. "You've just got to hear what I have to say!"

Sean thought the cloth gag in his mouth was going to tear his face off. His hands, tied behind his back, were bound with wire and bleeding. His ankles were crossed and strapped to the chair. All Sean could think of now was his life. Nineteen years of his life. Scenes kept running in front of his closed eyes. The good times. The bad. The chances he took, and the ones he let slip by.

"Wraps it up," the big guy with the slick black hair was saying. Sean stared numbly as the guy stepped into a blue coverall that looked like a moving company uniform. The other four guys were doing the same. The tags on their chests read Acme Moving and Rental.

"Yeah, except for this bozo," another guy added.

Wiry-haired and nervous, he gave Sean a look of pure resentment. "What are we gonna do with him, Briggs?"

A larger guy with a blond crew cut walked over to Sean and pushed his chin roughly to the side. "Why'd you have to go and walk in on us—scumbag? You wrecked our party."

The dark-haired Briggs twirled a toothpick in his mouth as he zipped his uniform on. Then he put his hands in his pockets, stepped forward, and looked at Sean. His eyes, cold and blue, were half-closed. His lips curled downward in an expression of pure hate. "Put the rest of the stuff on the dolly and get ready to leave nice and businesslike, Taylor." His eyes remained fixed on Sean. "While I figure out what to with this jerk."

Sean felt sick. The guy was only half human. He'd heard of thieving rings like this one. Most of them were into drug dealing, too. Gambling. He knew they wouldn't hesitate to blow the head off anyone who happened to stumble in their path.

"He's a witness, man," one of the crew-cut thugs was saying.

Another guy laughed. "So was our blond bimbo. And our surfer boy. So—what—are we gonna off them, too?"

"Shut up," Briggs snapped, lacing his fingers together and bending them back until his knuckles cracked. He sauntered forward, his arms crossed over his broad chest, until he was inches from Sean's chair. "They're not gonna talk." He started to laugh. It was a high-pitched chuckle that made Sean's blood run colder than ever. "They're gone. And they're gonna want to wash their hands of this operation. No. Not them. But this punk's gotta go."

Sean's heart pounded. Instinctively, he struggled in the chair. Saliva ran out of the sides of his mouth, soaking the gag. KC Angeletti's face began to float in front of his mind. For some reason, he could see it in great detail. The full, soft mouth. The dark curls that tumbled about her face. The eyebrows—so stern above the shining gray eyes. It was the kind of face he understood as well as his own. It knew about pain. It knew about keeping all the secrets safely inside. He'd seen it. Why hadn't he taken a chance with her? Why hadn't he just walked up to her table and . . .

"Forget it, Briggs," the wiry-haired guy objected. He put a hand to his forehead nervously. "We're outta here tonight. By the time he gets out of those ties, we'll be at least five hundred miles—"

"Shut up!" Briggs shouted.

"Come on . . ." one of the crew cuts started to protest before his gaze met Eric's. His expression changed and he stepped back, shaking his head.

Without saying another word, Eric walked toward the window and grabbed the telephone with one hand. Then, in one swift movement, he ripped the cord out of the wall jack, then tore the other end out of the receiver. Taking up a length of cord, he quickly spun each end around his thick thumbs until it was taut.

Sean shook his head, and with a violent thrust tried to shove his chair into the wall.

"No," Briggs was saying in a calm voice, stepping forward, his eyes glued to Sean's. He drew his thumbs together, then jerked them apart again so that the wire vibrated. "We've come this far—and I want this job clean. Very clean."

"Get outta here, Briggs," the crew cut objected. "Why complicate things? It's not our style."

Eric jerked the wire again, then looked over his shoulder. "You want this guy talking? He's got a big mouth." Sean jerked his shoulders back and forth as Briggs suddenly stepped forward, pulled the wire around his neck, then moved behind the chair and began to tighten it. "How's that feel, McGlofflin?"

A deep, choking pain shot through Sean's neck and shoulders. He dropped his chin, hoping to ease the pressure. But Briggs pulled tighter. He twisted in his chair, hoping to overturn it. His lungs begged for air. He could feel the heat of Briggs's body behind him and the two taut forearms that continued to squeeze the cord into the skin of his neck.

Sean sagged a little as he weakened. He had a sudden, desperate wish to understand what was happening. His life—was it possible for it to end so suddenly? Without purpose? He felt the wire squeezing harder as Briggs twisted it brutally in his fists. Sean's lungs seemed to cramp up, begging for air. The room became a blurry vision and his mind, a swirling, hopeless well of thought.

Everything in his body began to grow weak, and in a flash he saw clearly what was never obvious before: His life had a beginning and an end. And if by some miracle he had it back again, he knew it wouldn't be so full of hesitation and doubt. If he had another chance, he'd walk right up to KC's table. He'd take the white rose from her hand and . . .

There was a loud pounding somewhere in the distance, then shouting as his head hit the floor. The wire loosened, and his gasping lungs began to fill up with a rush of air.

"Police!" a deep voice shouted. *"Against the wall with your hands up. Get them up."*

"He's got a weapon, Brightly."

Sean fell sideways onto the floor, just as he recognized Officer Brightly running into the room. He watched as the heavyset policeman grabbed Briggs's arm and twisted it behind his back. Eric struggled violently, shoving Brightly backward against the big paned window, nearly smashing it open.

A second policeman held the rest of Eric's thugs at gunpoint, while a third grabbed Eric from behind again and pulled him away from Brightly.

"Stop or I'll shoot!" the policeman shouted.

Sean's head fell back onto the floor with relief as Eric quit his struggle. The next moment, an officer was snapping handcuffs on him and frisking his pockets. "Okay, Briggs!" the officer shouted, pulling his knife out of his pocket. "You're under arrest."

"Sean," he heard a female voice. A hand slipped beneath his head, and when he opened his eyes he could see KC's friend, Faith, hovering above. Slowly, he began to focus. Behind her was the SnoPro rep, Davis Mattingly, talking with police and gesturing toward

Briggs, who was being hauled away by three armed officers.

Sean took the longest, deepest breath of his life. Tears flooded his eyes. He got his miracle after all. A second chance. And he knew his life would never be the same again.

Twenty-five

On the crowded train, Winnie stood impatiently in the aisle. Just in front of her, two women in full-length fur coats were struggling to stow their carry-on baggage. Her overnight duffel weighed a ton. Her bare hands were frozen, and her scalp was sweating beneath her duck-bill cap.

Outside, she could see the swirling snowflakes reflected in the station-platform lights. Over the last few hours, the snowstorm had worsened. All flights had been canceled, and the highway over the mountain pass was closed. The only way out of Crystal Valley that night was the train.

"Excuse me," Winnie spoke up, finally spotting a

seat next to the window. She placed her overnight bag on her head and squeezed in. Then she collapsed on the seat and stared out the window, her heart heavy.

"All aboard!" a voice cried out. Below, the snowy platform was jammed with hundreds of people, all desperate for a way out of town. Skis banged. Luggage piles collapsed. Sprays of snow blew in through the platform's open end.

"Ladies and gentlemen," the conductor's voice crackled over the tinny loudspeaker. "We'll be delayed a few minutes while crews take snow-removal equipment off the track."

Winnie fell back into her seat. She'd been waiting since yesterday morning to leave, and her nerves were frazzled. Her night in the chain motel had been anything but restful. The Jacuzzi was out of order, the room smelled like disinfectant, and the bed was way too lumpy. She'd spent the night listening to the wind howl. It had been the loneliest, coldest night of her life.

". . . got to let me on," she heard a voice outside the window on the platform. ". . . let me just check?"

Something inside of Winnie woke up. She recognized the voice. Twisting to the side, Winnie made a frantic effort to rub the steam off the window. Finally, she caught sight of the guy behind the pleading voice. She saw the soft brown bangs and the big red jacket. She saw the pleading green eyes and the long, lanky body she loved. She squinted just to make sure, then she grinned and sprang up from her seat. It was Josh.

"Excuse me," Winnie called out, pushing against the incoming crowd. The hard edge of a suitcase jammed into her knee. The train whistle blew.

Winnie thought her heart would explode. Josh was out there. He was trying to get to her. "No. Wait!" she shouted, throwing her pack ahead and climbing past two crying children in the aisle. "Stop."

By the time she reached the front of the car, the seats were full, but the conductor was hanging out the doorway, arguing with someone on the platform below. "Sorry, fella. This train was booked solid yesterday."

Wwwhhhhhoooooo, the whistle blew one more time.

Winnie pushed forward, just in time to see Josh's desperate face behind the conductor.

"But you don't understand," she heard Josh yelling over the sound of the engine and the roar of the wind. "That's my wife on the train. I can't let her go."

"Easy, pal." The conductor began to back off. He raised his hand to signal.

Winnie's eyes filled with tears as she heard Josh sobbing. "She's . . . she's the only girl I've ever loved. Can't you understand that? I'll love her always . . . until the day I die."

Winnie gasped as the conductor's hand went down and the train began to move.

"And . . . and if I don't talk to her right now," Josh cried out, jogging alongside the train, "I'm going to lose her. I have to tell her. She has to know how I feel."

"Josh!" Winnie screamed as she moved toward the door, grasping the metal handle along the steps. "Wait!"

The train was beginning to pick up speed, but in

the instant it took for their eyes to meet, Winnie knew that she would never be apart from Josh again. And with one glance at his outstretched arms, Winnie leapt off the train.

"Josh," Winnie cried as his arms caught and encircled her. Behind them, the train rushed on into the black, snowy night.

"Win," Josh was sobbing. Still holding her up in his arms, he buried his face in her neck. "Win, I'm so sorry. I've been waiting, but . . ."

As he lowered her to the ground, Winnie put a hand on each side of his freezing face and looked into his dark eyes. His hair was covered with snowflakes, and his nose was red with cold. Tears flooded her eyes. "I heard what you said, Josh Gaffey," she said with a catch in her voice.

Josh pressed his lips together and nodded. Then he drew her close until his arms were completely surrounding her. The side of her face pressed deep into the front of his down jacket. "I should have told you that a long time ago, Win. But maybe I didn't realize it until now."

"I know, Josh," Winnie sobbed. "I know."

Josh suddenly grabbed her arms and pulled away. Then he gave her a long, deep look, full of love. "I want to start over, Win."

Winnie felt her heart grow calm. Even in the swirling chaos of the stormy train station, she felt as if she were already home. "Yes," she whispered back, her heart full, as Josh lowered his face toward hers, and their lips gently touched in the sweetest kiss of Winnie's life.

Twenty-six

KC struggled to wake up. She felt as if she'd been swimming through a long, dark tunnel. Someone was at the other end, calling her . . .

"We're back," she heard Faith calling. Someone sat down next to her on the couch, and KC opened her eyes. She was in their apartment, the snow had let up a little, and her watch read ten o'clock. Faith's face hovered over her, bright and flushed. Her hand smoothed KC's forehead.

"Everything's going to be okay, KC."

KC struggled to sit up in the couch, her thoughts gradually coming into focus. After she'd tried to call 9-1-1 a few hours ago, she'd collapsed on the floor.

But when she finally woke up and made it back to the couch, she could see that the police had burst in on the thugs attacking Sean. Minutes later, Faith had rushed in to tell her the news. Davis had known about the planned robbery, but had tipped off the police in time. Still, when it was all over, Davis wasn't out of danger. The police had taken him into headquarters for questioning.

KC rubbed her eyes and and blinked to clear her vision. She looked vaguely across at the elk-in-snow picture, the cluttered coffee table, and the skis leaning up against the far wall. She must have been asleep for several hours. Slowly she realized that Faith's face was radiant and that Davis Mattingly was standing right behind her. Across the way, Condo 1029 was dark.

"What happened?" KC whispered.

KC stared as Faith stepped back toward Davis and slipped her arms around his waist. Davis gave the top of Faith's head a tender, grateful kiss. He sighed and looked at KC. "Your friend Faith here just saved my life."

Faith grinned and shook her head. She turned on the tacky lamp next to KC's couch and gave Davis a playful punch in the side. "You saved Sean McGlof-flin's life."

KC quickly drew in her breath and bit back tears. Sean. It was Sean she'd been dreaming about all along. Would she ever see him again? Did he know the truth about her?

Faith knelt down next to KC and leaned her elbows

on the velveteen pillows next to her. "Davis told the police everything—"

Davis gave her a tired smile and lowered himself onto the gold ottoman across from the couch. "You made me do it."

"—all about how Eric Briggs tried to set him up," Faith continued. "Davis even admitted starting to go along with the robbery. But the police didn't care. They were so overjoyed to finally nail this thieving ring, they were ready to give Davis a medal."

Davis stood up, walked over, and put his hands on Faith's shoulders. Then Faith quietly stood up and slipped her arm around his waist.

KC bit her lip, feeling suddenly shy. "And Sean? Is he . . . okay?"

Faith and Davis gave her mysterious smiles, and KC heard a soft knock at the door.

"Look, KC," Faith said with a pat on her shoulder, "Davis and I need to talk. And I have a funny feeling there's someone out there in the hall who really wants to talk to you."

KC's hands flew to her mouth as Faith opened the door and Sean suddenly appeared. Davis and Faith slipped out discreetly while KC gasped with surprise. "Sean."

Pale but smiling, Sean walked toward her. A white bandage was wrapped around his neck, and below his sweater sleeves she could see white gauze covering his cut wrists. His blue eyes were soft and direct, and KC could tell at once that there was something about him that had changed. She felt her heart beat faster as he sat down on the couch and gave her cast a silent, pained look. Then, shyly, he pulled a floppy rubber rose from behind his back and handed it to her. "Better late than never."

KC stared at him in shock, then down at the rubber rose. For a moment, it was difficult for her to put Sean McGlofflin the Wise Guy and Sean McGlofflin the Mysterious Romantic into one package. But there he was, sitting in front of her. Two people, suddenly one.

"You broke your leg, and I nearly broke my neck," Sean cracked softly, slipping his hand into hers, "but here we are."

KC felt laughter bubbling up inside her. Everything seemed to hit her at once. The confusion. The terror. The truth. It was all too crazy to take in at once. And for the moment, all the two of them could do was laugh.

She felt the side of his hand on her cheek. Sean's face was suddenly serious. His eyes, once flashing with anger and contempt, were full of feeling. "KC? Why didn't you tell me?"

KC looked into his eyes, biting her lip. Sean bit his lip, too, as if he was searching for the right words. He glanced down at her leg cast.

KC giggled and let her head fall back. Then she threw one of her pillows at him. "If I'd only known it was you."

"You would have had a wonderful time with that information," Sean declared. "You would have made my life miserable."

KC nodded. "You're exactly right. I would have

driven you crazy with false leads and humiliating set-ups."

Sean's eyes were shining. "Who did you think I was?"

KC gazed back happily. She could almost feel the mysterious guy with the paper-white smile fading into the back of her mind. Reality was kicking in like a gust of fresh air, and she realized all at once it was better than a thousand fantasies. "I thought you were someone, Sean, who doesn't exist."

His expression turned thoughtful. "You were so different, KC . . . when I saw you through this window. I feel like I saw a part of you . . . well . . . that not many people get to see."

KC looked down. "I know I'm impatient, controlling, and horrible. You saw that right away in me and . . ."

Sean gave her a gentle smile. "And . . . what?"

"And I didn't like it," KC said simply. "So there. I know it's wrong, but I can't always help myself."

"Neither can I," Sean agreed.

Sean looked down pensively. Then he looked up again, his face suddenly ecstatic. "But you're great at icicle fencing."

KC giggled, flipping the rose in the air and catching it again. Sliding into the couch next to her, Sean gently lifted her cast and placed it in his lap. "It was strange, KC. I kept thinking about you as the noose tightened around my neck. I kept thinking, how can I die now? I've taught her about icicle fencing, but she still has baseball-bat icicle bashing and snowball hoops to learn—"

KC laughed out loud.

"—at least before she leaves Crystal Valley . . ."

KC reached out and slipped her hand around the back of his head, pulling him closer. "I'm not leaving right away," she whispered before his face fell toward hers and their lips brushed in a brief, sweet kiss.

Sean closed his eyes and snuggled closer to her on the couch. KC's head rested on his bent elbow as they both stared out the window.

"These are Olympic sports in Crystal Valley," Sean explained. "We take them very seriously."

KC sighed happily and tickled the side of his freckled face. "You don't take anything seriously, Sean McGlofflin."

There was a long silence as they stared out at Condo 1029. "Yes, I do, KC," Sean said, turning to kiss her once again. "I take you seriously. And I'm not going to want to let you go."

KC gave him a challenging look. "Maybe I won't let you."

Sean ran a single finger down the side of her face. "Our universities are only two hundred miles apart. Four hours, easy," Sean said with a thoughtful glance at the ceiling. "We can give it a go."

"We will," KC said with a quiet smile, more serious than she'd ever openly admit to Sean. "I know we will."

"Two solid days of powder skiing," Winnie rejoiced, draping her wet ski sweater over one of the apartment's plastic dinette chairs. She shook her head in happy disbelief.

"In the sun," Faith added with a grin, delicately touching her red chin with the tip of her finger.

"Sounds great," KC added, hobbling in from the back bedroom on crutches. "But true bliss is sitting by the lodge fire watching you guys wipe out from the safety of my chair."

Faith grabbed a balled-up pair of ski socks and threw them at KC. "You haven't looked at anything but Sean McGlofflin for two straight days."

Winnie grabbed a hair dryer, found a plug behind the sagging sofa, and turned it on high. "Of course, it didn't hurt that KC fell for a member of the McGlofflin family," she shouted, "and got us all free lift tickets."

KC gave her a superior smile. "And a complimentary brunch in the lodge dining room."

"Sean's parents are cool," Winnie commented, twisting one of her spiky clumps of hair with a dreamy expression. "Josh says he wants us to be just like them when we're an old and gray married couple. Running a shop up in the mountains. Sipping hot cider and skiing all over the place with our zillions of kids."

KC laughed. "The McGlofflins were grateful to get their stolen merchandise back. They just felt like celebrating."

Faith turned her head upside down and began brushing her damp hair out. "Some relaxing winter break. I feel like I've been on an emotional roller coaster for a week. How am I ever going to settle down to studying again?"

"Yeah," Winnie cracked, tossing a pillow at her head, "especially with Davis Mattingly in town, distracting you."

Faith's face began to glow. "He'll be working in Springfield pretty soon, Win. But he'll be busy, too. And then he'll go back to Hawaii for the surfing circuit. That will take months. . . ."

"He'll be back," KC and Winnie said at the same time, jumping on Faith and tickling her.

KC stepped away, still laughing and trying not to trip on her crutches. "Notice how much fun we started having once we were minus one roommate?"

All three girls turned solemn.

"Tory," Faith breathed. "Didn't know it was possible for anyone to pack five suitcases in less than a half hour. She didn't even tell me where she was headed. I guess she's already been kicked out of school."

KC clenched her teeth. "She's just lucky she wasn't in Condo 1029 when the police showed up."

Faith laughed, perching on the edge of the tiny coffee table. "I'd say Tory was lucky she never saw you again. You would have killed her."

Knock, knock, knock.

All three girls looked up, then glanced at one another. Davis and Sean were back at the lodge, resting up for some night skiing. And Josh was supposed to be at the motel, packing. Finally KC limped forward and opened the door.

"Hi," a dark-haired guy said.

"Hi," KC replied, wondering why he looked so familiar.

The guy's smile stretched wider as his eyes traveled down the length of her body, then up again. "Hope you don't mind. I got your name from the manager."

KC felt something clutch at her throat. "You did?"

"Yeah."

KC stared at the dark head of hair. The red ski vest. The bronzed face, and the paper-white smile.

It's him. Mystery Man. KC couldn't speak. He was just standing there.

The guy's eyes shifted a little. Then he extended his hand. "I'm Brent Fairchild. My family has a condo on the other side of the complex. I've seen you around."

KC gestured for him to come in, unable to stop staring at the coppery quality of his suntan and the deep, handsome cleft in his chin. She found herself wondering if he'd used a tanning booth, bronzer, or long, authentic hours on the slopes to get that look. "Um, yes. Hello. I'm KC Angeletti. I've seen you, too."

Brent just stared, the blank smile never leaving his face. "You broke your leg."

KC cringed at the obvious statement. "Um, yes."

"Too bad."

There was an awkward silence while Brent continued to stare. KC chewed the inside of her lip. Did he want her to carry the conversation? She wondered if he was waiting for details of her accident. Instead, KC stared, unmoved, at the well-formed muscles in his thighs. Her heart sank a little, then rebounded. Up until two days ago, she'd thought about those legs every night since they'd arrived. The tan. The empty blue eyes. The chin. But now, up close, the guy suddenly seemed like a beautiful, two-dimensional photograph. Great to look at. But impossible to talk to. Desperate for something to say, KC finally looked down at her cast and pointed. "How do you like it?"

Brent frowned, staring at the dozens of cartoon characters Winnie had drawn on the plaster with a set of fluorescent markers. "Gee," he stammered, shifting his weight, "that's really . . . awesome."

KC cleared her throat and looked around, but Faith and Winnie had mysteriously disappeared into the bedroom.

"Well," Brent said slowly. "Would you like to . . . join me at the lodge? I mean, if your leg doesn't hurt too much."

KC's mind went into high gear, suddenly desperate for an excuse. "It hurts," she said quickly, reaching a hand out to lean against the nearest chair. "It hurts a lot."

"Oh." Brent's gorgeous eyebrows furrowed in a display of concern. "Well, then . . ."

KC felt uncontrollable bubbles of laughter welling in her chest. Her mystery man—suddenly demystified. This was the guy she thought she knew? She thought she loved? Next to Sean McGlofflin's lightning-quick banter, this guy seemed as alive as a telephone pole. "Oh!" KC winced, staggering back a little, suddenly desperate to make him go away. *"Ouch!"*

"Hey, take it easy!" Brent exclaimed. He stepped back, his blue eyes wide and vacant. Then, forcing an anxious smile, he retreated quickly into the hallway. "Well, ciao."

"Ciao! Aggghhhh!" KC called back, just before she shut the door and collapsed on the couch, laughing uncontrollably.

"You're awful!" Faith cried, bursting out of the bedroom, followed by Winnie, who did an exuberant cartwheel, hooting at the top of her lungs.

Winnie then hugged her stomach and collapsed on the floor, howling with laughter. "Why didn't you tell us you were in love with a tree stump all week?"

KC bit her lip, giggling.

Faith gave her a teasing look. "Why didn't you just tell him you were—well, you were gaga over Sean McGlofflin?"

"Yeah," Winnie taunted, hiking her leopard-print leggings up and catching her breath. "Why didn't you tell him you were attached at the hip to someone with an actual personality?"

Faith tickled the back of KC's neck. "Well? You are attached, aren't you?"

KC shrugged. "Sure we are. Until we decide we can't stand each other anymore. Luckily for him, our campuses are four hours apart."

Winnie stood up and grabbed her jacket. "That would never work for me and Josh. We're going to stay as close as possible to one another. In fact, we've decided on a very tiny married-students apartment with *no roommates.*"

KC and Faith grinned at her.

Winnie pulled out a tube of fire-engine-red lipstick

and applied it carefully. "Whenever humanly possible, we're going to take time off from our respective, high-powered university lives to spend with each other."

KC slipped her arm around Faith's waist and squeezed her.

"But most of all," Winnie declared, snapping the tube shut and turning around to face them, "we're going to believe in each other."

"I'm going to cry," KC wailed, stepping back and collapsing on the couch, where Faith and Winnie quickly joined her. The next moment, they were all sitting together, staring up into the violet sky through the window.

"Wish you didn't have to go tonight, Win," Faith whispered.

"Yeah," Winnie agreed. "But Josh and I wanted to take the train together." She checked her watch. "In fact, I should get down to the lobby now. Josh said he wanted to blow some money on one of those horse-drawn carriages to the station. We're going to leave this place in style."

"So it's good-bye for now, Win," KC said with a break in her voice. She grabbed Winnie's wrist to keep her from standing up.

Winnie gave her a tender look. "Don't get so choked up, pal. I'll see you guys in two days."

Faith gave KC a sideways hug. "KC doesn't like to admit it, but she hates good-byes and she's a pussycat at heart."

KC wiped a tear. "It's just that . . . I don't know. Look at the three of us. I mean, since we started college together, it's been nothing but change."

"Turmoil." Faith shook her head.

"One crisis after another." Winnie sighed.

A tear slid down KC's cheek. "There's been one constant, though. One real thing we've been able to hang on to."

"Yeah," Faith said softly. "Us."

Winnie nodded, crossing her legs and bopping the toe of her hot-pink après-ski boot. "We three. When we're forty, let's have a reunion, right here, at this very spot."

Faith sniffed. "We'll bring our husbands and kids and dogs and ice chests and go skiing."

Winnie giggled, but KC could see tears brimming in her eyes. "I'll have my big psych degrees by then. I'll psychoanalyze all of you for free."

"I'll analyze your stock portfolio," KC offered, slipping her hand into Winnie's and looking over at Faith. "Hey, Faith? What will you do?"

"What else?" Faith said softly, drawing her knees up. "I'll get someone to produce a play about us. I could write it, direct it, and cast myself as one of the leading characters."

Winnie nodded. "Oh, that's a good idea, Faith. The stories you could tell about us."

KC laughed. "The show would go on forever. The plots would be endless."

"And unforgettable," Winnie added, raising her fist up into the air.

"Yeah," Faith said with a big smile, reaching her arms out and hugging Winnie and KC both. "Isn't that the truth?"

▦ HarperPaperbacks *By Mail*

They'd all grown up together on a tiny island. They thought they knew everything about one another. . . . But they're only just beginning to find out the truth.

BOYFRIENDS GIRLFRIENDS

#1 Zoey Fools Around
#2 Jake Finds Out
#3 Nina Won't Tell
#4 Ben's In Love

#5 Claire Gets Caught
#6 What Zoey Saw
#7 Lucas Gets Hurt
#8 Aisha Goes Wild

And don't miss these bestselling *Ocean City* titles by Katherine Applegate:

#1 Ocean City
#2 Love Shack
#3 Fireworks
#4 Boardwalk
#5 Ocean City Reunion
#6 Heat Wave
#7 Bonfire

Look for these new titles in the *Freshman Dorm* series, also from HarperPaperbacks:

Super #6:
Freshman
Beach Party

Super #7:
Freshman
Spirit

Super #8:
Freshman
Noel